The Dragon Keepers of Dumara

Book 1 of the Dragon Keepers Series

Jessica Kemery

Copyright © 2022 by Jessica Kemery

All rights reserved.

No part of this book may be reproduced in any form or by any electronic or mechanical means, including information storage and retrieval systems, without written permission from the author, except for the use of brief quotations in a book review.

Cover: **Covers by Christian**

Editing by: Ashley Smith-Roberts

Proofreading by: Horus Copyedit and Proofreading

Formatting: Hotmessexpresspublishing.com

ISBN: 979-8808458543

Map

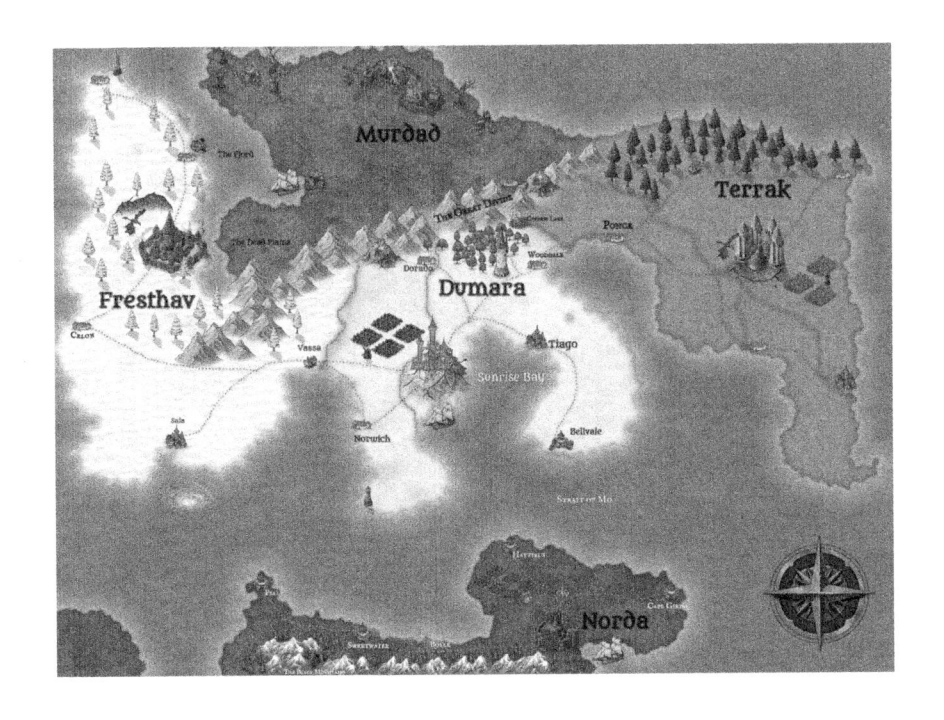

Chapter 1

Sunrise

Mila Fletcher moved down into the valley, following her father. Here and there, the remains of a charred black tree stump, still smoking in the morning dew, stood testament to the battle that occurred here.

Mila tripped over a tree limb that had fallen over the trail. Her father swung around, steadying her. "Watch out, Mila!" he said, rolling his eyes. His daughter was clumsy.

"Sorry, sorry!" she said, kicking the branch out of the way with her brown leather shoe. She was already out of breath. They had trekked since first light. The city of Dumara lay an hour behind them, bathed in the pink and golds of the sunrise.

A dragon in the distance roared, but it was not the usual roar of a dragon. This roar was filled with grief. Its cry shook their bones, rattling the teeth in their jaws.

Mila could see the dragon now, flapping its huge wings. Its shadow fell over their faces as they looked up. The dragon gave another roar as it passed over them and circled into the valley.

"He sounds hurt," Mila said, a look of worry crossing her face. "I couldn't see his coloring. I lost him in the sun."

Her father looked at her, concern clear on his face. "He probably is hurt. I suspect it might be his mate that fell last night in battle." The path took a steep decline now, and they practically had to scrabble through the loose gravel that lined the trail.

Aswin Fletcher, Mila's father, was the Dragon Keeper of Dumara. He worked for the King, and it was his job to care for the dragons and their younglings that lived in the cliffs below the castle. He tended them with great care, as his father had done before him, and his grandfather before him, and so on and so on for generations.

"There was a battle last night, and dragons usually fight to the death. Did you hear it?" Aswin asked as the path leveled out.

"I did, Father. I think everyone did. It sounded like it was right over the village," Mila said. The battle, and the flashing of magic and light, had woken her just before sunrise.

Another dragon's roar filled the air. "Hurry now, let's see what we can do to help," Aswin said, quickening his steps.

The clearing at the bottom of the valley became visible, and the body of a majestic, full-grown female lay on the ground, her eyes glazed over in death and her long-forked tongue hanging out of her mouth. Mila knew it was a female because it lacked the long, twisting horns of a male dragon.

Mila knew this dragon immediately by its coloring, a bright golden yellow, fading to white at the tail. This was the female drakaina Mila knew well. Her colors reminded Mila of the morning. She had named her Dawn.

"Hades," Aswin said. "She's dead, I think. And he has found her. This is not good."

The dragon that had flown over was lying next to her, his long neck draped over hers, and his wings cradling her like a hug. It was the enormous dark red dragon with the yellow underbelly who was the head of the dragon clan. Mila had named him Mace. He lifted his head and let out another tremendous roar as tears dripped from his eyes.

Mila had never in her life seen a dragon cry. She had also never seen a dead one this close before. She knew dragons mated for life and lived to be very old. Occasionally, they would fight. Sometimes one would die in battle, but then the other dragons would carry the body off and lay it to rest in their communal crypts under the castle.

Her father took one step forward. "She gone?" he asked urgently, not breaking eye contact with the red dragon. He felt for her heartbeat, and finding none, looked back at Mila and shook his head.

The dragon all at once rose from its bereavement, spreading its wings wide. The sun shone through them, and when he opened his mouth to roar, a brilliant beam of light flew into the sky.

They were so close, her ears rang, and the light blinded her for a moment. She could feel the beat of the dragon's wings, the air causing her brown hair to whip around her.

"You're hurt!" her father yelled above the roar. "You can't take her back with your leg like that! You won't be able to carry her!"

The dragon roared again, but this time Mila squeezed her eyes shut in time to keep from being blinded by the ray of light.

This wasn't the first time she had heard her father have a conversation with a dragon. She could see the necklace her father wore, the heavy bronze medallion with a dragon stamped on it. It was enchanted and allowed the wearer to understand dragon tongue. Mila wished she could talk to dragons. She was her father's only child, and as soon as she reached of age, she would inherit his powers and the heavy responsibility he bore.

"I'm sure they heard your call. Your sons will come. I'm sorry. I know she was your mate and the mother of your younglings. Let me look at that leg," Aswin said. Mila gingerly approached. Male dragons tended to be short-tempered, and could attack a person in a blink of an eye.

With a cry that sounded almost human, he settled down, folded back his leathery red wings, and sat on his haunches. He tossed his head, his long horns coming perilously close to her father. He stretched out his front leg for inspection.

Mila gasped when she saw the damage. The dragon's right front leg was torn to shreds. Deep claw marks ran from the dragon's shoulder all the way down to his foot.

His long sharp claws, nearly as long as Mila's arm, were bloody. So, he had joined the fight, but not in time to save his mate.

"I'm going to have to sew and bandage this later," her father said, shaking his head.

Mila heard a roar from behind her and was startled to see four dragons approaching. They must have already been in the area to arrive so soon. Two were male younglings but almost grown; the horns on their heads were half the size of full grown adults. Two older male dragons, respected warriors of the clan, flew with them. All four dragons circled a few times.

"We need to get out of the way," Aswin said, pushing her gently back up the path.

They stopped a bit up the path and watched the dragons settle in. The two younger ones Mila recognized as Dawn's own dragonlings. The oldest was golden yellow like his mother, and the youngest shared his father's dark red coloring. The two older males were hues of orange with white bellies. These dragons were members of the Sunrise Dragon Clan. They breathed powerful light rays that could burn anything they touched. Mila had heard in other lands, there were different colored dragons that breathed ice, a dark cursed magic, and columns of fire hotter than the sun, but she had never seen one.

"Watch, Mila. This is very rare," her father breathed in almost a whisper.

The four dragons came to rest next to Dawn's lifeless hulk.

They bowed their heads in deference to their leader. He roared again, this time joined by his younglings.

"It's so bright, Father," Mila said, squeezing her eyes shut.

"A great drakaina died. This is how dragon clans take care of their dead," Aswin said, pulling her closer to him.

The injured clan leader took a step forward, limping on his bad leg. Then he leapt into the cloudless sky. His body spun as it rose, straightening out like an arrow.

The four dragons gently, ever so gently, nuzzled the golden female until she lay on her back, her beautiful azure dragon eyes unseeing. Mila could now see what caused her death, as the dragon had a terrible rent in her side, and she had bled out. The ground underneath her was dark with dragon blood.

Each dragon took one of her legs firmly in a claw. With beating wings that struggled against the adult weight, they managed to lift her into the sky. Slowly, slowly they flew back east, toward their nests under the castle.

"That was amazing, but I feel so sad for the dragon and his younglings," Mila whispered, watching the enormous shapes retreat.

"Come, daughter. I still have a lot of work to do today. I need to go to the castle. There will be plans to be made, and questions to answer."

"And you have to go to the dragon lairs, to attend to the injured dragon? Can I go with you?"

Her father shook his head. "Not right now, but I need you to fetch me some supplies from the workshop. Based on his injuries, I don't have enough of what I need on hand to patch him up."

Sometime later, they reached the Drake River. It was deep here and fast-flowing as it curved past the dragon caves. Above them, dark openings dotted the cliffs. Normally, at this time of day, the dragons would be swooping out of their caves to go hunting in the northern forests, but now they were quiet.

Above the cliffs, the castle of Dumara loomed above, towering into the sky, its white limestone reflecting the morning sun like a lighthouse on the hill. The castle tower, which looked out to the south over the cliffs and river, normally flew a massive standard of Dumara, with light blue and yellow rays, and a red dragon in the middle. For some reason, the flag was missing.

"Father! They are raising a black flag! What does it mean?" Mila asked, pointing to the tower. She could just make out a form at the bottom, pulling the ropes. A black flag was slowly moving into place.

"That flag is only raised if someone in the royal family has died," her father said, sadly.

"Who died? Someone died?" Mila asked, confused. "Are they honoring the dragon that died?"

"Something like that," her father sighed. "I think you will find the Queen is dead also."

"What? I don't understand." Mila shook her head. Why would the Queen be dead on the same day as the dragon? Were they somehow connected?

Mila knew her father was headed to the secret path that led up to the caves. There was also an entrance into the subterranean tunnels from the castle dungeons, although Mila had never traveled that way with her father.

"I'm going across here," her father said, stopping at a series of stones, which he would use to cross the quickly flowing waters. "Head back home, and grab some more healing balm. I'm going to need more. That is a nasty wound on his leg. I'm also going to need some spider silk, about three meters of it. I believe I took the last two bottles of astragenica this morning. If you can't find any more on the shelves, mix up a batch quickly, would you? When you are done, hurry to the castle and deliver the supplies, I'll need them as soon as possible."

She nodded and watched as her father easily crossed the stepping stones and then began hiking up what looked like a faint mountain goat path. It was precarious, but he had done it hundreds of times, and Mila with him. When she was young, he used to put her in a backpack and take her with him, and she would play with the dragonlings while he worked.

The path wasn't so difficult once you made it past the first fifty feet. Soon, he had disappeared, hidden by the stone outcroppings, and Mila turned and followed the river road to Trader's Gate and the bridge that led into the city of Dumara.

Chapter 2

The Queen is Dead

The city of Dumara was the jewel of the south, and it hugged the base of the mighty castle. Trade from all over the world flowed through it, coming down the deep river and across the sea on boats that docked near the warehouse district.

The instant Mila stepped onto the main street, she knew that something was wrong. The normally bustling street was somber and quiet. The shops were shuttered, and not even their neighbor, Finn Gates, an extroverted old codger who ran the general store next door, was to be found. If not tending to his shop, Finn normally resided on a bench in the front, where he gossiped with locals and hawked his sales.

Her father's shop was on the corner, and the sign read "Dragon Keeper of Dumara." Her father sold everything dragon-related with a special permit from the King. Her father not only was the official Dragon Keeper of Dumura, but they were also the only ones legally allowed to sell dragon-related items. Anyone else was a fraud, pure and simple.

The shop had normal items, like dragon scales and leathers,

and more difficult to find objects, like bones and fangs. In the back was her father's workshop, where they created potions to sell to the public and to tend to the dragons.

Their most popular ointment, dragon balm, healed the worst burns in just a few days.

The sign in front of the shop read "CLOSED" but Mila could see Sam Arbuckle, the boy from town they had hired last summer for extra help, moving around inside. She opened the door, and he looked up from the shelf he was dusting.

"I had to close the shop. A herald came by earlier and gave us the order. He said it was due to the death of the Queen. What happened? Have you heard any news?" Sam was just about the same age as Mila, seventeen, and he was annoyingly naive and overly enthusiastic about nearly everything. He also had a terrible crush on Mila, which drove her crazy. His youthful face, flushed with excitement, and his short, russet-red hair made him look younger than his age.

"I'm not entirely sure," Mila said, plopping her bag down on the store counter. She pulled up a stool and considered the facts. She held her chin in her hand as her mind spun with the events of last night and this morning.

"Did you find the injured dragon? I wish Mr. Fletcher would let me go with you."

"Someone's got to tend to the shop," Mila chuckled. Sam loved dragons as much as she did. He spent time reading their encyclopedias and reference books when the shop was quiet and he didn't have any other duties.

"I suppose so." Sam looked crestfallen, and a frown crossed his face.

"We tracked the dragon north. Sadly, we found the drakaina dead. There was some kind of battle last night. Her mate, the leader of the dragon clan, was also injured. Father went straight to the dragon caves to tend to him, and he asked me to grab a few things and meet him there. The dragon's injuries were so bad, Father didn't have enough supplies in his bag to take care of them," Mila said, standing up. She grabbed an extra dragon keeper's bag her father kept fully stocked from under the register and quickly rummaged through it.

"All the astragenica is missing, but he did say he took them this morning. Do we have any more in stock?" she asked him, quickly looking at the stocks of potions behind her, all lined up neatly on the shelves.

She didn't even know what astragenica did. It wasn't a potion that they sold to humans, so it had to be a dragon potion, but she had never seen her father administer it to a dragon. All she knew was that he used a lot of it.

"Nope, all out," Samuel said, pointing to a bare spot on the shelves.

"Drat. I'll have to mix up another batch. Do we have clean bottles?" Mila asked. She moved to the back workshop and grabbed a thick canvas apron from the pegs that hung by the door.

"Yes, I cleaned and sterilized a batch yesterday," Sam said, watching her work.

"Thanks, Sam. You're the best!" she said, working quickly. He didn't say anything in response, and she looked up noticing a silly grin on his face. Now she could kick herself. She had to watch every word she said to him, lest he take it the wrong way.

Mila was aware that Sam had a crush on her, but she just wasn't interested in him at all. He was a friend, and that was that. She was never getting married, she had decided a long time ago. She would be the next Dragon Keeper of Dumara, and she had a feeling that Sam needed someone more conventional. Someone who would give him a passel of little ginger-headed children and stay at home and cook and clean. A girl that liked to wear dresses to go to church luncheons and potlucks. The thought of living that life made her physically ill. No, she didn't think marriage would ever be in the cards for her. She would adopt, probably.

Mila's problem was that she had never had a mother figure in her life, and her father just didn't care about raising a proper daughter. Her mother had died of dragon fever when Mila was just a year old. Her father had blamed himself for years, believing that he must have brought it home, that he must have been the cause of his beloved wife's death. But eventually, he forgave himself and set himself to raising their daughter.

He rejected all offers from townspeople to help him out, and he probably could have used the help. Mila was always a handful, more boy than girl, getting into scrapes constantly. She had been thrown out of school almost immediately because she refused to wear a dress.

Ever since she could walk, she only wore pants. She loathed dresses, fancy hair bows, and corsets. She didn't care, and the townspeople accepted her eccentricity. The Dragon Keepers had always been a little bit odd, they all thought.

Still, that didn't keep busy body matrons from suggesting potential suitors and contacting her father to suggest an arranged marriage. They were very wealthy after all, and many people seemed to think that Mila's husband would be the next Dragon Keeper, which made her furiously mad. Luckily, her father refused to even discuss such things, so Mila felt the freedom to be independent.

While she was thinking about all this, she grabbed the spider silk and stuffed it in her bag. Luckily, they had traveled to the northern woods just last month and had collected a large stock from the nests of the giant spiders that lived there, loading their old mule's back with as much as he could carry.

"Father asked for healing balm. Could you grab that for me, Sam?" Mila asked, tucking her unruly hair behind her ear as she pulled out a heavy stone mortar and pestle.

He grabbed a few tins of the balm, which were just over her head. These were packed for the public in a cheery turquoise tin box, decorated with roses and cherubs. These sold very well to housewives with children with scraped knees and minor kitchen burns. Sam stood with them in his hand, looking at her as she found the ingredients to make astragenica. Wormwood, nightshade, iodine, saltpeter, carbon, and dried or fresh astra flower petals. She never forgot the pinch of anise, which she assumed was to make it taste better. These herbs were mixed with two parts mineral oil to make it a drinkable potion. Then the mixture was poured into small bottles, one cup each, and stoppered firmly with a cork.

She ground and ground the ingredients, taking great pleasure in watching them come together. She looked up and caught Sam staring at her. "What, Sam?"

He cleared his throat. "Maybe this isn't a good time."

"What, Sam? Spit it out. I'm likely to be gone all day," she demanded.

"Well, ahhhhh, the church is having a picnic this Sunday, after services. Would you like to go with me?" he stammered. He moved over and placed the tins next to her, and he settled his hands on her shoulders, gently, as if he was afraid she would bolt.

"Sam." She groaned as she turned to him, away from her urgent work. He was uncomfortably close. He was holding his breath, waiting for her response. His hands moved to her waist, drawing her closer. He was looking at her intensely, his green eyes shining with hope.

"Well, what do you think? I asked your father if I could court you, and he said it was up to you."

"Sam, I don't date. You're a good friend. I'm not right for you. I'm not interested in courting or marriage. Why don't you ask Kiara? I think she likes you," Mila said. She didn't want to hurt dear Sam's feelings, but she was not interested, and Kiara Wright, the tailor's daughter who lived just across the street, really did seem to like him. She visited their shop nearly every day, asking for more balm, potions, and teas than a person could reasonably use in one lifetime.

He sighed and released her. He moved back, his face reflecting his hurt feelings. "I'm sorry. I shouldn't have asked."

"Go ask her now, Sam. While I'm still working. I'm sure she's at her father's shop."

"Okay," Sam mumbled, avoiding her eyes. He quickly left the room, embarrassed to be turned down.

Mila shook her head and sighed, grabbing the can of mineral oil from the shelf. She added it slowly, stirring it with a wooden spoon stained black from years of making this potion.

She made enough for a half dozen bottles and then corked them. The potion smelled strongly of licorice. She packed the bag quickly, placing the astragenica into the special compartments that held them upright and secure during travel.

Satisfied that she had everything her father asked for, she ran upstairs to their apartment to grab her warmer jacket. The caves were dark, cold, and damp.

Their living space was made up of just four small rooms. The largest room, overlooking the main street, included their living room, a tiny table and chairs, and the kitchen. The cast-iron stove was still warm from this morning, and their bowls from their breakfast were washed and dry on the counter. The living room was homey, with her father's rocking chair drawn next to the fireplace. The sofa where she liked to read her books was in the corner. Their black cat, Jinx, sat on the windowsill. He blinked his green eyes and stretched his long body.

She scratched behind his ears and he rolled over, blinking with contentment.

At the back of the apartment were the two bedrooms, which looked out on the back alley. A small bathroom with a vanity, a commode, and a washtub separated the two rooms.

She quickly went into her room, looking for her navy jacket. She found it hanging on her bedpost. She grabbed it and then leaned down to look under her bed. She found her study boots, the ones with good traction, that she liked to wear when going down into the caves.

She would be going to the castle, so she wiped the smudge of dirt off her cheek and brushed her wild and frizzy hair. If she ever bothered doing anything with it, it cascaded down her back in beautiful golden brown curls, but today she was satisfied with a quick braid.

In her one attempt at vanity, she dabbed a bit of astra flower perfume behind her ears. The flower only grew in the depths of the dragon caves. It was a small white flower that grew on mossy rocks. It was very rare and very pricey. The sale of one bottle of this perfume was a month's earnings in the shop. Her father had given her a bottle, lovingly made from his own precious stores, at midwinter last year. While most had been dried to use in the astragenica potions, he had enough left over for a dozen bottles of perfume, one of which he gifted to his daughter. The rest were already sold. It had been a good year at her father's shop.

Mila heard the bell tinkle on the door downstairs. She grabbed her things and ran downstairs.

"Kiara said yes," Sam said with a slight grin.

"I knew she would," Mila said, happy that the problem had been solved. "I'm going to the castle. If I'm not back by closing, lock behind you. Take your pay from the till," she said over her shoulder. Sam watched her go with sad lovesick eyes.

Chapter 3

Into the Caves

Mila made her way down the main street, passing Second and First Street until she came to Grand Avenue. She turned right, and the road took her straight to the castle's gatehouse.

Along the way, she heard the townspeople whispering.

"The Queen, she died unexpectedly in the night."

"No one knows what happened, the castle has made no statement."

"I heard it was dragon fever seeping up from the caves."

"How long do you think everything will be shut down? Until the funeral?"

The chatter and speculation filled her ears. When she finally arrived at the castle, she was not surprised to find the guards were grouchy.

A line of people stood outside the castle, trying to get in. Some were carrying bouquets of flowers, and others were openly weeping.

"No one is to enter at this time. Under orders from the King!" a guard bellowed, beating a gauntleted hand on his shield. He shooed the townspeople away, leaving Mila standing in the middle of discarded flowers.

"Except you!" The guard pointed at her. "Express orders to let in Mila Fletcher, Dragon Keepers' daughter. Come!" the guard said gruffly.

A couple of stragglers looked at her angrily. One old woman wearing her best hat and pearls hissed at her, "What makes her so special anyway? Why does the Dragon Keepers' sassy, wild daughter get entrance and audience with the king? She can't even dress properly! Wearing men's trousers, no less! The horror! What an embarrassment!" Mila tossed her head and paid them no mind, and she marched in like she owned the place.

Mila was rushed into the grand hall, and she tried not to stare like the commoner she was. She had been to the castle a few times with her father, and she was always impressed with the opulence of the main hall and throne room. The place was decorated in orange and red and featured heraldic crests depicting a dragon in flight. Tourmaline, sometimes called sunstone, shone with a copper hue from gilded picture frames and jeweled vases.

Thick rugs lined the floor, woven to depict dragons at battle. The rugs felt plush as she walked over them with her worn boots.

"Wait here," the guard demanded. She was left standing, staring at the artwork that surrounded her. Pictures of Kings past, and dragons aloft over the city, filled the walls. The castle around her was quiet as a tomb.

Mila was shocked when Prince Alex himself hurried into the room. The Prince was dressed shockingly casual, in a white peasant tunic worn unlaced. He had on a pair of riding trousers that had seen better days, and his long, golden-blond hair was messy. He had dark circles under his eyes. He had obviously been crying, but Mila supposed that was to be expected. His mother had just died, after all.

"Mila, we've been waiting. Please come with me," he said curtly, obviously annoyed at her delay.

"I'm sorry. I had to prepare the astragenica. We were out, or I would have been here sooner," she explained, clutching the bag with white knuckles. The Prince made her nervous.

His hard look softened. "Of course. We've been using a lot of it lately. Thank you."

She nodded and shifted the bag on her shoulder. "Where is my father?"

"He's down in the caves, attending to the injury. Have you been to the caves from the castle before?"

"No, we usually come from the river, up the path."

"Oh, quite treacherous, but your father does like that path for some reason."

"He says it keeps the neighbors from knowing all our business. You know how everyone in town is, they always have to know what everyone is up to. I'm sure a half-dozen people have already reported that Mila Fletcher waltzed up to the main gate and was let in while a long line was turned away."

Alex looked at her. He hadn't considered that. He supposed it would be more prudent for the Dragon Keeper to use that path, now that she pointed out the reasons. They neared a locked door, and the Prince fished a key out of his pocket. He unlocked it, and the heavy, wooden, iron-bound door swung open with a rusty squeal.

He looked into the gloom and sighed. "I suppose I should light a torch for you."

"You go down here without one?" she asked, horrified, the stairs descending into the inky black darkness.

"All the time. We have excellent night vision; it runs in the family." The Prince laughed at this, although Mila couldn't fathom why.

He lit a torch with a flint and steel that were hanging nearby, and they made their way down the circular stairs. They passed the door leading to the dungeons. Mila could hear the sounds of whimpering and laughter in the dark. "We keep all the mad and mentally deranged down here," Alex noted, hurrying past the doors. A thin man with wild eyes looked at them through the bars of the door and cackled madly as they hurried by.

The way down was a spiral, and Mila was getting dizzy. At one point, she almost lost her footing. "Steady," Alex said, taking her arm. "It can be a bit disconcerting. Do you know why the stairs are built like this?"

"No," Mila said, shaking her head. She had never considered the architecture of the castle. It just was, and always had been, a fixture looming over the town.

"To keep the dragons in the cave. They are too big to navigate this."

"Interesting. Were the builders afraid the dragons would rise up from the caves and attack the King?"

"Not the dragons who live down below. OTHER dragons," he said, with surprising venom in his voice.

Mila considered this. She knew other dragon clans existed, of course. They were in her father's books. The dragons below were sunrise dragons, all colored yellows, reds, and oranges, with light powers. Nightfall dragons lived to the north, colored black to deep purple, and they had dark energy magic. Summer dragons lived to the east, and they were shaded with hues of greens. They had fire magic. Winter dragons lived to the west, they were white and blue, and they had ice magic. She had never seen another type of dragon besides the sunrise dragons, but according to her father, they existed, as did other dragon keepers who cared for them.

Her thoughts were interrupted when in the darkness, a dragon roared in pain, and a hundred voices answered in symphony.

"Hurry," Alexander said. "Aswin is already with him. He is in a lot of pain."

They quickened their steps and reached the floor of the caves. It was a large room with entrances breaking off in multiple directions, every opening filled with darkness and dragon nests. At one end, an upper entrance was open, and the male dragons flew in and out at regular intervals. Some of the larger dragons were warriors, and they patrolled the borders of Dumara, protecting the kingdom from interloping dragons from other kingdoms. Some were hunters, and they deposited their catches into fresh kill piles near the entrance, so that the young, old, and nesting mothers could eat.

The torchlight danced on the smooth stone walls and gave the space an otherworldly feel. Mila knew it was a maze of tunnels down here.

She need not have worried. Without hesitation, the Prince picked a wide tunnel to the left. She realized she was now in an area she knew well. They were nearing the largest room, where she knew the leader and his family nested.

Mila could sense the dragons all around her now. She could hear the leathery rustle of the wings, the scrape of their scales on the stone, hear their cries, snorts, and roars of unrest.

Finally, they entered what Mila considered the great room. The leader lay in the middle of it, and Mila wondered where they had put his mate's body. It must already be in the catacombs down below. Two smaller nests were on each side, where the dragonlings slept. When they took a mate, they might move to their own nests, or they might stay in the family cave, depending on what the female dragon wanted.

The massive dragon was laying on his side, his long neck curled around his red body. The light reflected off his golden belly scales, making it look as if he was wearing a blanket of gold. His azure eyes blinked as the pair entered, and Aswin looked up from where he was packing healing balm into the dragon's wounds.

He was sitting on the dragon's injured leg, straddling it. His apron was covered with dragon blood, and he had a bone needle, nearly as long as his arm, clutched between his teeth.

Prince Nick, the younger brother, was standing off to the side watching, his arms crossed and an unhappy look on his face.

Her father shoved the jug between his legs and removed the needle from his teeth. "Mila, did you bring me what I asked for?" he asked urgently.

"Yes, of course," she answered, hurrying forward.

Alex pushed past his brother, shooting him an irritated look. He sat down on the floor and hugged the huge dragon's head. The Prince started crying, and he wiped his blue eyes with his sleeve. "It's going to be okay, the Dragon Keeper's daughter has arrived with more supplies. We will have that gash sewed up in no time."

Mila considered the odd sight. It seemed strange that Prince Alex was so invested in this one dragon. "Here is the spider thread you requested." She rummaged in the bag and handed over a bundle of it, neatly tied. Spider thread was the only thing that could hold a dragon's skin together.

"Thanks, I ran out about fifteen minutes ago, and I'm not even halfway done. This is a bad one. Real bad," Aswin mumbled as he quickly threaded his needle, which was made out of dragon bone, harvested from the oldest parts of the crypts. It was the only thing that could pierce a dragon's thick, tough skin.

"I need to clean this out better. I've already gone through one jug. This was a nightfall dragon attack. Their claws have a nasty venom to them. We need to make sure it's cleaned out. Hand me that unopened jug of spirits, will you?"

Mila picked up the heavy clay jug that lay at her feet. She uncorked it and took a sniff. "Yes. Pure grain alcohol. Blythe's Best." She wrinkled her nose against the pungency. Her father bought the cheapest spirits he could for wound clearing. Blythe's Best was the spirit of choice for the homeless and the poor.

"Boys!" Aswin bellowed, taking the fresh jug from her and

handing her the empty. "Distract him, please. He threw me off earlier. Sorry, buddy, this is going to hurt."

Mila took a few steps back just in case. Alex and Nick both crouched near the dragon's head, whispering something in his ears.

Her dad grimaced and poured Blythe's Best into the deep wounds. The dragon groaned, and his body writhed, but her father managed to hold on. His fingers quick as lightning, he began sewing up the leg, the needle moving quicker than she could follow. He grabbed the jug again from between his legs and poured another generous splash.

This time, the dragon roared, and a light beam flew from his mouth, hitting the far wall. Both Princes somehow managed to jump out of the way in time, although the back wall of the cave burst into rock shards.

Roars from the clan rose up around her, and their light joined his. The caves were so alight that she didn't even need her torch to see.

Her father continued to work as quickly as he could. Soon, he wiped the sweat from his brow and swung down from the dragon's leg, landing near his claws.

Mila hurried to repack the bag while Prince Alex picked up the jug and smelled it. "Ugh. Pure rotgut," he said, taking a sip.

"I don't use the best stuff for my dragon doctoring," her father said, shaking his head, and taking the jug from him.

"Father, you forgot the astragenica!" Mila pointed out. She was very curious as to what it was used for. She really wanted to know.

"We will let the old guy rest up first. He'll heal up better if he stays here for now. He's lost a lot of blood." Aswin patted the dragon fondly on an uninjured spot. The dragon gave a snort and looked at him with one blue eye.

"Yeah, I know. I'm just as old as you are," Aswin said,

nodding. "I'm sorry, I know the heartache of losing a mate. We will talk later. Rest, my friend."

"I should change and stay here with him tonight, to comfort him. I'm worried." Alex looked tortured as they turned to go. He put his hand to his shirt like he was going to take it off.

"Just wait, Alex," Nick said irritably. "Let him rest. We will change later. We will need to go out in the morning anyway."

"First, we need to talk, boys," Aswin said, taking off his heavy apron that was stained with blood. He poured some of the alcohol into his palm and rubbed his hands together to wash off the blood.

"Uggh," Mila said, fanning the smell away from her. "You smell like a drunk."

"But at least I'm no longer covered in dragon blood," Aswin said as he packed up his dragon keeper's bag.

"What about her?" Alex jerked his head toward Mila.

Her father sighed. "It's probably time we told her. She's almost of age."

"Tell me what?" Mila asked as they left the dragon behind in the dark and started moving back up the circular stairs.

"Family secrets," Alex said, his mouth set in a grim line, as he led them up into the darkness again.

Chapter 4

Secrets Revealed

They left Mila puzzling as they made their way back up through the dark.

Alex suddenly became interested in her day, asking her if she had been with her father that morning, what potions she had brewed, and what the townspeople were all saying.

"Of course, rumors are flying every which way. I'm sorry for your loss. Today has been a strange day," Mila said, touching his hand.

He looked at her and blinked back tears. "I tried to save her, but Father jumped in between. He wouldn't let me help, and now look what has happened."

"Of course Father didn't want you in the middle of it, Alex. You're the Crown Prince. I doubt he would have cared if it was me. Instead, I was left fending off two by myself," Nick said bitterly.

"Shhhh," Aswin said. "Unless you want the world to know." They were upstairs now, and servants bustled by, giving a quick bow to the Princes as they passed.

"Let's go to Father's study. It is more private," Alex said, leading them down the hall.

He led them to a comfortable study lined with books. Mila recognized some of the texts as originals of the books they had at home. All about dragons, of course. The Chuvash coat of arms hung on the wall, the yellow dragon shining bright with rays of sunshine depicted behind it.

Alex closed the door, and he and Nick sat directly across them on the matching yellow silk sofa. Aswin sat down with a sigh, patting the seat next to him.

Mila sat gingerly, looking at both of the Princes. Both were tall, with golden blond hair and those striking blue eyes so much like the dragons. With a start, she smiled as she put a lifetime of clues together in her mind. Alex's eyes went wide when he saw her make the connection.

"Which one are you?" she asked Alex, almost shyly. Aswin threw his head back and laughed so hard tears started coming out of his eyes. He clutched his chest.

"It's not funny," Nick said, throwing Aswin a dirty glance.

"I don't know. I do think it's funny it took her so long to figure it out. She's been coming to the caves since before she could walk," Alex said with a thin smile.

"Oh, you've hurt me from laughing. I needed that, my sweet clever child," Aswin said, pulling out his handkerchief and wiping his eyes.

Mila looked back and forth between the two. She was embarrassed, thinking of all the times she had rubbed Alex's belly and he had rolled on his back like a puppy. Or when she had called Nick a big selfish brute, or chastised Mace, who she suspected was King Rand, for being irritable. "I just figured it out …," she whispered, looking at them both with big eyes.

"It's true. We are dragons. You know, when not in this form," Alex said.

"Let's start at the beginning," Aswin said, sitting back to begin his tale.

In the beginning, the Dragon God came to this world and saw that it was ripe and full. The humans, dwarves, and animals were already here, but he desired the land for his kin. He remade this world, moving the earth, seas, and mountains to his desires. He created the dragons in his image and sent them out into this world.

But his brethren fought bitterly, and he tired of their bickering. He tired of them turning to him to solve every little problem, and he desired to leave. But his powers ran the world, and without the Dragon God, day and night would not come, and the seasons would not change.

To solve all his problems, he split the dragons into four clans and gave each clan its own Dragon King, with just one piece of his power. For he did not want one dragon to rise up and take over his own throne of the universe.

In the south, he gave Chuvash the power to bring morning and made them the color of the sun. He named their clan sunrise dragons. To the north, he gave Monserrat the power of the moon and the ability to bring night. He named their clan nightfall dragons.

Realizing that he had no way to change the seasons, he gave to Dayia the lands of the west and bestowed upon him the power of fire and heat. Those dragons he named summer dragons. To Stellen in the east he gave the power of ice and cold, and he named them winter dragons.

He bade the dragons to live in harmony and to rule together, for the only way for this world to thrive without the constant supervision of the Dragon God was for his servants to live in peace.

But he had almost forgotten the humans were still here. They were strange two-legged creatures who were quite clever and fierce and resisted domination by the dragons. So the Dragon God found four of the best, most loyal humans and made them Dragon Keepers. He gave them the knowledge of healing and medicine.

He picked out one human called him a sorcerer, bestowing great magic powers. The sorcerer would provide balance in this world.

He gave the Dragon Keepers a special potion that would allow his dragons to take the form of humans so that the humans would accept them. The keepers would be partners with the dragons.

To the dwarves, he gave his own caves, which he had found were filled with gold and silver. He then set the boundaries of each dragon's lands and caused the Great Divide to rise between them, mountains of rock and earth to keep their kingdoms separate. He sent them into the world and bade them to be fruitful and multiply.

But one human did not comply, He refused to be ruled by dragons, to give up his freedom for safety and security. He set off on a hand-built ship, with a large group of his people, to find his own land to live.

In anger, the Dragon God threw everything against him. He sent terrible storms, attacks by sea creatures from the depths below, and horrible sickness. But still, this man called Mo would not give up.

Out of pity, the Dragon God finally relented and caused a piece of earth to split and sink to the bottom of the world. The humans could live on their own, but they would have to share the land with the Dwarves. The boat landed, and there was much rejoicing.

To this day, there are no dragon clans on the southern continent. They still harbor resentment, and they have kept themselves pure, with no dragon blood tainting their human bloodlines.

And the dragon clans lived in peace. But then an interesting thing happened. The dragons slowly, one by one, lost their desire to shift into human form, preferring to live in their caves as dragons. Now, only their leaders, the most powerful dragons, retain that desire. The Dragon Keepers became necessary for this, and they maintain the knowledge of astragenica.

Aswin finished his story and looked at his daughter fondly. She was a smart girl and had followed along.

"I know it's a lot to take in. My brother and I were born as dragons, hatched from our mother's eggs," Alex explained. "We lived in the warm nest with the clan until we were five or so, but we have known who we are forever. Our mother prepared us well."

"And these battles between clans, that happens often?" Mila looked back and forth between the brothers.

"We skirmish from time to time, mostly on our borders for hunting grounds. But it rarely comes to death. My mother …," Alex said, getting choked up. "She went out alone, to greet the sun. Like we have ourselves gone hundreds of times. Sometimes we do it in a group. We had a clan meeting the night before and stayed up late. It's my fault—I wanted to sleep in."

"Anyone of us could have gone. We got complacent," Nick said sadly. "And now we have to live with the guilt."

The room was silent for a moment.

"The astragenica is used to allow the dragon to return to human form. Dragons do not need help shifting back to their natural form," Aswin said. "I know you have been curious, Mila."

She nodded, putting the pieces together. "And that's why we exist. Dragon Keepers, I mean."

"Yes, our family have been the Dragon Keepers of Dumara for as long as records have been kept. We were appointed by King Haver Chuvash. As you know, we tend the dragons, we heal them. Make sure they are healthy and help them transform. We gather the herbs and supplies necessary, and most importantly, we help hide the secret, for the general public must not know."

"Why not?" Mila asked.

Aswin gave a deep sigh. "People would not accept that their rulers are not quite human."

"When I'm in this form, I am as human as you are," Alex growled.

"My apologies. The public would not accept their rulers are

shapeshifters. They already distrust the dragons," Aswin said, looking over at Nick, who appeared bored by this conversation.

"And the other dragons, in the other lands. Do they share this same secret? You all know each other and coexist peacefully?" Mila was intensely curious. The puzzle of the dragons was slipping into place. She could see the whole picture now. All it took was that one key piece.

"Well, things have changed. Now there is a certain faction that wishes this world for themselves. They don't want to share anymore," Nick said, a warning in his voice.

Mila shivered and Alex turned his eyes to her. "You are right to be afraid. If we fall, daytime will never come again. The world will be plunged into darkness. Sunrise and summer will not come, and the crops will fail. People will die, dragons will die, and the world will become a dark wasteland."

"That sounds dreadful," Mila said, folding her arms around herself.

"And that would only be the beginning of the horror," Alex said. "We would all be enslaved, and all the joy and happiness would disappear from this earth."

"I doubt it would be that bad," Nick said, rolling his eyes. "You exaggerate, Brother. I think it's just that other clans want territory, wealth, and power. Isn't that what any disagreement is really about?"

Just then, a tap on the door broke the spell, and Mila jumped. A servant entered and asked for the King.

"He is not feeling well and is in his chambers. It has been a difficult day. He has asked not to be disturbed," Alex said, looking perturbed.

"It's the envoy from Norda. He requests an audience with the King immediately," the servant said fearfully.

"Tell the envoy he's just going to have to wait. Give him a guest room. Father may be able to make an appearance tomorrow. We will have to see," Alex said curtly.

"Yes, sir," the servant said. "Should I tell the other important guests the same thing?"

"Yes! We will not hold court until after the funeral. Advisors and diplomats can just bloody wait!" Alex said, anger rising in his voice.

Nick turned to Aswin. "Why don't you and Mila go home? Come back tomorrow morning, and we can care for Father then. Come up from the trail, as I'm sure the front gate will be blocked by well-wishers."

"That's a good idea," Aswin said, getting up, his hat in his hand. As they left the room, Mila turned back to look at the Princes. They both looked exhausted, tired, and heartbroken. She hoped they got a little rest themselves.

Chapter 5

The Funeral

Mila couldn't sleep. Her mind was racing, trying to absorb everything she had learned the day before. Finally, just before dawn, she gave up. She slipped out of her warm bed, grabbed her robe, and snuck downstairs. The shop was dark, and the gas streetlamp just outside on the sidewalk shone weakly through the front window.

She slipped out the door as quietly as she could, trying not to jingle the bells. She stood on the sidewalk and looked to the east, toward the horizon. She seemed to be the only soul awake at this hour. Every storefront was dark, and the street was empty of traffic. Her bare feet on the stones were freezing cold, and her toes curled up as her breath rose in the crisp morning air. An early frost painted everything with a shimmer of white lace.

"MEOW!" Mila heard behind her, and she nearly jumped out of her skin. She turned around to see a cat disappear into the alleyway, holding a mouse in its mouth.

She shivered and hugged her robe tighter to her body, still looking toward the east, not wanting to go in until she saw the dragons. Just then, the door opened, and her father stepped out, carrying two steaming hot mugs of tea. "What are you doing up at this hour?" He handed her a mug and then blew on his, looking at her as if she was crazy.

"I want to see the dragons," she said, wrapping her hands around the mug of tea. She welcomed the warmth.

"Hummm," her father said, not wanting to point out they would see the dragons in about an hour anyway. He turned and went inside abruptly, leaving her standing in the cold.

The sun was just peaking over the horizon when the door opened again a few minutes later, and her father joined her again. This time, he had her jacket.

"Put this on or you'll catch a cold," he demanded as he held it out to her.

"Thanks, Dad." She slipped it on, happy to have it.

He sipped his tea with her in silence. They watched the horizon intently. About ten minutes later, six fast-moving specks appeared on the horizon. The sky blazed orange, yellow, pink, and deep red. The sun rose inch by inch as the dragons grew larger and larger. Finally, she could hear the roars above them.

Father pointed. "Here they come! It's always an awesome sight, and this is a big group today. It's too bad few are up at this hour to see it."

"Wow!" she said, waving and grinning like a schoolgirl. She doubted they could see her, but who knew?

"They sent out six today. I'm assuming those are the Princes with four clan dragons." He held his hands over his eyes, following their forms as they began to circle over the cliffs, then dropped down and disappeared into their caves. "How much astragenica did you make yesterday?"

"Six bottles," she said, nearly jumping up and down with excitement. "Do I get to see the transformation today? This is what you do most mornings, isn't it? You go to the caves to turn them back into humans."

"Yes, and you can come today. The King should be feeling

better this morning. Dragons heal remarkably fast. We will go as soon as Sam arrives, which should be in about an hour or so. Just enough time for you to find some shoes and real clothes," Aswin said dryly.

"I can't wait!" Mila was glowing. She was finally going to see the magic and learn the final pieces she needed to be the next Dragon Keeper of Dumara.

———

Mila felt the cold ground under her fingertips as she scrambled up the path to the dragon caves. It had warmed up enough in the few hours since sunrise that she didn't need her jacket.

Her father was ahead of her, making good time, as she struggled to keep up with his pace.

"Come on slowpoke," he joked, shifting the strap of his keeper's bag to his other shoulder.

She didn't give him a response. It was easy to call her slow. He had taken this trek every day for the last thirty years. She only came up here every other week or so. Now that she knew the big secret, and they had Sam to take care of the shop, she hoped she could come along more often.

After a good thirty minutes of hiking up the cliff, they reached the first entrance. The smell of dragons hit her, musky mixed with the scent of astra flowers. It was strong, but not unpleasant. They passed the first opening and proceeded further up to the second entrance. There was actually an even higher third entrance, but that one required a bit of rope climbing and was precarious. It was rarely used by Aswin.

They entered the caves. The edge of the entry was rubbed smooth from centuries of use. Claw marks were clearly visible at the edge where the dragons stopped, spread their wings, and caught the air currents before hurling themselves into the air.

A clan dragon, this one an almost completely red female with an orange face, lumbered past them, her wings folded tight to her body. She blinked her black eyes at them and lowered her head in recognition. Aswin listened closely as she hissed.

"Yes, it is a fine morning. Greetings to the new day," he answered, and she spoke to him again.

He nodded. "We are headed to see the King. I'm glad you all went out in a group this morning. Probably best for the time being."

She roared in agreement, swung her head toward the entrance, found the edge and then dropped off into the air. She spread her wings and was off, headed to the west to hunt deer.

They continued on, passing several more dragons of various sizes and temperaments making their way to join the hunting party.

Soon, they reached the King's chambers and found the two Princes, in their dragon forms, laying next to their father.

Alex raised his golden head, his blue eyes staring into Mila's. She thought he looked like he was smiling. Aswin was already talking to him while looking over the stitches in Mace's leg. "Yes, we watched the sunrise today. You saw us?"

Mila smiled. She wondered what it was like to have the ability to talk to dragons. It sounded amazing.

"Yes, we brought it. You boys first," Aswin sat down his bag and started rummaging inside. Mace turned his red head and watched Mila intently. He snorted and shook his head. His golden mane flipped around violently.

"Oh, we told her yesterday. It was time she knew. She's your next Dragon Keeper after all," Aswin said, pulling out three bottles of astragenica. He handed one to Mila. "Just put it in their mouths, stand back, and maybe avert your eyes for privacy's sake. No clothes."

Mila suddenly became concerned, noticing a stack of clean clothing folded in the corner. Her father moved to the young red dragon with the yellow streak down his back. She assumed this was Prince Nick. He uncorked his bottle with his teeth and spit out the cork. "Well, hurry up, we haven't got all day!"

She hurried over to Alex, uncorking her bottle. She struggled with it at first, and then tried opening it with her teeth like she had just seen her father do. It popped out first try. The dragon lowered his head and batted her on the shoulder. "Hey!" she exclaimed.

He opened his mouth wide, his long, forked tongue flicking out. His rows and rows of razor-sharp teeth gleamed. With a firm hand, she poured the contents of the bottle into his maw. Her father followed at the same time.

The dragons both threw their heads back and swallowed the potion with a gulp and a snap.

Mila couldn't take her eyes off Alex. He looked at her with his azure eyes, as he started to shimmer with a golden glow. Suddenly he began to shrink, and for a brief moment, he was half-man/half-dragon.

Then he was crouched at her feet, completely naked. During his transformation, his eyes never left her, challenging her to watch.

She blushed and turned away. She felt like a voyeur, so she stared at the stone cavern wall while the Princes quickly dressed.

Aswin chuckled to himself at the awkward silence. They all would get used to it, after a while. They would have to. One day, he would be gone, and Mila would take on his daily responsibility.

"Do you think Father is going to be able to walk?" Nick asked as he tucked his black silk shirt into his trousers.

Alex was standing next to him, wearing the same simple linen shirt he wore yesterday and the same raggedy pair of riding pants. He gave her a knowing grin, noticing her flush.

Aswin moved over to the injured dragon. "He should be better today. He might need a sling for that arm though."

"I brought a bit of cloth we can use for a sling like you asked," Mila said, pulling the length out of her bag.

Mace was standing impatiently, holding his mouth wide open. He already looked better today and wasn't even favoring his front leg. Aswin poured the potion into the dragon's mouth, and he greedily licked his lips with his long tongue.

This time, Mila turned her back immediately, and when she turned around again, she found Mace gone, and King Rand in his place, gingerly putting his arm into his brocade jacket. He stared at her, almost angrily. "So we have ourselves a new Dragon Keeper, do we? Itching to retire, Aswin?" the King said with a hint of sarcasm.

"Your Majesty. A sling for your arm?" she offered, holding the cloth out.

"Yes. Thank you, Mila," he said, gruffly. She began to put it around his neck, gently positioning his arm.

"Oh, of course not, Rand," Aswin said. "You be nice to her! She's almost eighteen. She knows a lot, but not everything. I've got to finish up her training. What would happen if I dropped dead tomorrow, hum?"

"You're not going anywhere, old man," Rand said with a chuckle. "Unless it's with me to sort this all out."

"We can make plans later. How are you doing?" Aswin looked at him with concern, taking note that he was moving very gingerly.

"Fine, for a man who fought off two nightfall dragons, but failed to save his mate," he said. Reminded again of his failure, he slightly deflated.

"Let's go upstairs. Think you can make it, old man?" Aswin tilted his head and looked at his King with a professional eye.

"Of course. Come on boys," Rand said, brushing past Mila. It was apparent he wasn't quite on board with her being around more, but he hadn't outright banished her, which was nice.

They again found themselves in the study. King Rand put a guard on the door with instructions they should not be disturbed. They fell into familiar positions on the yellow silk couches, except the King was behind his heavy wooden desk, with his back turned to them, looking out the window at the glorious fall leaves turning color. Colors of red, yellow, and orange reminded him of his wife, lying dead in their dragon caves below. She rested peacefully in the crypts with their ancestors.

He held a glass of Isciki in his hand, and he looked like the world was on his shoulders. He was an older man, in excellent shape. While his sons looked like their mother, Rand Chuvash had auburn brown hair, just now speckled with gray. He held his chin in his hand, and his azure blue eyes were filled with pain. He took a slow drink of the spirits, relishing in the burn, and then he turned and placed it gently on his desk.

His arm still throbbed, and he was glad for both the sling and the alcohol, which was dulling his pain, both mentally and physically.

Nick was drumming his fingers impatiently on the arm of the couch, looking at his father intently. Alex was examining his fingernails. They were dirty and black, and they badly needed trimming. In fact, the man really needed a bath. He had a streak of dirt on his chin, and his golden blond hair was limp and greasy.

Nick's eyes flicked to the Dragon Keepers, who sat waiting patiently for the King to fill them all in. He wasn't feeling so patient. He wanted answers. "What exactly happened, Dad? Mom went out to greet the sun and the next thing I knew all hell was breaking loose. The patrols came back roaring about a large force of intruders, and then the next thing I knew, you were gone without a word. It would have been nice if you had shown a little leadership."

Rand's eyes narrowed at his youngest son. He could feel his dragon temper rising. "Listen, Nick. I know you don't understand, but I had a sense of foreboding. Every cell in my body screamed to go protect Cassandra. You know dragon mates have a strong bond, and I could feel her distress. I headed to meet her, but I heard the battle before I even reached her. When I saw her, she was fighting two dragons, but she was already badly wounded. I fought them with everything I had, hoping that she would be able to make it home so that Aswin could heal her. I jumped on the nearest dragon, tearing his wing. He broke away, turning to the west. I hope I injured him enough that he didn't make it home. While I was fighting that dragon, the second dragon struck the death blow. I lunged at him, drawing his attention away. That's when he got me because I was watching Cassandra fall. She fell in a rain of blood, and that's all I could see. I was late… too late to save her." Rand's voice broke, and he put his hands over his face. He cried silently, his shoulders shaking.

Aswin rose and crossed the room. He put his hand on Rand's shoulders. "It's okay to grieve, Rand."

The King nodded and put his hands down. He pulled out a handkerchief and blew his nose. His eyes were red and bloodshot, his face blotchy. Aswin sat back down, looking at his friend with concern.

"We were too late ourselves. We fought them, but then they retreated," Alex said quietly. Tears were streaking down his face also. "The nightfall dragons need to pay for what they have done."

"They saw an opportunity and took it. Mother should have never gone out alone," Nick said impassively.

"Are you defending our enemies?" Alex growled low in his throat; a sound that made Mila's arms break out in goosebumps. He sounded dangerous.

"I'm not defending, I'm explaining. Mother never should have died," Nick's voice rose. "She should have never been caught in the crossfire. She was innocent."

"Let us gather the clan and take our revenge," Alex said, hitting the couch with his fist.

"It's not going to be that easy," Rand said, looking at his sons. They were both so angry. He didn't feel anger yet, but he knew it would come. "There were two dragons. One was a nightfall dragon, and the other was a winter dragon. They were working together. I think their target was me, but of course, I'm sure your mother was just as good."

The words fell like a bomb. Never in their history had two dragon clans conspired against the other, never had they purposely tried to assassinate a member of another clan. Yes, sometimes hunters clashed on the borders, but it had never led to the death of a dragon king or any of his family.

Aswin shook his head. "Unbelievable, what's your plan going forward? This was obviously planned out."

"First, we will have a funeral for Cassandra, to put her at rest and say goodbye." Rand pondered what his next step should be. A plan was starting to form. He looked at his sons, and then at Mila. It was very convenient she was coming of age. She would be needed.

"We will be there," Aswin said, "and we will pay our respects. I know both Mila and I will miss her deeply. She was special."

Mila nodded. The Queen had been her favorite dragon. When she visited, Dawn had always been playful, licking her hair flat, or pushing her toward Alex and Nick, encouraging the younglings to play with the human. She had never minded when Mila had used her as a jungle gym, and many times as a child, she took naps either on top of Dawn or between her two front legs. She really would miss her. Dawn almost felt like a mother Mila had never had, even if she was a dragon. It was hard to reconcile that Dawn was Queen Cassandra, and that she was gone forever.

Rand's azure eyes turned on her, and she felt like he was staring into her soul. "Yes, please bring Mila. She is important to the next phase of my plan."

"Me? Why me?" Mila asked, suddenly self-conscious.

"Your father can't be in two places at once, can he?" Rand asked, turning his attention to the globe on the table. He tapped the outline of the Kingdom of Murdad, where the nightfall dragons lived, ruled by King Ibis Monserrat. "And I plan on getting to the bottom of this."

―――

The funeral was Saturday, and Mila desperately looked through her wardrobe for anything that would be suitable.

"Listen, Mila," Aswin said. "You've going to need something to wear. This will be a very formal event. I'll wear my dark suit, and you need to go to the tailors and have something made. I don't care what it is, just make sure it's appropriate for a funeral. And for god's sake, do something with your hair! You've got leaves in it!" her father grumbled.

She touched her hair. It was a frizzy mess. She had pulled it back this morning because it was so tangled, and she hadn't had time to sit and brush it all out. She realized that her parched trousers and threadbare shirts wouldn't do at all, so with reluctance, she headed across the street to the tailor shop.

Franklin Wright's shop was a place she had spent a lot of time. The front room was filled with bolts of colorful cloth. She let her fingers trail over the fine fabrics. The scent of textiles filled the air, and the tailor's daughter and wife sewed in the back, the machines thumping with the movement of their feet on the pedals.

They were good friends with the Wrights. Kiara and Mila were almost exactly the same age, just a few weeks apart actually, and their mothers had been best friends growing up.

Mila walked toward the front counter as Kiara's mother, Judith, fed black silk through the machine with deft fingers. She looked up and smiled, catching Mila's eye as Mr. Wright hurried forward to greet her.

"Mila Fletcher! Long time no see, my dear. You are here for a dress for the funeral, I take it? Good thing you're here early this morning, we have been very busy."

"My father and I will be attending in our official capacity, so I really do need something new. But no dresses, please," she implored.

Franklin Wright chuckled. He was well aware of Mila's hatred of dresses. "Well, I was just in Tiago for the annual Tailor's Guild gathering. There is a new style in the city, a kind of fitted jacket and trousers for women. I think it would be nice on you, my dear. I thought of you when I saw it. You do need a foundation garment though." He looked over her chest and she blushed. She had tried to wear a corset years ago, but she had found it dreadfully uncomfortable.

"I can help you with that," Mrs. Wright said, hurrying forward. "We have some new styles that I think will suit this one better. We also have some more ... feminine shoes we just got in stock from the cobbler. We will get you fixed up in no time, Mila."

Judith had been waiting to get her hands on this one for a while. She had been good friends with Mila's mother, when they were younger, and knew her friend Leah would be aghast at the state of Mila's wardrobe if she were still alive.

"Fine," Mila said in resignation. "Dad said to charge it to his account. I'm afraid how much this is all going to cost."

"Well, he might regret that, when we are done with you," Franklin chuckled, knowing how much Aswin hated to part with a good banknote.

The next few hours were spent being measured and poked

with straight pins. Mila found herself in a changing room with Kiara, where they were giggling like schoolgirls.

"Sam asked me to the church picnic," Kiara said through a mouthful of pins, crouching down and pinning up the hem of the trousers.

"I know. I told him to ask you!" Mila laughed as she tried to stand still. It was hot and stuffy in the booth, and all she wanted to do was be done with this chore.

"You did? What did you say, exactly?"

"I said it was more obvious than a mole on a spinster's nose that you liked him, and that you two were perfect for each other, and your future children would be adorable."

"Mila Fletcher! You did NOT say that!" Kiara said, blushing bright red.

"Well, maybe with not so many words. I hope it goes well. I need Sam off my back. If he becomes obsessed with you, that's okay with me," Mila said, trying to stand up straight.

"He really likes you, I think," Kiara said, sadly.

"He's like a brother to me, Kiara. Honestly, I hope you two work out," Mila said fondly. She would like nothing better than her best friend to end up with Sam, who was hard-working, kind, and loyal.

"Well, after he tastes my apple pie, he will come to his senses. You can barely cook canned beans," Kiara joked.

"That is a fact," Mila nodded. "Totally unsuitable as a wife or mother. I lack all the necessary skills or the temperament. If I ever have kids, they will be like wild dragons in the streets," she smiled, looking at her reflection in the mirror.

She had picked out a dark, midnight blue velvet for a jacket. The jacket fit her like a glove, ending tapered at her waist. The matching pants were made of gaberdine fabric and were form-fitting, with a thick waistband. Under the suit, she would wear a silk shirt that was a bit more flowing than she really cared for. It had a soft cowl neckline that plunged and showed off her graceful neck.

It was obvious that she needed a corset. She couldn't hide her figure with bulky sweaters and scarves with this outfit. Mrs. Wright brought in a soft garment she called a brassiere. "Much more comfortable. No laces. It will hold everything in place and make this outfit look wonderful on you. You are going to have to fight off the men."

"I'm not looking to fight off men, Mrs. Wright," Mila answered curtly. She acknowledged that it was comfortable, and it did make her look polished.

"Now, let's do something with that hair," Mrs. Wright said. Instead of brushing it out, she wet her hands, running them over Mila's head. "You have beautiful curls, just like your mother, Leah. Don't brush these, Mila. That's what you've been doing wrong. Use a wide-tooth comb when it's wet. Less is better in your case." Mrs. Wright pinned back a few curls.

"Oh, Mila. You look gorgeous. Who knew how pretty you looked under those old clothes and wild hair?" Kiara said, clapping her hands and smiling.

"I love it! It's a whole new me!" Mila said, smiling at her reflection in the mirror. She had never felt pretty before, and now she felt grown-up, like a woman, and not a little girl.

"You look like your mother," Judith said, wistfully.

"It's so sophisticated. I feel so grown up. Can I have a few more of these outfits? Maybe in a more durable fabric. With a few more shirts, but maybe just cotton with a plain collar," Mila said, her eyes sparkling as she looked at the new her in the full-length mirror.

"I'm so glad you like it! You do look good, and all the ladies are going to want this style. Tell them you got it here!" Mrs. Wright was happy she could help.

Mila quickly picked out a few more fabrics. A brown, grey, and dark green, and just to be a little daring, a dark wine color.

The bill would be expensive, but she figured she had saved her father a lifetime of dress bills.

She took the receipt and planned to pick up the suit before the funeral tomorrow. While she was at it, she picked out a tie for her father, in the same midnight blue silk. The color was nice, and he should have something new to wear himself. He was the Dragon Keeper of Dumara, after all.

She was humming when she went back to the shop, still closed for the rest of the week. Sam was in the workshop with her father. Aswin had been busy all this week, gathering a copious amount of raw materials used to make potions.

He had Sam running all over town, knocking on back doors, procuring bits of this and that. Sulfur and coal from the blacksmith, chicken feathers and eggs from the farms, and mercury from the hatter.

Aswin and Mila had even gone to the dragon caves yesterday, collecting the last of the summer astra flowers. They were drying now on every rack they owned. Sam poured over his notes while her father told him how to brew up a batch of quicksilver syrup to treat dragon fever.

"I'm sorry, Father. I ran up quite the bill at the tailors. I apologize in advance," Mila said sheepishly.

He chuckled, "It's about time. No worries, you need some new clothes."

Mila nodded and grabbed an apron. "Anything I can help with?"

"Grind some bones, would you? I want that jar filled before you go."

"Go? Where are am I going?"

"You and Alex are going to be making a little fact-finding trip."

"What? Where to?"

"We will fill you in later. We are still working it out."

"Father! I just can't leave!" Mila was horrified. She had never left Dumara without her father by her side.

"You can and must. You know everything now, and we have Sam here to run the shop. I have confidence you and Alex, working together, can manage anything."

"But Father! You have the dragon medallion! How will I talk to Alex if you aren't there? He won't be able to tell me if he's sick, or hurt."

"I've already considered that. A Dragon Keeper usually gets their medallion when they turn eighteen. You are just a month away from that milestone. So we will make a little trip, just a month early. To see my brother."

"Really? We are going to visit Darius? I've never even met him, I've only heard your stories."

"Family disagreement?" Sam asked, looking up from his work, interested. Aswin so rarely talked about his family, Sam often wondered if the man even had parents.

"Yes. We stopped talking years ago. He blamed me for my wife's death, but we need him now. As far as I know, my brother is the only sorcerer in this world, and the only one that can bestow a Dragon Keeper's medallion with its powers. Rand is having the crown jeweler make you a medallion now, so you can talk to dragons."

"Great. A family reunion. Based on your stories of him, he hates me."

"He doesn't hate you, my dear. He hates me. You are a reminder of what he couldn't have. I'm not looking forward to it myself."

"When are we leaving?" She brushed her curls out of her eyes. She noticed that Sam was staring at her. She had hoped he had gotten over her, but nope, apparently still obsessed.

"Monday. We will leave Sam in charge of the shop for the

day. King Rand wants you two to leave as soon as possible," Aswin said.

Kiara took it upon herself to drop the new clothes off at the Dragon Keeper's shop the next morning.

"Hi, Sam," she said shyly, giving him a little wave.

"Hey, Kiara. Ready for the picnic tomorrow? I'm glad it wasn't canceled because of the funeral." Sam grinned at her as she laid the packages on the counter.

"I am," she said happily. "I've been looking forward to it all week."

"Thanks, Kiara. I was worried you guys were too busy and wouldn't get it done," Mila said, running down the stairs from the upstairs apartment.

"No worries. Mom and I were up all night finishing your order, and several other orders as well. We got everything done, and Dad said we could close the shop today and take a break. We all need it."

Mila grabbed the packages and hurried up to change, leaving Sam and Kiara chatting below. For once, Sam wasn't staring after her with lovesick eyes.

She hurriedly changed, and did her hair, wetting it and lightly combing it as Mrs. Wright had taught her. She grabbed the tie and took it to her father's room. The door was closed, so he must have been getting ready. She knocked on the door.

"Come in," his rough voice said, and she pushed the door open.

She found her father, sitting on his bed, holding a small painted portrait of her mother in his hands. He had a faraway look in his eyes.

"Father, I bought you a new tie. I thought you might like to wear it today."

With a sigh, he sat the painting down on his nightstand and wiped away a tear.

"Thank you, Mila," he said, taking the package. "It's a lovely color, and it matches your suit. I like it, very classy, my dear."

"You miss her, don't you?" Mila stated the obvious and sat down next to him. He started putting on the tie slowly and methodically.

"I do. Losing a loved one is something you never get over. King Rand and I have been talking about that a lot lately. Today will be a hard day for both of us, but for him especially because he has to say goodbye for the last time."

"And hard for you because it brings back memories. I'm sorry, Father. I wish I remembered her." Mila looked at the picture.

"Don't be sorry, Mila. She was the best wife and mother there could be. One day, I'll pass on, and we will be joined in heaven."

Mila and her father walked the five blocks to the castle gates. He looked distinguished in his black suit, with his new tie. His salt-and-pepper hair was neatly brushed, his shoes shined and his Dragon Keeper's medallion was freshly polished and gleaming on his chest.

Mila was wearing her new clothes, and her father was shocked at the young woman on his arm. Her hair was held back with a few well-placed pins and cascaded down her back like a river of brown curls. Her outfit was smart, sophisticated, and perfect. She would turn heads, even if this was a funeral.

They arrived at the main gate and pushed to the front, showing their official invitations to the guards. The others would have to wait here until the gates were opened later for the procession.

The inner keep was silent and somber with black buntings

hung above the doors. The servants and guards all wore grim faces.

Aswin and Mila made their way around the outside of the keep, finding the chapel doors thrown open. Honored guests of the King were starting to take their seats, and the room was filled with the upper crust of Dumara. Wealthy lords and ladies, advisors, the elite of the Trade Guilds, and even a few commoners who were personal friends of the Queen.

A closed casket sat up on a dais under the huge stained glass window, which depicted the Dragon God, a pure white dragon, with wings spread. Yellow and red roses covered the top of the coffin. The only explanation given was that the King could not bear to look upon his dead wife. In reality, it had been filled with rocks and nailed shut.

Aswin reached out and hugged Rand tightly. If anyone was shocked at the familiarity shown between the Dragon Keeper and the King, no one dared say a word. Mila was surprised to find they were sitting in the second row, right behind the King and the Princes. Alex looked tortured, and Nick avoided her eyes, concentrating instead on the choir, which had just started singing.

King Rand looked ashen and grey. Mila noted that he had discarded his sling, and he seemed to be moving his arm easily, reaching out to shake each guest's hand as if he were never injured.

"All hail the Dragon God. Righteous and mighty," the choir sang, repeating the refrain again and again as the music soared up into the high ceiling.

The priest, in funeral black robes, stepped up to the altar. He began to give the funeral mass. Mila tried to pay attention, but she had never been one for church.

She looked over at Alex, who was staring at her with those azure blue eyes of his. It was hard to believe really, that these men had the power of dragons and a bit of power direct from the Dragon God. She understood then why they hid their true identities.

All this talk about the Dragon God sending four Kings to rule the world made a lot more sense when you knew the descendants of these Kings still roamed the world and ruled over their kingdoms to this day.

They stood again as the priest gave his blessing and then joined the procession as they exited the church.

Mila found herself walking next to the Crown Prince. "Mila, thank you for being here," Alex said, sadness in his eyes.

"Well, I had to be," she pointed out awkwardly. Immediately, she wanted to kick herself for sounding so callous. She added hastily, "I am sorry for your loss."

They walked in silence, then found the line waiting for the casket to pass. Queen Cassandra's casket would be buried, with the rest of the coffins filled with rocks, in the cemetery of the chapel.

Alex wanted to comment on how pretty she looked today, but he felt it would be awkward, considering they were at his mother's funeral. He found himself thinking a lot about the Dragon Keeper's daughter this week. She was an intriguing mystery. He had grown up with her, yet he found she was a stranger.

After the casket passed, carried by six servants all dressed in white, the King and his sons milled around, thanking the guests for coming.

Finally, it was just the rest of them, and Rand looked at his Dragon Keeper. "Now, it's time for the real funeral. Let's go. The clan has been gathering below."

Mila noticed the sky above the castle was empty today, which was rare.

They made their way down the twisting stairs, weaving through the caves. Mila could feel the dragons all around her in the dark, waiting for them.

"We will change here," Rand said as they neared the entrance to the outside. Already dozens of dragons filled the halls, looking at them expectantly.

"It's rare to be invited to these events, let alone be asked to participate. I've only been one time before, when King Royce died. It was the first time I rode a dragon, and today will be your first time as well."

"Wait? I'm riding a dragon today?" Mila asked, surprised. She knew her father rode Rand often, and she understood now he was probably accompanying the King on trips. But she had never even dared to dream of riding on the back of these beasts.

She longed to ride as a child, even climbing on Alex's back a few times before he threw her off in disgust. She was glad she was wearing pants, for how did one ride a dragon in a gown?

Her father touched her arm, and she turned around with him.

Behind them, the King and his sons slipped off their clothes.

"Let's go. We'll fly for Queen Cassandra Chuvash!" Rand proclaimed, standing in his bare skin, with both sons at his sides. He began to shimmer, surrounded by a golden glow. Rand felt the warmth and power start to flow through him. It was exhilarating, and it was something of which he never tired.

His body started to change, his legs growing thicker and longer. Scales appeared, and his jaw grew. He felt his teeth grow long and sharp, and his hair turned into a golden mane. His horns sprouted from his head, and he felt their weight. His vision sharpened, and his tail grew long. Finally, he ballooned in size, rising like a loaf of bread.

His sons, morphing beside him, took their final form.

"It is done, Dragon Keeper. Collect the young one, and let's go. I want to send Cassandra on to the Dragon God before sunset."

Aswin nodded and touched Mila's shoulder. "They are ready. Go get on Alex, he is probably less likely to throw you off."

"What? How?" she asked, suddenly fearful.

"Grab his mane, sit at the base of his neck and hold on tight. Don't worry, you won't hurt him."

"Umm, okay," she said hesitantly. She approached Alex, and he blinked at her and lowered his head.

Right then, Mila decided to put her fears aside. This is what she was born for. With a grin, she climbed onto him, feeling a thrill as his considerable bulk shifted.

Under her, Alex was pleased she had chosen him. His brother would not take so kindly to being ridden, considering it beneath him to carry a human like a pack horse.

He could feel her hands digging into his mane, and he shook his head a bit. She laughed behind him, and he realized his mane had flicked into her face.

He wished he could talk to her like his father did with Aswin. He would have loved to tell her not to grab him so tight, and to relax a little, but he supposed she would learn.

"How does it feel to be a beast of burden?" Nick snorted to him, flicking his tail in irritation. "You actually look like you're enjoying this a little too much, Brother. Remember, our mother is dead."

"I'm very aware," Alex roared at his brother, flicked his own tail back at him.

"Boys!" Rand bellowed, stomping his foot. His claws raked the edge of the opening. "Stop fighting, and let's go!"

They moved up to join him, and the rest of the sunrise dragons started to appear. Soon, a line of orange, yellow, and red dragons stood at the edge, the river far below them.

From her vantage point on the back of Alex's back, she was dizzy. She clutched his mane, his golden hair twined in her fingers. The cool air from below hit her. She wanted to close her eyes but did not want to miss a single moment of this.

She saw Rand unfold his wings. They rose up behind him majestically. He had a wingspan of almost 40 feet across. The afternoon sun shone through them, and she could see the intricate pattern of blood vessels through the paper-thin skin. She was interested to see that his injury had completely healed, leaving only a faint scar running from his shoulder down his leg.

The Princes opened their wings and stepped to the edge. Mila saw her father touch his necklace, and then he said, "With the fading light, Cassandra Chuvash is called to the Dragon God. We fly with her on her final journey home."

And with that, Rand stepped off the edge and dropped. She had just enough time to see his wings catch an updraft and go soaring into the sky before the two Princes stepped off themselves, followed by the rest of the dragon clan.

She wanted to whoop and holler with joy as Alex caught the wind, and then turned, following his father over the river, but she held herself back. It didn't seem fitting to celebrate her first flight at a funeral. She watched the rest of the clan, now taking flight, a good two hundred dragons strong.

Below, the townspeople, gathering at the graveyard to lay their own flowers and pay their respects to their beloved Queen, would point and mention that the dragons seemed to be making some kind of display for the funeral.

With the wind on their faces, they turned west toward the setting sun. They would fly for hours, only landing when the last rays of the day disappeared below the horizon. For a moment, she could have sworn she saw a faint specter of Cassandra, flying by Rand, just a few seconds before the light faded into night.

Chapter 6

The Sorcerer

Darius Fletcher was a sorcerer; he had a tower and everything. He liked living alone, and he hated visitors.

His ascension to serving the Dragon God as the one and only sorcerer was a long story. It involved a wager with the previous sorcerer, which Darius had lost spectacularly.

It seemed these days he had too many guests. Someone was always turning up at his door, wanting him to remove curses, open hexed treasure boxes, or enchant some piece of jewelry. It was quite vexing actually, but it paid the bills, kept his stomach full, and his fire hot.

He chose to live in his master's tower, mainly because it was free. He could have lived with one of the many Dragon Kings, he had his choice, really, but he preferred his independence. He could go tell them to stuff it if he wanted.

The only threat was then they could return with their entire clan and reduce his cozy little tower to a pile of smoking rubble. He tried not to anger the Dragon Kings, as you really didn't want a dragon with a grudge against you.

It was rainy, and he had elected to sleep in today, reading a new book he had just purloined from the library in nearby Wooddale. His one weakness was stealing books. He couldn't resist. It was just so tempting and easy to slip one into his pocket.

His early warning spell activated, and an annoying shriek filled his ears. "Dingbat dragons!" he grumbled, scrambling to his feet and grabbing his staff. He was in no mood for visitors today, especially not Dragon Kings or their keepers.

Cursing under his breath, he made his way down the stars. At the bottom, he grabbed his wizard hat and slipped on his sandals.

"Temptus Reductius!" he shouted as he threw open the door. The rain stopped suddenly, and the clouds disappeared from the sky as if they had never existed. He didn't like to play around with the weather too much, as it could have long-term consequences, but stopping a light drizzle wouldn't cause too many problems, except maybe the wheat yield to the west would be slightly lower this year.

He watched as the two dragons landed, yellow and red. Sunrise dragons, then. "Interesting," he thought, as he was rarely visited by the Chuvashes. He spied two figures on their backs. Go figure, his brother, and probably his niece. They had decided to pay him a visit after all these years.

"Fantastic," he thought sarcastically, "Just who I wanted to see today."

He stomped outside, making sure to stand on top of the small hill that led to his tower, in order to appear more imposing.

He watched as the dragons folded their wings, were given their potions, and began to shapeshift in front of him.

In a few minutes, the four figures walked up to his tower, stopping just short of him.

His brother spoke first. "Darius," he said curtly.

"Aswin." He narrowed his eyes. "What do you want?"

"That is no way to greet your King. Or do you forget your

tower lays in the Kingdom of Dumara?" Aswin demanded, raising his voice. No matter how hard he tried, he and his younger brother never managed to get along.

Darius rolled his eyes and turned to King Rand. "Your Majesty, my apologies. I was so surprised to see my brother after all these years, I forgot my manners."

"I can see it's a warm reunion," Rand said dryly.

"And who did you drag along today?" Darius asked, his eyes turning to the people beside him. He looked at Mila with a slight smile. "You must be Mila."

"Hello, Uncle," she said, looking at him with green eyes that looked so much like her mother's it tore his soul.

"And this is my son, Crown Prince Alex. It's been a while, hasn't it, Darius?" Rand asked, looking over the tower with a keen eye. "You pay your taxes like a good citizen, so I'm happy to leave you alone."

"What do you want?" he asked grumpily.

"We just want to talk to you," Rand said. "And we want this necklace enchanted so Mila can talk to dragons."

"Of course. It's always an enchanted necklace. I don't work for free, you know," he said, irritably waving them inside.

Sadly, this looked like it was going to take a while.

Darius led them up a floor to his workshop. It was a messy place, the tables covered with jars filled with all sorts of strange things. Mila saw specimens floating in liquids of various colors and mysterious unlabeled herbs and powders. Books spilled off a shelf, onto the desk underneath it. Test tubes, cauldrons, and stacks of loose notes tumbled out of drawers, and everything was covered in a thick layer of dust.

Star maps and element charts covered the walls. A tiny little window let in the only light, and the room was dim.

"Lux Lum," Darius said, pointing to a black obsidian bowl. It erupted in bright yellow flames, illuminating the room with its glow.

Mila looked at her uncle in his wizard robes. He was a tall, skinny man, with a very long beard. His dark eyes were flinty under his wizard's cap.

He considered a workspace and finding it lacking, he swept a table clean with both hands. Papers and bits and bobs flew across the room. "Let's see it then," Darius grumbled, knocking on the table in an inpatient manner.

Rand nodded and pulled out a necklace from his jacket pocket. He laid it on the center of the table, and they all looked at the piece of art.

"I had this made especially for Mila," Rand said.

It was a nice piece of work, worthy of enchantment, Darius thought as he considered the pendant. It was completely round and about four inches wide. Made of gold, it shone brilliantly. The design was a delicate filigree, with a golden dragon on the front. A strong chain was attached.

"Let me see yours, please," Darius said, holding out his hand to Aswin.

"I hate taking this off. I rarely ever do. It's hung on my neck since my eighteenth birthday. Hard to believe it's been almost thirty years, Darius. You recall when your master made it for me?"

"How could I forget," Darius said with a sarcastic tone.

Aswin took it off, laying it next to the new piece meant for Mila. It was a thick disk of bronze, with just the etching of a dragon fully in flight. It was heavy and much larger than the delicate thing meant for his daughter.

Darius touched it, feeling the spells that bound it. "What ever happened to our father's medallion, Aswin?"

"I buried him with it, as is customary with Dragon Keepers.

You would know this if you had come to the funeral," Aswin said crossly. This visit was making him remember old hurts.

"I had my reasons, as you know," Darius said, sighing. It had been a while since he had made one of these. The last one had been for the Dragon Keeper of Fresthav, who paid for her necklace by spending the night in his bed. A night he would remember fondly. Her necklace had been made of silver, and the dragon emblem was set with sapphires. A lovely piece.

He looked over at his niece. She was so much like her mother, Leah, who had been his first love. They had all grown up together, and he had loved her since he was a child. Leah's father was a paper maker, with a shop a few streets over. But as they had grown older, her attention had been given to his brother, and he acknowledged that it drove a wedge between them. When she had died of dragon fever, he had maybe unfairly lashed out at Aswin. They hadn't spoken since.

"Let's discuss payment," Darius said curtly, pushing down his resentment.

Rand crossed his arms. "What's your going rate?"

"Well, it varies. For you, it's one hundred pieces of gold and a good horse. I haven't had a horse in a while."

"How about we forgive your taxes this year?" Rand asked blandly.

"Fine, I guess I'll buy my own horse. Now let me work. I need Mila and your son. I'm assuming that's why you brought him?"

"Yes. Aswin and I are bound already," Rand said, looking over to his oldest son. Alex was confused, as he hadn't really known why his father had asked him along today. He had figured it was so he could meet the sorcerer, arguably an important person for him to know, once he took his father's throne.

"What do you need me for?" Alex asked, looking back and forth between his father and Darius.

"A dragon medallion needs to be attuned to a dragon before

it will work. His medallion was made with my power. It binds the dragon and the keeper together."

"I see," Alex said, although he really didn't.

"You'll understand soon enough. Mila is going to be your Dragon Keeper. The connection between you two will be strong. You will be able to speak to each other across great distances, and she will gain the ability to understand dragon tongue."

Mila's eyes were wide as she listened to this conversation. She knew that her father's medallion was enchanted, and it gave him the ability to talk to dragons, but she never knew about the connection with the King. It explained how he knew things ahead of time, and always seemed to know what was going on at the castle.

"Now, you two, step right up. You probably aren't going to like this, but you don't have much choice in the matter, do you? None of us has a choice," Darius said cynically.

Mila and Alex looked at each other. Uncertainty lined both of their faces.

Meanwhile, Aswin and Rand watched, holding their breath. They both remembered vividly, so long ago, when Sorcerer Ezra had enchanted the necklace that Aswin now wore, and how the world had turned upside down for them both. For one, Mila and Alex were in for the world's biggest headache. But, it was probably for the best they weren't told of the side effects from the spell beforehand, or else they might not consent.

At the very least, the ability to read each other's thoughts would be initially disturbing.

"Mila, dear. I'm sorry in advance," Darius said.

"Why?" she asked, her green eyes growing wider.

"You'll see soon enough. Now, place your hand on the medallion," Darius ordered firmly.

She complied hesitantly, and then Darius looked at Alex and demanded, "Put your hand on hers."

She noticed that he had recently trimmed and cleaned his

nails. His hand covered hers completely. Darius grabbed his staff and placed it on top of their conjoined hands.

"Whatever you do, don't move your hand, no matter how much it hurts," he ordered sternly.

Fear filled her. What was this spell that would cause her pain? She supposed it was too late to turn back now. She looked over at her father, who nodded at her, his face composed.

Darius began to utter the spell. A long and complicated ancient spell passed down from the Dragon God himself.

"Custodis cor tuum in manu regis draconis," Darius said in the old language.

As her uncle spoke, his staff began to glow with a bright blue light. She felt a power flow from the staff, to Alex's hand, into hers. The medallion under her fingers became warm to the touch, and then hot, and then burning. Eventually, it felt like her entire hand was on fire, and a searing pain suddenly ripped from the medallion to her hand, up her arm, and then settled deep inside her brain where it twisted like a knife. She cried out in pain, and stumbled, but she managed to keep her hand on the metal. Next to her, the pain twisted up Alex's arm. He grunted as it settled in between his eyes, and the room seemed to shift in front of him.

"It is done," Darius said, throwing his hands in the air. "The words in the ancient tongue mean 'Keep your heart in the Dragon Kings hand.'" He took a step back and looked at the two.

Alex lifted his hand, looking at it suspiciously and flexing his fingers a few times.

Mila picked up her own hand. The heat was gone, but her head felt like it was in a vice. She grasped the table for support. "My head," she said weakly, holding her hand to her temple.

"Yeah, it really hurts," Alex said, closing his eyes against the light.

"It takes an hour or so to adjust," Aswin noted. He moved

forward, rubbing his daughter's back. "Your necklace, dear." He picked up the delicate chain and fastened it gently around her neck. "You can understand dragon language now, and you two are forever bound. Going forward, you will be able to communicate with just your thoughts, if you so desire. You'll be able to hear him, like a whisper in the back of your head. It does take a little getting used to. It's jarring at first. Eventually, you'll learn how to tune each other out."

Jarring was an understatement. "She's in my head," Alex exclaimed, looking at her in horror.

"And you're in mine." She flinched, holding her hands to her ears. "Get out!"

"I promise, you will learn to block each other out. Although a stray thought will slip by now and then," Rand said dryly. He considered Mila and his son. He knew there had been female Dragon Keepers in other lands. Fresthav's Queen had one now. But never in the history of Dumara had the Chuvash Kings had a female Dragon Keeper. The title had always been passed to a male son of the Fletcher line.

Rand thought it would be odd to be in a woman's mind, but that would be Alex's challenge.

Mila's mind was flooded with too many things at once. "Why is she here? She shouldn't be here. My thoughts are my own!" She clearly heard Alex's thoughts pulsing through her own head.

In his own separate hell, Alex was having the same problem. "It hurts. Make it stop! I don't like this!" He clearly heard Mila's complaints in his thoughts.

"Maybe they should rest a moment," Darius said, "In separate rooms. Alex can stay here, and Mila can go upstairs to my room."

"That might be a good idea," Aswin said, looking at his daughter. He took her hand and led her upstairs, where she laid on the settee with her eyes closed.

"Why didn't you tell me?" Mila cried at her father, her face scrunched up in pain and tears dripping from her eyes.

"Would it have changed your decision?" he asked gently.

"No, I guess not," she admitted.

"This will pass. In time you'll forget what it was like to have your mind to yourself," Aswin said, remembering how he had struggled at first. "I'll let you rest."

Downstairs, Alex found a ratty old armchair shoved in the corner. Stacked on top of it was firewood. He removed the logs and sat down, putting his head in his hands. He could clearly hear Mila and her father upstairs like they were in the same room as him. He looked at his father, who was watching him closely.

"So this is how the Dragon Keeper knew where to find Mom and got to her so quickly. You told him you were under attack, didn't you?"

Rand nodded. "This power is special between a Dragon Keeper and the King. I've called Aswin from afar many times. It's a tool that can be used."

"And now we have two Dragon Keepers," Alex said, realizing what an advantage this would give them.

"Yes. It happens occasionally. We hurried Mila along a little bit because you both have a trip to take."

"What? A trip? Where are we going?" Alex asked. He could feel Mila in his head, listening.

Aswin stepped back into the room. "You two will be traveling to Terrak. We need you to contact King Dayia and find out if he knows anything about Fresthav and Murdad working together. It's really just a diplomatic trip, but your father and I can't leave right now, especially with these new developments."

"What developments?" Mila asked in his mind. Alex turned to his father and asked, "What developments?"

"I would like to know why a dragon from Murdad and a dragon from Fresthav were seemingly working together. I would like to see if we are dealing with rogue dragons, or if there is some larger, more nefarious plan. Unfortunately, you know I can't just reach out to King Monserrat of Murdad due to his persistent aggression. And I am hesitant to reach out to Queen Stellen of Fresthav without some answers. She is a little unstable," Rand said, pondering.

"And we will need to have more sentries on our northern borders, which may mean more skirmishes. I can't leave, in case of injury or sickness. It would leave the clan vulnerable. So that's why we needed to speed up Mila's little coming-of-age ceremony. She is now a full Dragon Keeper, bound to you, which means you two can go to Terrak. It should be relatively safe, as long as you stay away from the northern border," Aswin explained.

"If this is my coming of age, I want a cake," Mila said in his head, and Alex smiled.

———

After an hour's rest, Mila felt calmer. She was already feeling better about this. Always having Alex in her head would be difficult, but it was just a matter of attention. She found if she concentrated on something else, like the clock for example, his thoughts faded to the background.

Downstairs, Alex was discovering the same thing, but he found himself fascinated by the female mind. He had never been one to pay much attention to girls, or female dragons, known as drakaina. He now found he wanted to explore her every thought, especially about dragons. But out of respect, he held himself back.

He was thinking about the upcoming trip when Mila's thoughts intruded. "How do you think it's going to be to fly together, now that I can communicate with you?" she asked.

He sensed her exhilaration and chuckled. To him, flying was second nature, but he supposed if he had been born without wings, he would find it pretty fascinating himself.

"It will be nice to be able to tell you not to pull my mane so hard," he said.

"I don't think you'll have to tell me. I think I'll be able to tell."

"True," he thought. He was ready to go. This sorcerer tower was dirty and dingy. They had gotten what they needed.

He stood up and shook his head, his long, golden hair swinging. "We are ready, Father."

"Good, let's go," Rand said, abruptly turning and exiting the room without saying goodbye to Darius. He was just as anxious to leave as his son. This place stunk, literally.

"This is how it is, they come, they get what they want, and then they leave. It's almost as if I'm not a good host or something," Darius smirked at his brother.

"Well, Brother, it's been a fun little reunion. Stop by next time you are in Dumara. You are always welcome."

"Yes," Mila said, emerging from upstairs. "Thank you, Uncle, even though you have given me the worst headache of my life."

He shrugged and looked at his niece fondly. "At least SHE has manners. Takes after her mother, I suppose."

"It wasn't my fault, Darius. She could have picked up dragon fever from anywhere," Aswin insisted sadly.

"I kind of enjoy hating you, Brother. Let's not ruin it by making it nice, hum?"

―――

Alex and Rand were waiting impatiently at the top of the hill. They had both shifted back to their dragon forms.

Mila smiled and touched her new medallion. It glowed warmly at her touch. "Hello," she said shyly, looking at Alex.

"Hello, Dragon Keeper," he said. In her head, his voice sounded the same, but deeper, with a warm grumble.

"Come, my children. We will all talk on the flight home," Rand said as Aswin settled onto his back.

Alex lowered his golden head and smiled as she took her place. She was careful to not pull hard on his golden mane.

"You are learning, Dragon Keeper," Alex growled.

She gave him a squeeze with her legs. It really was much like riding a horse. "Let's go, Alex. This should be fun."

"If it's fun you want, then let's go!" Alex said, spinning to the sky. Mila felt joy welling up into her, then gasped as she felt Alex's same joy at flying. Their connection at this moment was so strong, it took her breath away.

"Feels good, doesn't it? This is so strange," Alex thought as he flapped his huge golden wings into the wind.

His father, with his dark red scales and golden underbelly, watched as the young ones rose into the sky. "Kids," he rumbled to Aswin, leaping into the sky to follow.

The wind was blowing through her hair, and the fall day had turned warm after raining this morning. She could feel Alex shift in the wind as he flew west, and she caught sight of her father and Rand just behind them out of the corner of her eye.

"There are deer down below," Alex said helpfully, tipping to the left slightly. Just down below, she could see a large group of deer racing through a field.

"What, you want to go hunt?" she asked, feeling the medallion grow warm under her fingers.

"I would, if it didn't take so long to stop and eat," he said dipping back to the right and leveling out.

Rand and her father caught up with them. She glanced over at Rand, his red body shimmering in the sun. His wings beat the air gracefully, and her father gave her a little wave.

"You will be leaving in a few days. We will go over plans, but do you two think you will be able to handle it?"

"Yes. I've got this." Alex said, "Besides, I get along well with Kip and Sadie."

"Who are they?" Mila asked.

"The Prince and Princess of Terrak. Both are just a little younger than me. We've always gotten along."

"Yes, but you are going to be trying to convince their father, and he's a different sort. You're going to have to prove to him we need his help, and it's in his best interests. I trust you two will not fail me," Rand said.

"And Mila, you will need to appeal to Tyson," Aswin said. "He's not one for risks. I'm unsure how he will receive you, but you must get him on our side. The Dragon Keeper is just as important as the King in this case."

"Yes, Father," Mila said, wondering if she was ready for such an important task. She was determined to do her best.

They flew on to Dumara. When they arrived over the castle, they circled above, then swooped down so suddenly her stomach jumped. They landed just inside the cave. She slipped off, suddenly exhausted. But they still had work to do. Rand and Alex needed astragenica, and there were the normal rounds to make through the cave to make sure any minor injuries and ills were taken care of. They set to work, and Aswin was glad he now officially had a second set of hands.

It took longer than it should have because every dragon wanted to speak now with Mila. There was a sense of excitement, as the girl they all knew and loved could now talk to them!

"Mila!" A female dragon she called Spice called out to her. "Welcome, Dragon Keeper." She nuzzled her, and Mila laughed.

An old elderly dragon, bright yellow with a mane that had turned white with age was looking at her sharply. "You are the fourth Dragon Keeper I've had the privilege to know. When I was born, it was your great-grandfather William. He was all business, never wanted to chat, or maybe he just didn't have time for inquisitive dragonlings. Your grandfather, Liam, was a musical soul, always signing through the caves. Your father is a friend to everyone. And now you, the first woman of your line. I look forward to knowing you more," he wheezed.

"Thank you, Brightsun," she said, patting him on the flank. "I am happy I can speak to you now."

"You know, Mila, you are the only Dragon Keeper that has named us. It's your little quirk. Only Kings had names before you. We liked it so much, we have adopted the practice, and dragons from other clans have as well. It is a great honor to be given a name by Mila."

Mila was touched. "Well, I'm glad then," she said. She had even given Alex a name. She had called him Ryker, and Nick she had called Quince, which he had loathed. "Nick never liked the name I gave him."

"Well, Nick doesn't like much of anything. Very disagreeable, that Prince, but don't tell him I said that."

"Of course not," Mila laughed. She found her father down the hallway, checking out two newly hatched dragonling twins. They were about five feet long and just born this morning to a dragon named Ginger, who looked over her babies protectively from her nest. "They are healthy and fine. Make sure you feed them well, and they will be full grown by spring," he chuckled. Ginger picked up both dragonlings up by the back of their necks, like a mother cat would, and lowered the babies back into her nest. They were making little shrieking noises.

Mila found them adorable. "Congratulations, Ginger," she said with a smile. "May we collect the eggshells?"

"Of course, Mila. And congratulations to you, new Dragon Keeper. Would you name my younglings?" Ginger asked.

"Of course." She considered the boy, who was orange with red streaks, and the girl, who was yellow with orange streaks.

"The boy we will call Blaze. The girl reminds me of a summer treat, so let's call her Lolly."

"Fine names. Thank you, Dragon Keeper." Ginger nodded her head and rolled over with a mighty heave so the dragonlings could tuck in next to her warm body.

Mila and Aswin departed, as the King and Alex had already gone upstairs. They made their way down the mountain path in the dark. Mila slipped a few times, and her father had to steady her. "We should have brought a lantern; the days are getting short."

"If Alex and I are going to leave soon, we need to start planning and packing right away," Mila said, worry crossing her face.

"We will worry about that tomorrow. It's been a long day. First, we rest," Aswin said, rubbing a hand over his eyes.

They arrived back at the store. Sam was still there. He had stayed late, he wanted to hear of their day.

"I've made you dinner. It's just beans and rice, but I figured you both would be too tired to cook," he said, sitting the still-warm pot on the table for them.

"Bless you, Sam," Mila said wearily. She sat down at the table, which had already been set. Her father sat down, slipped off his jacket, and said a quick grace. Sam took the extra chair and gazed at them both as they dug into the simple meal.

Mila could barely keep her eyes open as her father told Sam about their day, including their meeting with the sorcerer. The entire time, she could hear Alex's thoughts in her head. He had gone back upstairs in the castle and was now eating his own dinner of venison and mashed potatoes. It was extremely distracting to hear two conversations at once.

"Mila, focus," her father said, noticing her glazing over. "I know it can be distracting. Focus on the here and now."

Sam looked at her curiously. She shook her head. "I have a headache, Dad. I've had one all day."

"I know, dear," he said, patting her hand. "Look at me, focus on me."

She looked at him, as he spoke, and it did help. Her father's words became sharper, and Alex faded into the background.

"Sam, Mila is going to be going on a trip for the crown. You are going to have a big task," Aswin said. "I'm going to need you to do even more here. I know you will be up to the task."

"What! Where is Mila going?" Sam asked, looking at her with concern.

"She is going on a diplomatic visit to Terrak with Prince Alex. She is now his Dragon Keeper, and it is only right that they start working together."

"Dragon Keeper? Wow, Mila," Sam said in awe, gazing at her.

"Yeah, but I didn't know what a headache it was going to be," she said, holding her hand to her head.

"VERY FUNNY, MILA," she heard Alex say in her head.

She shook her head and continued on. "Sam, you are going to have to make potions for Father, but you know how to do it, and I'll leave you my notes."

"And you are going to have to man the store, every day. I might need some help in the caves on occasion, and you'll have to come with me. We will just have to close the store on those days, it can't be helped," Aswin said.

"I understand," Sam said, excited to have more responsibilities.

"Sam, since I took you on, you have done a fantastic job. We ask a lot of you, and you are here every day. I always anticipated you stepping into this role when Mila came of age. I hope you will consider staying with us, well, forever."

"I would be honored to work for the Dragon Keepers of Dumara as long as you will have me." Sam's heart was jumping. They had never talked about this being permanent, but Sam had hoped that would be the case. He was starting to dream about a future here, after all.

"That being said, I'm going to offer you a very generous salary. Three hundred notes a week. The shop has been very profitable, but we can't do it without you, Sam. We want you to be a part of this for a very long time."

Sam's head swam. That salary was twice what he made now. Sure, he really was only part-time, and now he would be expected to be here at all hours, but he could afford to move out of his parent's squalid house, and rent or buy a little place and start his own family. Pretty good for the son of an unemployed ex-soldier who was always lost in his cups. "I'll take it, sir, thank you for the opportunity."

"It's my pleasure, Sam," Aswin said. If he had had a son, he would have wanted a boy like Sam.

Chapter 7

Dreams and Schemes

Mila slept poorly that night, tossing and turning in her bed. Her mind filled with not only her own dreams, but those of Alex as well. It was a confusing muddle of grief about his mother mixed with their experience with the sorcerer.

At the castle, Alex got up very early in the morning, after his own restless night of sleep. He lit his fire and sat staring at the flames. He attempted to push Mila's dreams of her father, and of being a new Dragon Keeper, out of his head.

Finally, he sensed that she was awake. "Good morning, Mila," he thought.

"Good morning, Alex," she thought back.

"Since you are up before dawn, do you want to come greet the morning with me?" he thought. He stood up and started getting dressed. He would head downstairs and shapeshift soon.

"I have much to do here this morning. Sam is coming, and we are going to go over some last-minute details. Dad said he would be up this morning."

"Okay. I'll see you later, then," he thought, with a hint of sadness. He rather enjoyed flying with Mila yesterday.

"I liked it too," she thought, picking up on his sadness.

"Eavesdropper," he teased back.

"You were in my dreams all night. Who is the eavesdropper?" she thought.

"You have a point there. This is so difficult," Alex thought, heading out of his room. He was so caught up in his internal conversation, he didn't notice his brother, standing in the dark, looking at him intently.

"Brother," Nick said, putting a hand on his arm.

Alex jumped. "Nick. What are you doing standing out here in the dark like a specter?"

"I wanted to go with you this morning," Nick said, turning and walking with him down the hall.

"Thank you," Alex said, nodding his head. "I wonder if Father will come?"

"I told him last night to sleep in today. He appears strong, but I know his grief is eating him inside," Nick said simply. They opened the door that led downstairs, nodding at a guard who stood sentry. Neither of them bothered with a torch, as their night sight was very good.

"We will take a group. I don't trust the nightfall dragons. It would be just like them to attack again," Alex said.

"I think it's fine. They won't attack again now," Nick said, shrugging.

"I have a lot to do today when we get back. I don't know why Father thinks it's important we go to Terrak, but I worry that they won't listen to Mila and me. We are just messengers from our fathers."

"Well, you are the Crown Prince, and you will be the next King. That has to have some weight," Nick said, getting irritated. He was still mad at their father for not suggesting he also go. He could have seen Sadie.

"I hope so," Alex said.

They entered their family nest and changed quickly. Alex transformed into his golden dragon form. He shook his head and stomped his feet. His brother was taking too long, making sure his clothes were folded just so. Alex nudged him to hurry along.

Finally, Nick transformed into his red dragon body with a golden mane. He roared, cross with his brother for rushing him. "Don't boss me, Alex," Nick growled.

"Come, Nick. Let's go," Alex said. He was already moving out of the caves to the entrance, where a group of six clan dragons roared their greeting and joined them as they took off to meet the sun.

As they flew in formation eastward, they began to feel the power of the morning. Roaring their powerful light blasts into the sky, they encouraged the sun to show itself. Once it did, they circled tightly back west, guiding the sun higher and higher.

"I need to do something," Nick roared to his brother. "I'll meet you back at the castle."

"What? A little morning hunting?" Alex growled back as his wings beat the air next to his brother.

"Don't worry about it, Brother. It is just a small task. More of a moment of meditation really. There is a little place up ahead I like to go to think," Nick said, not looking his brother in the eye.

"Fine," Alex said, glaring at his brother. Just like him to go sneak off somewhere so he could be moody and mysterious. "I'll see you later."

Nick watched his brother and the rest of the clan dragons fly away to the west. He flew in circles until they were out of sight, and then he immediately turned north, flying until the peaks of the Great Divide came into view. He was close to Murdad now, and any dragon would be wise to pay attention.

He flew until Cypress Lake shone below him. It was fed by a mountain river that tumbled over a ledge, it's waterfall splashing with great force into the lake below, before exiting out the Cypress River at the eastern end.

He smiled a toothy smile as he spotted a female summer dragon moving in his direction. She had a deer in her claws. She was dark green, with a black underbelly. Her orange eyes blinked at him as he met her in flight, and they both circled around the lake.

Sadie Dayia, Princess of Terrak, settled on a small island in the middle of the lake. She threw down the deer carcass and blasted it fiercely with a long flame of fire. Summer dragons had heat and fire as their power.

He landed next to her, taking a powerful stance. He nuzzled her affectionately with his nose, and licked her neck, which amounted to dragon kisses.

"My love," she growled softly, blinking her orange blazing eyes at him. She licked him back and entwined his neck with hers.

"I've missed you, Sadie," he said breathlessly, his claws raking her gently.

"And I you," she said, bowing her head. "I brought us breakfast, for after."

"Thank you, my love," he said as she dipped her head submissively to him. He roared with lust and nuzzled her neck roughly.

After, they shared the deer, lounging for a few moments in blissful silence as they ripped it apart with their teeth.

"My mother is dead," Nick said sadly. "It was supposed to be my brother, but she went that morning instead."

"I heard the news. Our diplomat attended the funeral," Sadie Dayia said.

"An unfortunate causality. My heart is sad," Nick said, a few tears dripping from his dragon eyes.

"How does this impact our plan?" she whispered. She moved closer, so she could feel his warmth.

"It's not good. I wanted my brother out of the way, without throwing suspicion on me. I will be King. The power will be mine. You and I will rule the east, and our child will ascend to Emperor."

"Father has been bothering me to pick a summer dragon as a mate. I told him I was not interested."

"You are mine!" Nick roared.

"Well, maybe you should ask for my hand," Sadie said, turning her back on him.

He growled and spit out a bone. "There have never been dragons from two different clans that have taken each other as mates. But if we can achieve it, then our children may have both fire and light, and we will be able to conquer the lands of Murdad and Fresthav. We will wipe their evil from the lands, and every day will be light and warm."

"Soon, my love. But you know, these things can take some time," Sadie said.

"I have to handle Murdad very carefully. They only know me as the traitor. They think I work for them, but I only work for myself."

"Well, you work for us, right my love?" she purred.

"Yes. For us. Tell me again how you love me," he demanded.

"You are my mate. For now, it's a secret, but it will soon be known to all," she said, rising to her feet.

"Soon, my love. When can I see you again?" he asked, rubbing up against her green scales.

"The sooner the better."

"As you wish. My brother is going to be visiting your father soon. I wasn't invited, but maybe I can follow him and make a surprise entrance. He's bringing our new Dragon Keeper, Mila Fletcher. You can play her easily. She is stupid and naive. She will believe anything you say."

"I will befriend her. It may prove useful later. I already have our Dragon Keeper under my spell," Sadie said. She picked up the scraps of the deer and threw them into the lake, where the local sea serpent would enjoy the leftovers. The serpent kept the humans away from this island.

Chapter 8

Connections

Sam carefully packed Mila's bag. He made sure she had extra bottles, all the herbs and ingredients she could need, and two tins of dragon balm. She ran down the stairs with her own small bag, packed with everything she would need for the trip.

Even though she had spent the week planning with her father, it seemed like there just hadn't been time to pack, so now she was rushing around at the last minute to get everything together. They would be leaving this morning. "Sam, thank you so much." She gave him a rare smile.

"I've barely seen you, Mila. You've been so busy," Sam said sadly.

"I know. I'm sorry, Sam. Everything's fallen on you. Thank you," Mila said fondly. She sat down at the counter. "Tell me, how did the picnic go with Kiara?"

"It was great," Sam said with a smile.

"Great? That's it? Come on, Sam. Spill the beans. I'll get it out of Kiara anyway."

Sam blushed. "If you must know, we are going to keep seeing each other. She's very nice."

"That she is, Sam. Well, I'd best be off. Duty calls. Dad is already at the castle this morning."

"I'll be here, as always." Sam sighed and watched the girl he loved slip out of the shop and down the street. His face brightened again with the bells on the door tinkled back open.

"Kiara!" Sam said, delighted to see her.

"Hi, Sam," Kiara said shyly. "I was wondering if you wanted to go for a walk after work today? It should be a nice fall day."

"Of course, Kiara. I don't know what time Mr. Fletcher will be back, but as soon as he gets home, I'll come across the street and we can go for a stroll up merchants' row."

Mila walked up the streets, swinging her bags. The streets were busy today, with farmers flooding into Dumara with their fall crops to sell in the markets. Some of the wheat would be stored, but much of it would be sent on to other kingdoms, loaded into the boats and shipped off to Norda and Fresthav.

"The streets are busy today," she thought to Alex.

"Really?" he asked. He was down in the caves with his father, and this morning, when he had greeted the sun, he had seen many wagons on the roads, headed to the city of Dumara.

"Farmers are in with the fall crops. Looks like it was a bountiful year," Mila thought.

"Your father is here. We are going over our plan. Will you be here soon?"

"Yes, just a few minutes. Are you still all in the caves?"

"Yes. I didn't bother to change, as we are going to be leaving soon."

"I'll come up the cliff paths then, it's a little quicker," Mila thought. She turned down the street, barely missing getting run over by a draft horse pulling a wagon loaded with potatoes.

"Pay attention, lady!" the farmer yelled at her, snapping his whip over his horse's head.

"Sorry, sorry," she said, giving him an apologetic wave.

"Careful, Mila!" Alex thought in exasperation.

Soon, she was climbing up the trail. It was easier now, she had done this every day since becoming a Dragon Keeper, and her body was getting used to the climb.

Soon, she reached the top, and she was surprised to find Nick waiting for her at the entrance. He was in human form, and he leaned against the rock wall with a scowl on his face. "Mila," he said sourly, "glad you could finally make it."

"I had to pack!" she protested.

"Yeah, whatever. I wanted to talk to you before you left. Alone."

Suddenly, she was curious. "What is it?"

Nick looked around, as if he was afraid someone had followed her up the cliff. "Not a word of this to anyone."

"Uhhh, okay." She realized that Nick didn't know about the mental connection that she and Alex shared. She almost said something, and then figured that it was a secret for a reason.

"I'm talking to your brother. Are you listening?" she thought to Alex.

"Yes. I didn't know where he had gone. I wonder what he wants," Alex mused in her thoughts.

"Listen, Mila. You and Alex are going to Terrak. I wanted to let you know something that may come in handy in your negotiations, and I need your help."

She looked at him in concern. "Of course, Nick. But what could be so important that you would tell me, and not your father, the King?"

"It's love, Mila. He wouldn't understand. You're a woman, you can certainly understand love."

"Love? I've never known love, Nick. I don't know if I'm the right person to talk to about this. I've pretty much sworn off ever getting married."

"Listen, I need your help. The King's daughter, Sadie, and I are in love. But neither of our fathers would approve. I want you to suggest to my father that an arranged marriage between us two would be beneficial for both kingdoms. My father has been pushing my brother and me to pick a mate. I want to be with my true love, but if I suggest it, it will be dismissed outright. Will you help me?" he pleaded.

Mila's head was spinning. She could feel Alex's anger. She reached out to him, "You're listening to this, right?"

"I can't believe my brother. That's where he has been going when he sneaks off!"

"What do I tell him?" Mila asked Alex.

"I don't know, I've got to think about this. This is crazy," Alex said. "Just tell him you will see how they respond to our initial proposal. My father will hate this idea, along with Aswin, which is why he is trying to go through you. He's taking advantage of your inexperience."

Mila considered Nick. He looked so sad, and his blue eyes pleaded with her for help. "I don't know, Nick. I just became a Dragon Keeper, and I don't know if I have much pull in all of this. I'll have to see how they react to a proposal of an alliance."

"That's all I ask. I had planned to go to my father, but frankly, he has a lot on his mind lately. I don't want to burden him with affairs of my heart," Nick said, following her closely as they moved through the lower caves. He was walking uncomfortably close to her, and she didn't feel quite safe. She felt like he was threatening her with his presence.

Meanwhile, Alex was cursing out his brother in his mind, and of course, Mila had a front row seat. When they arrived at the Chuvash nest, King Rand and Aswin were there, along with

Alex, who turned his dragon head and looked at his brother as they approached.

"We've gone over the plan. You should get a good reception from King Dayia at least. I don't know if he's going to want to help, to be honest, but he's always been friendly," King Rand said.

"I have an idea," Mila said. Nick looked at her in alarm. "What if you suggest an arranged marriage?"

Rand laughed, slapping his leg in mirth. "This one here doesn't seem to be interested in marriage," he said pointing at Alex. "Besides, it's never been done. I don't know if it's even possible …," he said, thinking hard. "Although, I have heard legends of half-breed dragons. In the stories, the Dragon God is always angry, and he smites down the sinners."

"No, Father, me!" Nick said in exasperation. This girl couldn't even do this right. He should have realized telling her would go wrong. He would have to remember she wasn't good for anything. He silently glared at Mila. This is not how he expected this conversation to go. He had hoped for her help, but not like this. Now his business was getting pushed into the open.

Rand stopped and looked at his son, his mouth hanging open in shock. "You would marry a summer dragon? Sadie Dayia?"

"Why not? If it will help us, I would. Besides, Sadie and I get along fine on the times she has visited our kingdom with her family."

"Or perhaps you've been sneaking away to see her?" Alex roared.

Nick turned and blinked at his brother. "Well, I admit it. We have met a few times, when I was hunting on the eastern border. It was a matter of accident at first, she was hunting in the area, as was I. A friendship has grown between us, one could say, a very good friendship. I consider her a friend, and frankly, I like her better than any drakaina here in our caves."

"Oh, Nick," Rand said, shaking his head. "This is a terrible idea."

"Why? If we had children, they would have both light and fire. It would only make our two kingdoms stronger and cement our strength."

"In his writings, the Dragon God explicitly says, 'The Dragons are to rule their lands and their clans, they shall keep to themselves, and not intermingle their lines.'"

"It's just historical writings, Father. Come on, do you really believe the ramblings of fourth century monks?" Nick sneered.

"We will see. I'm not sold on your idea, Nick. You can find a mate here, and we won't have to worry about angering our God," Rand said, shaking his head.

"Pssst. Just old stories. I don't believe in the Dragon God. He's nothing more than an origin story."

Just then, the earth started trembling. It was minor at first, but soon, the floor was visibly rocking. Somewhere deep in the caves, rocks crashed.

"Earthquake!" Rand roared. Soon though, the floor stopped shaking. They all looked at each other in disbelief.

"That was a sure sign from the Dragon God, Nick. You do not know the powers you are messing with," Aswin said, looking alarmed.

Nick rolled his eyes. "It was a coincidence, nothing more."

"Aswin and I will go and make sure no dragons were hurt when those rocks fell. You two, fly fast, and try to avoid the northern border. If you spy any nightfall dragons, turn south immediately with great haste. They shouldn't chase you too far into our territory," Rand said.

They made their way to the exit, and Alex stood at the edge while Mila secured the bags and her dragon keeper's case. He was wearing a belt that went around the middle of him, from which she could attach their bags. She clamored up on him, settling in as he stepped to the edge.

"I'm a little heavy with all this luggage," Alex complained. "I won't be able to fly as fast."

"Sorry, I tried to pack light," Mila said to him.

He dropped off the edge without warning, and Mila grabbed his golden mane as he took flight. Alex's golden scales glinted in the sun as he fell straight down, gaining tremendous speed until he spread his wings and leveled out. Then, with a chuckle at Mila's reaction, he turned due east.

"I can't believe my brother. I bet he's been having an affair with Sadie. They aren't just friends. He has an ulterior motive."

"It's so weird that he was waiting for me at the entrance. He doesn't know about our mental connection, does he?"

"No. He doesn't. Just like your father, my father never told us of it. It's a handy little trick to have, I suppose."

"Alex, when we reach the tower, can we stop at my uncle's?" Mila asked.

"Sure. Why?"

"I need to talk to him about my mother. I couldn't do it in front of my father. I need to know some things."

When they arrived at the sorcerer's tower, Darius was standing on his hill, waiting for them. He wore a scowl, but his face softened when he saw Mila.

"Mila. Is everything okay?" he asked with concern, gripping his staff tightly. He seemed surprised that it was only her.

"Yes, Uncle. I wanted to stop and say hello. I'm sorry I couldn't tell you in advance."

"No, problem. Uhhh, do you want to come inside?" he asked, glancing at Alex.

"I'll stay here. No sense in changing for just a few minutes of chat with your uncle. Besides, his tower is a dump," Alex thought to her.

"You know, I can understand dragon. It's a little perk of the job," Darius said, grinning at Alex.

Mila gave an awkward laugh, "He'll stay outside, but I would love to talk to you for a few minutes." Mila slid off Alex's broad back.

"Well, I can't say I usually like unexpected guests, but you are an exception. Come, my dear," he said, leading her to his tower. "We will have some tea. Tell me, how are you adjusting to being a Dragon Keeper, with the mental link and all that?" They went inside, and he pulled out a simple wooden chair for her at his small table. He took a kettle of hot water off his stove and poured some into a smaller tea pot. "I think you will like this. Astra tea. Very rare." He smiled and smelled the steam, taking in the fragrant vapor.

"Thank you, Uncle," she said, picking up her mug and blowing into it. "It smells amazing. I didn't know you could make astra tea."

"Yes. Although with the price of astra petals, it is very rare and costly. I happen to have a cave nearby where they grow. It's by Cypress Lake. Beautiful place."

"I didn't really come here for your tea." Mila said, blowing on the tea and turning the cup in her hands nervously.

"And how are you feeling?" Darius gave her a knowing smile.

"I'm adjusting well. Alex is listening now, of course. He says that using astra flowers for tea is a horrible waste," she giggled.

"And your headaches are gone?" he asked, with concern on his face. "I'm sorry you had no warning. The connection between keeper and King is a secret that's been kept for generations."

"The headaches are all gone," she said with a smile. "And I understand why it's a secret. It can be a powerful tool, can't it?"

"Yes. A very powerful tool. They are full of secrets, those Kings. And they can be quite vicious. I suppose it's their nature."

Mila closed her eyes for a moment and smiled. She nodded

and then looked at Darius. "Alex says he's never hurt you or anyone else for that matter, and he considers that slander, but he means it in a humorous way."

A little smile turned the corner of Darius's mouth. "So everything is going well. What else brought you here today?"

"We are headed to Terrak, on a diplomatic mission. But I knew we would be flying by here, so I wanted to stop and talk to you, alone. I don't have any other family, and as you know, you haven't really been around much since I was little."

"Your father and I had a deep disagreement. But that is not your fault, dear. I'm sorry I'm a terrible uncle. No presents at midwinter, no cards at your birthday. I've never been good with that kind of thing. It's probably for the best I never married and had kids."

"Can sorcerers get married and have kids?" she wondered aloud, looking around his messy kitchen.

"Yes. Why not? It's not like I take an oath or anything. I've only ever loved one person in my life, and your father stole her from me," he said bitterly, looking at Mila.

"Oh," she said softly, feeling sad for her uncle. "I'm sorry that happened."

"You had nothing to do with it. Although you do look so much like your mother it hurts me." He sighed and took another sip of his tea.

"If it's any consolation, my father loved my mother very much. He still grieves for her," Mila said sadly, remembering how downhearted he had seemed the day of the Queen's funeral.

"Well, I should just let it go. It's been a long time since she's been gone. We were childhood sweethearts, your mother and I. We did everything together. She was the first girl I kissed on the playground at school. But then we grew up, and she only had eyes for Aswin. Funny story, Mila, your mother is partially the reason I became a sorcerer."

"Really? I've never heard what happened. You grew up in town, right? In the same place I live now."

"Oh yes. Above the store. Aswin and I shared what is probably your room now. He always was going to be the Dragon Keeper, follow in pop's footsteps and all that. I was supposed to run the store, which was fine by me. Mother did it when I was little, and I helped out. That's how I learned how to make my first potions, of course."

"Oh, that makes sense. I wondered what Grandpa Liam did about the store. It's so much work. We hired a local boy, named Sam, to help us now."

"Well, Leah fell in love with Aswin. I grew bitter, and we fought. I decided that if I could just make a love potion, and slip it to her, she would remember that she loved me first. Ridiculous really. I see now how stupid my plan was. It ended very badly, but you'll see that soon. I had met the old sorcerer before, he had come to the shop a few times. I knew he lived out here, so I borrowed a horse from the livery and rode out here and met Erza. He was ancient then. He lived to be one hundred and three, but he was in his nineties at the time, hunched over and bent. But his mind was still sharp."

"He lived out here all alone?" Mila asked, looking around the place. Some of the furniture did look quite old, and she thought Erza probably had been a bit of a mess himself.

"Yes, he had never married. Being a sorcerer out here is a lonely life. Not a lot of eligible ladies around, if you know what I mean."

"I guess I can see that," Mila chuckled, pouring herself another mug of tea. It really was quite nice, and it left her feeling warm and comfortable.

"I asked him to teach me how to make a love potion, and he refused, saying that nothing good ever came out of love, and that love was a foolish notion." Darius sighed again, and played with his spoon, spinning it in his long fingers.

"I don't think it's foolish," Mila quipped. "But maybe trying to make someone love you who doesn't love you back is." She thought of Sam, and how he annoyingly wouldn't get the point.

"Well, he made me a deal, and I took it. Again, dumb on my part. Never make a deal with a sorcerer."

"What did you agree to?" Mila asked, curious. This was a good story.

"He told me he would teach me to make a love potion, but that if it didn't work, I had to leave Dumara and become his apprentice."

Mila laughed until her sides hurt. "Oh dear. That does seem like a bad deal. I guess you lost then?"

"I lost, spectacularly. I made the love potion and gave it to Leah in some astra tea. She fell in love with me, forgetting Aswin. Of course, he didn't understand what was going on. He was heartbroken for an entire week. Leah was mine, and she slept with me. I asked her to marry me, and she agreed. I was so over the moon happy."

"And then the potion wore off," Mila surmised. "And I bet that went poorly."

"It did wear off, seven days later. She was furious with me, she threw things at me, she called me names and told me she never wanted to see me again. Of course, she gave me back the engagement ring I had given her. She went back to Aswin, and told him what had happened, and begged him to take her back."

"Oh dear. I can't imagine my father was happy with you."

"No. We actually got in a physical fight. He beat me to pulp and might have actually killed me with his own two hands, if not for our father. He broke it up, physically getting between us. He told me he was disappointed in me, that I had done an evil thing, and that I was no longer welcome in his home."

"And then you became the sorcerer," Mila said, thinking that drugging her mother and forcing her to love him had been a terrible thing. Her uncle probably did deserve to be thrown out of town.

"I did. I came to Erza with my tail between my legs. He took me as his apprentice, and the rest is history, so they say."

Mila and her uncle continued to chat. He found that she was smart and well-educated.

"Mila!" The note of alarm in her head caused her to startle. "We need to go! I see nightfall dragons on the horizon!"

"Uncle, I must go. You have more unexpected guests," she said, jumping up. She ran over and gave him a quick hug and a peck on the cheek.

He stared off into the distance. "I do. Nightfall dragons. Well, you had better leave now. I would hate to have a dragon battle in my front yard."

She sprinted across the yard, watching the nightfall dragons, black and purple shapes, clearly approaching from the distance. She swung onto Alex's back in one swift move, and he leapt into the air. She quickly waved at her uncle and then bent over Alex's neck, holding tightly onto his mane and neck as he beat his wings furiously, heading due south.

Mila threw a quick glance over her shoulder, and she could see four dark nightfall dragons getting closer. "Four dragons, Alex! Do you think they are going to visit my uncle? What could they want?"

"I don't know. Keep an eye on them, I'm just trying to put some distance between us. They have probably been flying a while, and I'm fresh, so I don't think they will catch us. Good thing you had that good long talk with your uncle."

"Sorry, we got to talking and …," she said, feeling guilty.

"No worries," he said shortly. He was going as fast as he could, and he had caught a tail wind.

She turned again to see where the nightfall dragons were. She could see them circling over the sorcerer tower. "I think we are good. They are landing. I guess they really did want to see my uncle."

"Oh, thank goodness. Four against one isn't a fair fight," Alex said.

"Hey, don't I count?" Mila asked, crossly.

"Do you have a weapon?" he grumbled.

"No. I guess I don't. I could chuck things at them though," she added helpfully.

"Mila," Alex said, shaking his head. "Maybe we should get you a weapon. Do you know any archery?"

"No, I can't say I do," she admitted sheepishly.

"And some training," he added, with a chuckle. He made a course adjustment, and soon they crossed the river that separated Dumara from Terrak. They were now in relatively friendly territory.

Chapter 9

Visits

Kai Monserrat, nightfall dragon and Crown Prince of the Kingdom of Murdad, flew over the mountains that separated them from their nemeses, the sunrise dragons in the Kingdom of Dumara.

He glanced with his yellow eyes down below and saw mountain goats frolicking on the steep, snow-dusted slopes, which reminded him that he was hungry.

He turned to snatch one with his razor sharp claws, but Doyle, his kingdom's Dragon Keeper, smacked him on the neck. "Not now, Kai! Can't you think of anything but eating?"

"Hit me again, old man, and I'll dump you off and leave you on a mountain top," Kai hissed.

Doyle laughed, knowing that the young Prince would do no such thing. It was cold, and Doyle wrapped himself tightly in his dark purple robe. With his robe on, he was effectively camouflaged on the back of most nightfall dragons, who tended to have dark purple scales. Some of the females were a light lavender color.

"Where is this sorcerer? I see no tower," Kai grumbled as

they reached the border to the Kingdom of Dumara. The land below was so unlike the bare and dead landscape of Murdad. Below his purple wings, the peaceful woodland forests of north Dumara stretched green into the distance. Farther south, he could make out farmland dotted with small holdings, barns, and the King's Road, which ran along to the east and west.

"He is just a little farther south, at the edge of this forest. If you think I'm grumpy, wait until you meet Darius. Be respectful, Kai. He is the sorcerer of the land, and we need his assistance. Make him mad, and we will get nothing done your father sent us here to accomplish."

"My father, sending me as his errand boy. He should have just come himself," Kai hissed. He spotted a tower in the distance.

"It's time you meet the sorcerer. Besides, he has an important meeting with Fresthav he cannot miss."

"Doyle! Look there, it's a sunrise dragon, taking off! Should we give chase?" Kai spotted the golden dragon leaping in the air.

"No, there is no need to instigate the Chuvashes more than we already have. But it is very curious. If I'm not mistaken, that must be young Mila Fletcher on his back. I think that may be Alex Chuvash. I wonder ...," he mused, watching the dragon streak south. Alex and Mila were flying fast. They must have spotted the nightfall dragons and cut their visit short. He wondered what the two had been speaking to Darius about. Perhaps she was already a Dragon Keeper? Very curious indeed.

Kai turned to begin his descent, and they spiraled down, landing with a gentle thump at the bottom of a slight hill that led to the tower. Darius stood, both hands on his smooth, ash staff, looking at them in distaste.

"Well, my old friend, it's good to see you again too," Doyle chuckled, swinging down off Kai with more grace than one would expect from a man in his eighties.

"What do you want today, Doyle? Another potion of life? Still no heir I assume?" Darius asked sarcastically. He was very annoyed at having two visitors today. He hadn't worked this hard in he didn't know how long. He enjoyed his little visit with Mila, but he could have left it at that. Besides, the nightfall dragons always wanted something highly complicated and risky.

"You've got me pegged, as always, Darius. Let me get Kai here turned, and then we will all talk," Doyle said, dropping his bag. He started rummaging through it, all the various potions and herbs a Dragon Keeper would need, plus a few extra little surprises he kept up his sleeve. He pulled out a flask of astragenica and turned to Kai.

Kai held his mouth open, and Doyle touched his medallion. His was made of a dark iron, and it had the image of a dragon in full flight in front of a moon. "Good boy! Just like that!" he said rudely, dumping the flask as quickly as possible into Kai's maw.

Kai threw his head back quickly, the dark scales under his chin showing, his dark mane flipping back. As soon as the astragenica was down his throat, he felt the burn begin. He hated this part, slipping back into his human form. He rarely did it, except when he needed to address a human for some reason. He preferred to stay in his nest, alone, which was tunneled into the volcano, at the base of which their castle lay.

His legs and arms shortened, his claws receded, his body shrank rapidly, and his spine groaned in agony as it compressed. He stood on his hind legs and finished transforming. Soon, he stood, in his human form, nearly seven feet tall, rippling with muscles. His eyes remained yellow, and he blinked as he pushed his long black hair behind his broad shoulders. Doyle handed him a simple linen shift out of his bag, and he slipped it on and tied it at the waist. He did not plan to stay in this form very long, and he never cared much for human clothes. He found them scratchy and just as awkward as his body.

Darius sighed and invited his second group of guests inside. Once inside, Doyle noted that the table was still set for tea.

"Did I interrupt your little tea party, Darius?" Doyle asked, dripping sarcasm.

"My niece was visiting. She thought it prudent to leave when you approached," Darius said, picking up the dirty cup, and then setting out two clean ones for his guests. He poured more tea, and then found another chair, shoved in the corner.

Kai looked around the tower kitchen with disgust. "You live like a pig."

"Didn't anyone teach you not to comment on other people's homes? I'm not royalty, you know. I don't have a slew of servants catering to my every whim. In fact, I'm quite busy. You know, a constant stream of Dragon Kings wanting this and that and the other. Now, what do you want so I can get on with my very busy day?" Darius asked, his voice dripping with sarcasm. The best thing about being an all-powerful sorcerer is that you could talk back a little bit, at least to the young Crown Princes.

Kai had it in him to at least look slightly abashed. He cleared his throat and stared at the floor, not knowing what to say.

Doyle chuckled. Kai was hotheaded and rude. He was glad Darius had put him in his place. "Well, I do need that potion, Darius. And before you ask, no, I still don't have a successor."

Darius rolled his eyes. He stood up and went over to the corner, where he had a small cauldron and a few bottles of a blue liquid. He picked up two of them and then placed them on the table. "Same price as always."

"Here is your payment," Doyle said, thumping a bag of gold on the table. "I don't plan on dying. I can live indefinitely with these potions. I don't feel a day over thirty."

"As always, I warn you, that potion has risks as well as rewards. You really should think of taking an apprentice. What if you finally kick the bucket? Not that I care, but we can't have a repeat of the Fresthav incident," Darius said his brown eyes narrowing.

"Queen Stellen shouldn't have eaten her Dragon Keeper.

Then, she wouldn't have been without one. Although the new female Dragon Keeper, Gayle, is quite a handful," Kai said.

Darius didn't respond, but his mouth twitched and his eyes sparkled "Anyway, enough gossip. What else do you need from me today?"

"I want you to make me noctum," Kai said with a slight smirk. "I have something you might want." He took a fist-sized deep purple stone out of his pocket and placed it on the table. It was rough, and it still had dirt on it from where it had been pulled from the ground.

"Is that a veta stone?" Darius put down his spoon and picked up the rock. "An uncut veta stone! Humm, very interesting. I've never seen one this big." He smiled and put the stone in his pocket. He looked at Kai intently. "I'll do it. But why do you want noctum?"

"All you need to know is that I need it. Perhaps I have a hard time sleeping at night. Perhaps I desire to see visions of the future. Perhaps I want to poison my enemies. Perhaps I desire all of the above. But what I do with it is none of your concern, sorcerer. Remember, you serve the Dragon Kings. All of them. If I ask you for noctum, I expect you to deliver, or there will be consequences."

With a sigh, Darius stood up. "I have none in stock. It will take me a few hours to brew. Go outside and do something else for a while. Get out of my tower. I would rather keep my secrets to myself, thank you."

"As you wish," Doyle said, standing up. He looked at Kai hard. He frowned and stood up. They strode out of the kitchen.

For the next several hours, Kai paced back and forth outside the tower, impatient, waiting.

Doyle sat in the shade under a tree. He knew that Darius wouldn't ask too many questions, as a veta stone of that size was quite the treasure. King Ibis Monserrat's throne was set with a dozen of the smaller stones. Veta stones were said to increase a dragon's power, and they were only found in the volcanic mountain of Murdad. Most nightfall dragons wore at least one or two somewhere on their bodies, usually around their ankles as a type of cuff. But most veta stones were the size of pebbles. It truly was a great treasure the sorcerer had been given, and Doyle wasn't sure it had been a smart move to give an already powerful sorcerer a stone that would only amplify his power.

While he pondered the veta stone, Doyle fingered the potion in his pocket. His potion of life. He would take it tomorrow, alone in his chambers. The side effects would incapacitate him for a day, but by the next, he would feel young again. He was nearing his eighty-fifth year of life, and he had no plans to retire anytime soon.

Inside his tower, Darius placed the veta stone on his shelf. The stone, for certain, would be his next project. He would polish and shape the stone, and put it in his collection of smaller veta stones he had inherited from his master, Erza. The stones amplified his power greatly, and he often used them when doing difficult spells. With this stone, he thought, those difficult spells would become much easier. He was excited about the prospects. Who really cared what Kai Monserrat did with this noctum potion? If he wanted to see visions, or sleep better, what did Darius care? Although Darius suspected, due to the gift of the priceless veta stone, the Prince might have more nefarious purposes. Well, what was Darius to do? Kai was right, he was the sorcerer for all the Dragon Kings. The nightfall dragons could destroy him easily, if they wanted. He should play no favorites.

He gathered the ingredients. Nightshade, valerian root, passionflower, root of poppy, and the venom of the poisonous stoor worm. He put the ingredients in his large mortar, and then ground and ground until his arms ached. He was left with a fine, black powder. He took the powder and put it in his copper cauldron, along with the dried, mummified body of a moon spider and a half cup of water. He brought the potion to a simmer, being careful not to inhale any of the vapor.

He took the mixture off the flames and considered the concoction. Years ago, as part of his sorcerer training, he had taken just two drops of the liquid on his tongue. He'd had the most powerful visions of his life, and afterwards, he had slept for nearly three days straight.

While the potion cooled, Darius looked out of the window. Doyle rested in the shade of his apple tree, and Kai paced restlessly. Darius began having second thoughts about delivering this potion. Kai was slightly unstable, and his father, King Ibis, was an evil and villainous worm. He enslaved the humans of Murdad, and he ruled his kingdom with an iron fist. On the few occasions they had met, Ibis had sent shivers down Darius' spine. The man wanted to rule the world and become emperor of the dragon kind.

Darius glanced again at the veta stone and then shook his troubled thoughts away.

Once the potion cooled, it turned a deep black color. Darius took a funnel and a clean glass bottle and carefully poured the liquid into it, making sure to spill no drops on his skin. He didn't want to die today. A few drops would give you visions, but more than that would kill you. He stoppered it tightly and tucked it in his pocket.

He poured fresh water in his copper cauldron, and then he brought it back to a boil to clean the pot. He dropped the funnel, his mortar and pestle, and the spoon he had used to stir the concoction in the boiling water. He added a bit of the root of the soap plant and left it to soak.

He headed downstairs and stepped out through his heavy wooden door. He walked over to Kai and handed him the potion. "As you ordered. Keep in mind, this is very poisonous. One drop will help you sleep, but you will have strange dreams. Two drops will give you powerful visions, and you may sleep for days. Any more than that will possibly kill a person. Use it very carefully. I am not responsible for any accidents," Darius said firmly.

"Thank you, sorcerer. I trust you will not mention this to any other Dragon Kings who happen to visit you. I demand your silence on this matter," Kai said, holding up the bottle and looking at its black contents with a smile. He handed it off to Doyle, who, with a sigh, rose from where he had been sitting under the apple tree and tucked it in his Dragon Keepers bag.

"You have my word," Darius said with a nod.

"Goodbye, sorcerer. Thank you," Kai said. He took off the robe, and he began to change in front of Darius's eyes. Darius took a step back as Kai began to swell and lengthen, turning deep purple in his dragon form. Kai dipped his head, his black mane blowing in the breeze. His bright yellow eyes glared at Doyle.

"Let's make haste for the border. We can meet the clan to the east and greet the night before delivering the noctum to your father," Doyle said, touching his dark medallion.

Darius lifted his arm to wave goodbye, but they were already off, Kai's purple scales shining so brightly in the afternoon light. "Well, that was a day wasted," he thought, heading back upstairs to his workshop. He considered his brand new veta stone with a smile. He could perhaps set it into his staff. He couldn't wait to test out some of his spells with it. He then turned to the still steaming pot of cleaned instruments. He had an idea. There still should be some noctum residue in this water. He picked up the bowl and, with a shrug, took a sip.

The power of the noctum residue left in the bowl hit him immediately. He found himself sinking to his knees, his eyes glazing over. The visions started to flash in front of his eyes, of the past, the present, and the future.

As the future began to play in front of his eyes, he saw a bright figure sinking to the ground in front of him. It was too bright to look at, and he was blinded. The light exploded around him, and he saw the end of the world. In the void, a voice spoke to him, "You have put the pieces in motion. Everything will be undone. The Dragon God will return." One boom of a drumbeat exploded in his head, shattering his vision into pieces that dissolved into rainbows.

"Oh no. What have I done?" This was his final thought before the darkness descended.

Chapter 10

Terrak

It was cold up on Alex's back. Mila thought maybe she should have dressed warmer.

They were up so high that they were above the clouds. Every once in a while, Alex would come upon a flock of birds, and they would become alarmed, squawking like crazy and breaking up their flock in two as he powered through them.

"You're cold," he said softly, sensing her discomfort. "It can be chilly up at these heights."

"It's very cold," she said. Her hands felt numb, and she tucked them further into his mane.

"I think we are out of danger. I was sort of using the clouds to hide, and it's easier to fly up this high with the tailwind," he said. He dived abruptly, and Mila giggled as her stomach dropped suddenly.

"You didn't have to go lower just for me," she said. The air was warmer here, below the clouds, and she could see the land of Terrak below her. In the distance, the four towers surrounded a deep crater, with a castle right in the middle. A tall wall surrounded the crater, and a few green summer dragons circled the towers.

"You're my partner, Mila. We have to work together if we want to succeed. I am a dragon, you are human. I think it's going to take us a bit to figure this all out."

"Yes. Tell me, Alex, why don't you and your brother get along?" Mila asked.

He chuckled, and the deep sound reverberated through his body. "Nick only cares about himself. He is very jealous of me, and although he has never said anything, he wishes he was Crown Prince. He thinks I am not as smart as him, not as good a hunter. He thinks he is a natural leader. My father probably favors me, although he has never said as much."

"I remember when you two were little, always fighting," Mila said.

"Yeah, nothing really has changed, and now my mother is gone. She used to make us get along. If we fought, we were both in trouble. Father doesn't want to deal with it."

"What do you think of my uncle?" Mila asked. The castle of Terrak was still so far away, the plains underneath them filled with herds of cattle and ranchlands. Terrak was known for its ranching and textiles.

"I think your uncle is dangerous. Darius has always been somewhat difficult. The fact that he seems to like you could be a powerful tool," Alex said carefully, thinking about his past interactions with the man.

"It's sad, but I can't say I approve of his story about my mother. She didn't love him, and yet he forced himself on her."

"Well, look where it got him. Living alone in that dump of a tower. He didn't have to make the choices he did, Mila. That's all on him."

"Do you have anyone you care about?" Mila asked. This whole concept of love was so foreign to her. Of course, she loved her father, but she couldn't imagine meeting a man she wanted to bind herself to.

"No. It vexes my father. He would like it if I would pick a mate. I know it's important, securing the future and all that rubbish, but honestly, I just have never met another dragon that I connect with. They are all rather basic. They just worry about hunting and caring for the clan. I need to meet someone who will be my equal. What about you, Mila? I already know you don't like that Sam boy your father hired," he chuckled again, dipping down even lower. The castle only looked slightly closer, but now Mila could see a group of green summer dragons headed their way.

"No, Alex. I'm dedicated to being a Dragon Keeper. *Your* Keeper. I've never had time to meet anyone, and the townspeople don't understand me anyway. Even Sam doesn't get it. I'm going to be forever alone," she said sadly.

"Mila, you have me," he said softly. "We can be alone together, forever."

She was quiet when he said this, and he wondered if he had insulted her.

"Alex! Those dragons headed toward us, are they a threat?" she said, concerned. The dragons were moving fast, and they would soon be upon them.

"I'm going to land, and we will talk. They shouldn't see me as a threat. I'm not here with a big group, and we have always gotten along with the summer dragons." He scanned the ground below, looking for a good spot to land. He spied a large hill with a flat top. It was perfect. There would be no humans around, and there was plenty of room for them all to land.

He flared his wings, bringing his legs down, his claws reaching for the dirt. He landed with a soft thump and folded his wings carefully. "Stay here, Mila. Don't say anything unless they address you. I don't expect any problems, though."

She placed her hand on her medallion as the green dragons

began circling. Evergreen, fern, kelly, mint, jade, lime, and emerald shades whirled above. They were so close she could feel the wind from their wings. The dragons landed, one by one, surrounding the visitors, their orange eyes examining them curiously.

"I am Alex Chuvash, Crown Prince of Dumara. I come in peace to speak to King Dayia. I come alone, with only my Dragon Keeper."

A jade dragon approached them, sniffing the air. "This is not Aswin. Who is this female child? His daughter? What is your name, Dragon Keeper?" he asked. He was just meters away, and his eyes looked at her dangerously.

She tried to not show her anxiety, but her palms were sweaty as all six dragons turned their eyes to her. With a firm voice she answered. "I am Mila Fletcher. Daughter of Aswin and his heir. I have reached adulthood, and I have taken the position of Dragon Keeper, as it is my blood right."

"Very well. Welcome, Alex and Mila. I see you come in peace. Follow us to Terrak. We will extend our hospitality," the jade dragon said. One by one, the dragons launched into the air, and Alex joined them, following at a respectful distance. One by one, the summer dragons surrounded them. Mila realized this was more for defense, as Alex would be unable to deviate from his path.

Mila watched the summer dragons fly. Unlike the sunrise dragons, they were slightly shorter, with a smaller wingspan. The males had larger horns on their heads, and their manes were longer. Soon, they were circling the city, and Mila wondered where their dragons lived. There were no mountains here to make caves in.

Soon, she had the answer to her question, as she saw a large, gaping hole in the middle of the crater, just below the central keep. It was wide enough for them all to enter at the same time.

Mila nearly gasped as they dived in, sure she was going to hit her head on the stone ceiling.

They landed in a deep underground cave, so vast and filled with darkness Mila couldn't get her bearings. Her human eyes had not adjusted to the light.

They seemed to have landed in some type of central square, and Mila could hear dragons all around them. When she saw a flash of fire in the distance, she got a sense of the vastness of the space.

"Welcome, Chuvash," a voice said from in front of them.

"Tyson. We come in peace. We wish to visit King Dayia," Alex said, lowering his head.

Mila slipped off his back, managing to land on her feet in the dark. "I am Mila Fletcher, Dragon Keeper of Dumara," she said in the direction that the voice had come from. "It is a pleasure to meet you."

"Oh!" Tyson said in a surprised voice. "I was expecting Aswin. I did not realize … Well, welcome, Mila." He lit a torch, and Mila was glad. Tyson looked to be about the same age as her father. He was wearing a green vest with white sleeves rolled up to his elbows. He was of average height and stocky. He wore brown, knee-length boots with trousers tucked into them. He smiled, and Mila sensed he was a kind man.

"You can change me now," Alex said.

"Oh yes." She turned back to him, pulling off their two small personal packs, and then her Dragon Keeper's bag. She placed the bag on the floor and rummaged hastily for her astragenica. She had plenty for this trip, six bottles. She grabbed one, uncorked it, and delivered it to Alex.

As he changed, she opened his bag and pulled out his clothing. A simple black silk shirt with the emblem of Dumara embroidered in golden thread on the left shoulder, a pair of black pants, his belt, and a pair of black leather shoes and socks. She turned and was startled to see him standing there, fully nude.

Without a word, she handed him his clothing. She was getting used to this, and if he wasn't going to be embarrassed, why should she?

Soon, he was ready, and he offered her his arm with a smile.

"Come, I'll take you to the ascender," Tyson said.

They followed him through the dark, and Mila was happy she had Alex's arm. There was a path, but it was hard to make out. She could hear the summer dragons chatting in the shadows. It was all about them, of course.

"There is a new Dragon Keeper in Dumara? She's a girl? Are you sure? I didn't see her wearing a dress," the voices chattered.

"I wonder why King Chuvash sent his son? Could he not come himself?" the voices wondered.

And then she heard another interesting note, "Our houses will be joined as one, just you wait."

"Did you hear that?" she pointed out to Alex through their shared link.

"I did. Gossip about Sadie and my brother must already be circulating. I don't know about all this," Alex thought.

They reached an underground stream, the sound of the quickly moving water echoing off the stone walls. They seemed to be near the center of the crater. Stone walls, descending from the keep above them, reached all the way down here, their foundations set into the very bedrock of the dragon caves below.

"We use this stream to power what we call the ascender," Tyson said, pointing to an opening in the walls. "We have the luxury of having the river above to power it down, and this stream here to power us up. It is truly a wonder of science and engineering."

They stepped into a metal room, and Mila could feel the power of the underground stream pushing against the floor. Alex smiled at her and then held her tightly with one arm while bracing the other against the wall. "It's a bit of a wild ride," he said, having visited before with his father.

Tyson nodded. "That it is. The power of the water will push us all the way up to the castle in just seconds as soon as I release the clamps that hold the ascender in place. At the top, this chamber is moved over to the down position, where it will stay until someone wants to descend."

With wide eyes, Mila watched as Tyson grabbed a bar on the side of the metal room and then touched a button. The door closed, sealing the room tight. All at once, a heavy thunk sounded as the clamps released.

They shot up so fast Mila stumbled, falling into Alex's arms. He grabbed her and steadied her, chuckling. In seconds, the roar of the water stopped, and they bobbed a few times before the clamps at the top moved into place. Tyson waited a moment and then hit the button again. The door opened, and they stepped out into a beautiful open room.

"This is the lower level of the castle," Tyson said, leading them out.

Jade and marble tiles covered the floor, and a multitude of halls led many directions. Servants on various errands bustled through the space. This was truly the heart of the castle, and all the service rooms lay here. The kitchen, the laundry, the castle stores, and the servant's barracks all resided here. They headed to the far end, where two gleaming white marble staircases led upward to the main entrance and hall.

Attempting to take it all in, Mila looked around breathlessly. She was glad she had worn one of her nicer pantsuits today. She smoothed her hair with one hand. "How do I look?" she whispered to Alex.

He appraised her. She was dressed nicely, and her sandy brown hair fell in gentle curls down her back. He reached up and tucked a stray lock behind her ear. "You look lovely, Mila. I hardly recognize you without overalls on. Your hair isn't even wild. But I warn you, Queen Shayla Dayia is very sophisticated. She has probably already started planning a formal event, which we will all have to attend and pretend to enjoy," he chuckled.

Mila looked horrified but realized this was part of the job. "Okay, thanks for the warning."

"Yes, the minute the Queen heard you were here, she started planning an elaborate dinner party. So we do have that to look forward to," Tyson said dryly. He directed a servant to take their bags, although Mila insisted on keeping her Dragon Keeper's bag close. No way she would let anyone touch this bag. Tyson seemed to approve of this, giving her a small smile and a nod.

They were led into a glimmering throne room. It was decorated with green silk wallpaper printed with a golden floral pattern. Crystal chandeliers hung from the ceilings, and plush rugs, a specialty of the kingdom, covered the deep green tiled floors. At one end sat the King and Queen, and to their sides sat their children, Princess Sadie and Crown Prince Kip.

"Welcome, Prince Alex of Dumara. It is a pleasure to see you today. To what do we owe such a prodigious visit?" King Cleon Dayia asked, his voice echoing through the throne room.

"Your Majesty, thank you for the gracious welcome. I know I have come unexpectedly. I have come to discuss some private matters with you. But it is with great sadness I share with you the passing of my mother, Queen Cassandra Chuvash."

"I have heard of her passing, and we share our condolences," Cleon acknowledged sadly. Cleon had black hair and green eyes. He wore a tunic of green, embroidered with dragons in a fine silver thread. A cloak of black sable with a large emerald brooch was clasped at his neck. His hands were dripping with emerald and gold rings, and he had a long black beard, meticulously groomed. His green eyes seemed kind but guarded. He wore a simple silver crown with a large green stone set in the middle.

"I am so sorry, Alex. You know your mother and I shared a special friendship," Queen Shayla said, offering her hand. Alex took it and gave it a courteous kiss. She was dressed in an elaborate dress of green silk. Her hair was piled high on her head, and she wore a simple gold circlet on her forehead.

"How did she die?" Sadie asked with a slight smile. Alex turned to her, with his eyes slightly narrowed. He had never particularly liked Sadie, having thought she was snobbish and aloof.

"That is a matter I need to discuss with your father in private," Alex said curtly.

"And this must be the Dragon Keeper's daughter? Mila, is it?" Shayla asked, looking at her simple but tasteful pantsuit inquisitively. She noted that the girl was pretty but definitely unconventional. She was a diamond in the rough.

"Yes, Your Majesty. I am Mila Fletcher. I am now a Dragon Keeper. I have finished my training," she said, bowing her head in respect.

"So Dumara now has two Dragon Keepers. What an advantage you have!" Cleon said, looking at Mila with interest. "Tyson's son is still a young lad. We have many years to go before he will be ready to step into his father's footsteps."

"The disadvantages to marrying late in life, my liege. I was too busy in my youth serving you, Your Majesty, to think of frivolous things like love."

"That is so. Tyson is a very dedicated man. It is a wonder he ever married. I don't think he would have, except I reminded him of the importance of having an heir," Cleon remarked, a twinkle in his eye.

"Let our guests get settled in, and then we can have dinner. Perhaps you men can discuss your private matters after dinner," Shayla said, looking over them with a smile. "Sadie, Kip, please escort our guests to their quarters."

They were led to a large suite of rooms. There were two small bedrooms connected by a common sitting room, where there was a fire already blazing in the grate.

"Mila, the Queen requests formal dress at dinner," a servant said snidely, looking at Mila's pantsuit.

"Oh, no worries, I brought something more formal. It's here in my bag," Mila said with a smile.

"Oh. Well, I will send a maid in about an hour to help you dress," the servant said, closing the door on them.

"Oh, we are sharing a room?" Mila asked, looking at Alex, who had settled into a plush chair next to the fire.

"This is the guest suite. You can have the bigger bedroom, I don't really care." Alex said, pointing to the door on the left.

"Oh," she said, looking around. These accommodations were certainly comfortable, and she supposed it was common for Dragon Keepers to stay nearby.

"What did you bring to wear to dinner?" Alex asked with a slight smile on his face.

"I brought a pantsuit of course. It's black velvet and jade. Kiara made it for me, especially for this trip."

"I don't think a pantsuit will please the Queen, but I'm sure she will adjust. After dinner, we will have a discussion with Cleon. I will want you there," Alex said, turning and looking into the fire.

Mila could sense his unease. "What bothers you?"

"Can't you tell?" he asked, turning his eyes back to her.

She opened her mind to him and felt his grief. "Oh. You are missing your mother."

He nodded. "The last time we visited, she came with us. She and Queen Shayla were good friends. Being in this room reminds me of that visit."

Mila came and sat down next to him on the sofa. She took his hand in hers and gave it a squeeze. She didn't have to say anything. She let her own feelings of sadness about Cassandra's death wash over her. Together, they sat for a while, sharing their feelings and emotions without saying a word. The only thing that broke the spell was a knock on the door.

"Miss Fletcher, I'm here to help you dress for dinner," a maid said, bustling in. She looked at the pair, lost in thought, holding hands and staring into the fire. "Oh, I'm so sorry, I can come back."

The spell was broken, and Mila rose. "No, we should get ready. Let's go to my room."

Alex looked after her, closing his mind off. They were both getting used to this. It was nice to sit with her and share his feelings without saying a word.

He changed for dinner himself. Hopefully, their task here would be done, and they could leave in the next few days. It would depend on how resistant King Dayia would be to an alliance.

Chapter 11

The Alliance is Sealed

Dinner that night was a pleasant affair. Alex looked dashing in a black dinner jacket with the coat of arms of Dumara on his breast. His golden hair was slicked back, and he moved with ease and grace. He grinned at Mila, who had emerged from her room looking stunning.

The jade-colored suit was the perfect color, and the cut was perfect. It managed to look feminine and also set off her green eyes. Her sandy brown hair had been twisted and braided intricately. A few curly wisps trailed down, framing her face.

"You look beautiful," Alex said, finding it hard to take his eyes off her. He didn't know what was happening to him. He was having feelings for Mila, and it was alarming him. They had to work together; he shouldn't be falling for his Dragon Keeper. He shook his head and offered her his arm.

She smiled and took it, and then the maid led them downstairs to the grand dining hall.

It seemed like the entire court was there. Advisors, lords, and ladies of the kingdom. Mila and Alex were seated at the head table, next to Tyson, Princess Sadie, and Prince Kip.

The main course arrived: venison with a rich, red wine sauce, with roasted potatoes and a salad of cold carrots and beets.

A light and sweet white wine from Terrak vineyards to the south was served with dinner. Not used to having such luxuries, Mila was thoroughly enjoying this dinner.

"Easy, Mila," Alex thought to her as she picked up her second glass. After his admonishment, she sipped the wine more carefully.

They chatted with the Prince and Princess. They had known Alex for years, so they weren't so interested in him. He watched with amusement as they gave Mila the third degree, noting that Sadie seemed to be smug about something.

"So, Mila. You grew up in Dumara. How was it to grow up to be a Dragon Keeper?" Kip asked. The Crown Prince had the wisp of a mustache, and he was gangly, having just grown several inches. Like the rest of his family, he had dark hair and green eyes.

"I had a very unconventional childhood," Mila admitted. "I didn't go to school. I went with my father almost everywhere. When I got a little older, I ran the shop for him, and the neighbors looked after me while my dad went away on trips, or I spent the time playing in the dragon caves. I grew up with and around dragons, and I take my responsibilities seriously," she said, taking a quick glance at Alex. His eyes were sad again, remembering when his mother had watched her two dragonlings play with the young Mila. They had had some good times as children. It was a shame his brother had to go and ruin it by being an absolute jerk.

"Why the pants, Mila?" Sadie said, somewhat snobbishly. "I mean, I've got to say, that is a look. The cut and style looks quite nice on you."

Mila considered Princess Sadie. She was wearing quite an elaborate dress that dipped low to show a good amount of cleavage. It was cinched tight at her waist, and the skirts of satin were voluminous and covered with bows.

"With all due respect, Princess, I couldn't do my job in a dress. I have to crawl around caves, ride dragons, and be prepared for all sorts of environments. Just last month, my father and I visited the Northern Woods and collected bales of spider thread. That was quite the messy job, and it involved climbing quite a few trees to get what we needed."

"Humm, how very adventurous of you," Sadie said somewhat dismissively, tossing her black shiny hair.

Dessert was served: a towering trifle of chocolate pudding topped with raspberries and sauce. Mila enjoyed it, and even Alex seemed delighted. Dinner fare in Dumara tended to be much simpler, and desserts were saved for special events.

Finally, dinner was cleared, and the majority of the guests moved to the main hall for conversation.

The time had come for the real reason they were here, and Cleon stood up. "Come join me, Alex, and we will discuss matters in my study."

Tyson and Alex stood up, and Mila jumped to her feet. The King was startled as she moved to join them. "Well, might you want to retire for tea with the ladies?" he asked, raising his eyebrows.

"No, thank you. I'll join you, as I am the Dragon Keeper."

"Yes, I would like Mila to attend, Cleon. I'm sure you understand," Alex said, grabbing her hand and leading her with him down the hallway.

Cleon looked put out but nodded his head. Tyson gave a chuckle. He liked this girl already, as she was spunky. Definitely her father's child. She was just as stubborn as Aswin.

They went into the study, and Alex and Mila took a seat on a long sofa. Tyson sat in a wingback chair and King Cleon took the other. He pulled out a box of cigars and offered them around.

Alex took one and glanced at Mila, who shook her head. Her father smoked them occasionally, and she hated the smell of cigars. But, she would not object. She was in the King's study, after all. Tyson took one and then picked up a decanter of fine iseiki imported from Fresthav, a liquor made with star anise and elderberries. He held it up and looked at Mila with a raised eyebrow. She nodded. If they were all going to drink, so was she.

Tyson chuckled to himself and poured the spirits into four crystal glasses. He passed the glasses around, watching Mila closely.

"To good neighbors," Cleon said, raising his glass.

"Yes, to good neighbors," Alex said, raising his own. They all joined him, and Mila took the tiniest of sips from her glass.

She nearly choked but managed not to. The liquid burned as it went down. How the men managed to drink bottles of this, she would never know. With the cigar smoke now filling the room, she tried to ignore the stench.

"It's quite funny watching your reaction to all this," Alex said in her head.

She turned her green eyes on him. "Cigars are disgusting, and this iseiki is like drinking poison," she directed back at him.

"Well, to be honest, I don't really care for cigars, but you know, sometimes we have to do things for the sake of politics and making nice," he thought to her, taking an inhale of his long cigar, puffing the smoke in her general direction. She just glared at him.

Tyson was watching the two. He opened his mind to his King. "What do you think, Cleon? Mila Fletcher is an interesting development, is she not?" he thought.

Cleon smirked and took a drink. "She is like a fish out of water here, but she is holding her own. Let's see what else she brings to the table. She seemed intelligent at dinner, and she certainly is a wild stallion. I wonder if she can be tamed?" Cleon directed at Tyson.

Alex looked around the room as they all sat in silence. It was obvious that conversations were happening under the surface. He cleared his throat and began. "King Dayia. You have heard of my mother's death. The news has spread far and wide. I come to you today to give you the alarming details. My mother went out to greet the morning sun, alone. She was ambushed by two dragons. She called for help, and my father arrived first. My brother and I were able to reach them minutes later. We fought off the attackers, but we weren't able to save her. She was mortally wounded," Alex said.

"I was wondering what had happened. We only heard that she had passed from our diplomat. He gave us no other information," King Cleon said, puffing on his cigar. He sat up, realizing that he was going to get details. "What dragons attacked her?"

Alex looked at him solemnly. "Unsurprising, they were nightfall. You know how they instigate us all with their encroachment into our territories to hunt."

"Yes. I had a visit from a nightfall dragon about six months ago. He wanted us to ally against you."

"What?" Alex asked, shocked. "Why didn't you bring this to our attention?"

"I didn't think it was of importance. You know nightfall dragons, always looking to cause trouble. I declined and sent him on his way. I told him to stop harassing our borders, and thankfully, it has been quiet since then."

"That is alarming," Alex said. "But more alarming is that the nightfall dragons weren't working alone. There was a Fresthav dragon with them."

That piece of information sucked the air out of the room. Cleon put his drink down abruptly. "Are you sure of this?"

"We are sure," Mila said, all heads turning to look at her. "My father and I found the Queen's body. She had been viciously attacked, and a huge gash had killed her. There is no way that one dragon could have taken her. This was the work of many."

"And my father arrived in time to see the fight. He attacked a nightfall dragon, putting himself at risk. He was injured. My brother and I fought off two other nightfall dragons before the attackers realized they were outnumbered and retreated. We saw a winter dragon retreating with them."

"Rand's wounds were most definitely nightfall, as his injuries contained the poison from their claws. I helped clean the wounds," Mila said.

Tyson and Cleon looked at each other. Mila got the impression they were talking to each other. Tyson turned to her. "Mila, are you sure? How much experience do you have with dragon injuries?"

"I'm sorry, are you questioning my abilities?" she said, her eyes snapping. "I have been at my father's side since I was a small child. My own mother died when I was little, and he had no other choice than to bring me along. I am sure I knew more about dragons before I was knee-high than your own son knows now!" she said, her voice rising.

Alex was amused. Mila was holding her own, and he found himself filing with pride. "It is true, Tyson. Mila is practically a dragon already, and she did grow up at my side. I have no doubts in her abilities, or she wouldn't be my Dragon Keeper. We are bound."

Tyson looked startled, gazing between the two. Of course, they were bound. Aswin was bound to Rand. "I see." He thought he needed to start training his son.

"Nightfall dragons killed my mother, and may be working with the winter dragons. I ask that you join Dumara in an alliance, to keep the balance of power even. You know how King Ibis thirsts for power. I wouldn't be surprised if they have already tried to unite their clans. A dragon heir with both winter and night magic? Can you image the destruction that would bring to our kingdoms?"

"So, are you suggesting an alliance, or a marriage?" Cleon asked, stroking his beard. "A unity of summer and sunrise? Fire and light?"

"I am suggesting both," Alex said, finishing his drink and placing it on the table. Not to be outdone, Mila took a big gulp of her drink, managing to finish hers, also. She tried to keep her eyes from popping out of her head at the fire in her belly.

A knock came at the door. "Yes, what is it?" Cleon asked loudly.

"It's Sadie. I need to talk to you," a quiet voice said.

"Come in," Cleon said with a sigh, wondering what his daughter wanted.

She came in, and out of the darkness, Nick appeared. She grabbed his hand and led him into the room.

Alex looked stunned. He stood up, angrily looking at his brother. "Nick. What are you doing here?"

"I followed you, brother. I have some matters of my own to attend to here in Terrak," Nick said. He was dressed in an immaculate suit, a fine golden ascot tied at his neck. He looked like a much more refined Prince of Dumara. His shoes where shined to perfection, and his smile was big. He sat down on the sofa across from Alex and Mila, and Alex just glared at him. If looks could kill, Nick would be a dead man.

Just then, Queen Shayla entered the room without knocking. "Well, we have quite the little party here. I saw Prince Nick arrive, and frankly Sadie, I'm quite surprised at the welcome you gave him. That was quite the kiss," she said curtly, sitting down on the arm of her husband's chair. He leaned over with a sigh and put his cigar out, and Tyson and Alex followed suit.

"Well, we were just discussing an alliance between Dumara and Terrak. A traditional alliance, and a marriage alliance. I must admit my mind went to Prince Alex and Sadie, but it seems like there is something here I should know about," Cleon said, glaring at his daughter.

"As you know, Father, I like to hunt on the western border with Dumara. Nick and I have run into each other a few times, and we have grown fond of each other," Sadie said, looking at Nick, and grabbing his hand. He glanced at her and kissed it.

Alex rolled his eyes. This was not going to plan. He was livid at his brother for interrupting his diplomatic negotiations.

"Sadie. You could pick any summer dragon in the cave. There are many to pick from who would make a wonderful husband. But you dabble with a sunrise dragon?" Shayla said, her face flushing.

"Shayla. My dear. Let's hear this out before you dismiss it outright," Cleon said, his eyes darting to Alex. He sensed the tension between the brothers, and he knew that Alex had been caught unaware. This in itself was very curious.

Alex stepped in, trying to save the situation. "Well, this is not how I intended this conversation to go. But think of it; it would cement the relationship between our kingdoms. If they managed to have a dragonling, we would have the power of light and fire. That would counter whatever Murdad and Fresthav can come up with. And with you helping secure the northern border, we can pay more attention to the east and keep the threat of Fresthav down."

"Yes, brother. You want the alliance on paper, but I want an alliance of the heart. I ask for Sadie's hand. She will be my mate, and we will unite Dumara and Terrak," Nick said, bowing to Cleon. "We love each other, and we desire to declare it to the Dragon God in a ceremony of binding."

Just then, Kip stuck his head into the room. "What's going on? A family meeting? Why didn't you call me?" he asked.

"Come in, son. Close the door and lock it please. Prince Nick here just asked for your sister's hand in marriage. Tell me, my

Crown Prince, what you think of this idea?" Cleon asked, glaring at Nick.

"What?" Kip asked, looking at them all gathered. "I don't know …," he stuttered. "Has that been done before? Is that even possible? The children …"

"I am already with a dragonling," Sadie said with a smug smile, and Nick beamed down at her happily.

"I'm sorry, what?" Cleon roared. Nick looked stunned, and Alex dropped his head into his hands. This was turning out to be a disaster.

"Yes. I am with a child. I told you, we love each other. I will make my nest in his caves, and we will raise the child in Dumara," Sadie said.

"I promise you, I will take care of Sadie. We love each other," Nick said, putting his arm around her. She beamed up at him.

"It is against the prophecies of the Dragon God. You do not know what you play with. I was all set to agree to an alliance, but put aside the notion of marriage. It is forbidden!" Cleon roared.

"If Murdad and Fresthav decide to unite their houses, then we must be prepared," Nick said.

"Unfortunately, he is right," Alex agreed. "Although I wonder if our clan will accept this marriage. There will be hard feelings on both sides."

"Alex is correct. The summer dragons will be angry Sadie has turned away from her own," Cleon said.

"Don't I get any say in the matter? I don't think Sadie should leave Terrak," Kip said, biting his fingernails.

"So, you will allow us to marry?" Sadie asked, her voice taking on a pleading quality. Nick looked at her adoringly.

"Yes. Since you are already with dragonling. As a father, I really have no choice, do I?" Cleon growled. "I am not happy about it at all."

"Thank you, Your Majesty," Alex said, rising. "I have brought two copies of an alliance agreement. If we could both sign." He pulled a sheaf of paper out of his pocket and laid it on the table.

"I would have preferred YOU to marry Sadie. You are the Crown Prince after all," Cleon grumbled, picking up the paper and looking at it. He nodded and moved to his desk. He found a fountain pen and then signed the agreement with a flourish. Alex moved next to him and signed as well. They all turned and looked at Nick and Sadie.

"Well, then, I think Sadie and I want to be married as soon as possible. We will head back with my brother when he leaves, and we can plan the wedding in a month's time," Nick said.

"Fine. Now leave. I have matters to discuss with Alex," Cleon said, pointing to the door. His family shuffled out, and Nick with them. Cleon turned to Alex and Mila.

"Trust me when I say that was all unexpected, Cleon," Alex said, looking after his brother. He poured another round of iseiki and they all took another drink, even Mila, who was now feeling slightly drunk. She knew better than to talk now, as she was not thinking straight.

"You had no idea? I'm very upset at all this," Cleon shook his head.

"My brother just told me that they were friends. He has been sneaking off for some time now, and now I know he was meeting up with Sadie. I can't lie, we had discussed the possibility of a marriage before I left, and I was just getting ready to open discussions with you on that. I did not expect my brother to show up unannounced. He could have just traveled with me, if that was my plan." Alex sighed. He glanced over at Mila and could sense she was slightly drunk.

For another half an hour, they discussed defense of the borders. Alex promised he would try to visit Fresthav. While some tension existed, sunrise and winter dragons had always at least met peacefully before. "I don't sense any danger from them, and It's possible perhaps the Fresthav dragon that joined in the fight was rogue. I can feel them out and then send word to you," Alex said.

"That sounds like a plan. And regarding Murdad, I've always been able to have a good discussion with Ibis. We do have some trade between our kingdoms. I can go pay a visit myself on the premise of a trade deal, when the wedding is over," Cleon said, running his fingers through his black hair. He looked tired.

"We will retire for the night. We can discuss this more tomorrow," Alex said, getting up. He looked with concern at Mila, who looked very drunk. She stood up, swaying slightly.

"Come, Mila," Alex said with a bemused smile. He took her hand and put his other hand around her waist. She swayed slightly and blinked her eyes.

"Time to go?" she slurred.

"Yes. I think you have had too much to drink," Alex thought to her, steadying her as she stumbled.

"Goodnight," Tyson said, chuckling at Mila's state. He was quite taken with Mila Fletcher. She was a unique girl.

Alex led her out of the room, past the party still going on in the foyer. He saw that now a string quartet had set up, and people were dancing and enjoying drinks. Sadie and Nick were dancing, and by the joyous look on their faces, they were celebrating being allowed to marry.

Queen Shayla and Kip were in the corner, engaged in a rapt discussion. Alex felt sorry for the poor boy, as his mother obviously controlled every aspect of his life.

"Alex, I'm a little drunk," Mila said loudly, nearly tripping over the flower pot. "I don't think iseiki is my drink."

"I don't think it is, either, my dear," he said fondly, leading her to their suite. If it had been just him and his brother, they would have shared it, but he honestly didn't care where his brother ended up tonight. Knowing him, it would be in the arms of Sadie, but it's not like that even mattered anymore.

"You're going to be an uncle," Mila laughed, hitting him on the side.

Alex just shook his head, realizing that he himself would have no heir. He trusted his brother, didn't he? Maybe he should consider finding himself a mate, after all.

"You want a wife now?" Mila said, laughing again, picking up his stray thought. "Well, our little connection will make quite an awkward wedding night for you, won't it?" she asked, laughing and falling against the wall.

A servant passed and cast a disparaging look at the pair, mumbling something about unseemly drunkenness and wearing trousers.

Alex smiled down at Mila. She was really something. He opened the door to their suite, and she nearly fell inside.

"Come, Mila. It's bedtime. You will have a bit of a hangover in the morning, I think. I sure did the first time I had isciki." He led her to her bed, and she sat on the bed looking at him with her green eyes.

"Did I ever tell you that you have spectacular eyes?" she said drunkenly, standing up.

"No, but thank you," he said, bemused. "Your eyes are very nice as well."

"Really?" she hiccupped, and took a step closer to him. They were close now, and he read her thoughts before she did it. For some reason, he didn't stop her.

She looked at him, and the next thing he knew, her lips were on his, and they were kissing passionately. Soon, he pulled away. She was completely drunk, and she would probably have regrets the next day. "Mila, no. Not like this. It's time for bed," he said firmly.

She laughed and threw off her jacket. He was acutely aware of the shape of her body in the tight silk shirt she wore under her jacket. She pressed up against him, and it took all his willpower to gently push her away. He wanted to tear that shirt off her and throw her onto her bed. But common sense prevailed, and he cleared his throat. "Goodnight, Mila. Sleep tight," he said, stepping out of her room. He grimaced as he heard her stumble and crash into what must have been the dresser.

Shaking his head, he went into his own room and closed the door. He locked the latch for good measure. That's all he needed, a drunk Mila sneaking into his bed at night. He certainly wouldn't be able to summon his willpower if that happened.

Chapter 12

Hangover

The next morning, Alex awoke to the sound of retching in their shared bathroom. With a sigh, he swung his feet over the side of his bed, grabbed his robe, and went to the bathroom door. He tried the knob and found it open.

Mila was hunched over the basin, still wearing her clothes from the night before. Her hair was still braided, but it had come partially undone, and it was an absolute mess. She was sobbing and retching at the same time.

Alex patted her back. "Bit too much to drink last night? I bet this is the first time you've drank, isn't it?"

She nodded miserably, avoiding looking in his eyes. "Clean up, and you'll feel better with a bit of breakfast in you," he said. He peeked his head out of their bedroom door, spying a maid in the hallway. "We are feeling a bit under the weather this morning and won't be able to make it downstairs. Could we have a bit of breakfast and some tea here?"

"Of course, sir. The kitchen has already prepared many breakfast trays. I think everyone's feeling a bit under the weather. The party went very late last night, with the excitement and all."

"What excitement?" Alex asked.

"Don't you know? The engagement announcement between your brother, Prince Nick of Dumara, and Princess Sadie. It's the talk of the castle this morning." She smiled and hurried off to get their breakfast.

"What? He made an official announcement. Oh, what a disaster!" Alex said, closing his eyes and shutting the door. He turned back to Mila, who was sitting on the bathroom floor, looking green.

"I'm so sorry," she whispered. "I didn't know …"

"It's okay, Mila. You didn't. I shouldn't have given you a second glass of iseiki. That is some powerful stuff. You know now what your limits are," Alex said. He knelt down beside her and looked at her carefully. "Do you remember last night?"

"A little bit. Everything after the second iseiki is a little blurry. Your brother and Sadie are getting married, right?" she asked, trying to remember. Her brow furrowed. Much of last night was missing. The last thing she remembered was … OH, NO! She looked up at Alex with alarm. She had kissed him!

He smiled and then rose. He offered her his hand, and she took it, stumbling to her feet. She still felt sick, although she didn't know if it was from the drink or the realization she had thrown herself at Alex.

"I see you remember," was all he said. "I ordered breakfast for us. Maybe get changed? I think we will leave today. Our work here seems to be done. I've got the treaty on paper. My brother seems to have taken care of the rest."

She wobbled slightly, still feeling sick. She blushed deep red as she remembered kissing him. It was a great kiss.

He read her thoughts and grinned. "Yes, it was," he thought back to her, and blinked his eyes. He turned, left her in the bathroom, and went to his room to change.

She groaned and leaned over the sink. She opened the taps to rinse out the basin and splashed her face with cold water. She had to get herself together. What had she done? Thoughts rushed to her in a panic. Had she gone and ruined everything by her little indiscretion? She had no right to kiss Alex. She wasn't even sure what she had been thinking. She looked at herself in the fancy gilt scrolled mirror hanging on the wall. She looked sick, and she was rumpled from sleeping in her clothes.

Mila went into her bedroom and took off her clothes. They stank of cigar smoke and iseiki liquor, which she had accidentally spilled down her front. Apparently, she was a sloppy drunk. She took out a gray tweed pantsuit and a fresh shirt and started cleaning herself up. She considered her unruly hair. She unbraided it and laughed at the huge curls that fell around her shoulders. She went back into the bathroom, fighting nausea again, wet her hair, and tied it back with a simple bow.

She grabbed her Dragon Keeper's bag. Rummaging around, she found what she was looking for, an anti-nausea powder and a headache powder, wrapped in little packets of wax paper. Taking them with her, she went into the common room and found Alex already sitting on the sofa, perfectly collected and dressed simply in his white linen shirt and trousers. A tray of biscuits and steaming tea was waiting for her.

"Eat, you will feel better, if you can keep it down." Alex spread butter on the fluffy biscuit, and it smelled delicious.

"I found something in my bag that should help," she said, holding up the packets. She sat across from him and ripped open the packets, pouring them into an empty tea cup. Pouring them both tea, she sat back and sipped it, tasting the bitterness of the herbs. She hoped they worked soon.

Alex drank his own tea, looking at her intently. With a sigh, he picked up a biscuit and pushed one toward her. "Eat," he ordered.

She picked up a biscuit and nibbled on the corner. Her

stomach didn't seem to rebel, so she took another bite. "Are we going to talk about it?" she asked softly.

"Nope," Alex said, looking at her with a grin. "We are not. We are just going to pretend that never happened, okay? You simply had too much to drink. Happens to the best of us."

"Okay. Never happened," she said with a small smile. "And I'm never drinking isciki again."

After Mila started to feel better, they made preparations to leave. Heading downstairs, they found the royal family already gathered in the throne room, chatting away while the musicians still played. Guests from the night before loitered around, many looked as hungover as Mila felt.

It was like the party had never ended. Trays were now filled with light snacks, and fruit juice filled cups instead of fine wine. Nick and Sadie were in attendance, both looking immaculate. Sadie now wore a tight-fitting sheath dress, in a cream color, and Nick wore an emerald green waistcoat, with a black tie. His blue eyes sparkled as he looked at Sadie, and they held hands as they chatted with guests.

Alex's eyes were full of anger as he looked at his brother. There was no doubt Nick had upstaged him and put the negotiations at risk. He approached the royal family and gave them a slight bow. "Good morning. I see you are all up early this morning."

"I took Sadie out with me this morning to greet the sun. I think she found it fascinating. She promises to take me out at the change of seasons," Nick said, watching his brother closely.

Alex's jaw clenched tightly. He couldn't believe his brother had taken a summer dragon along to perform their sacred duty. "Did you happen to run into any sunrise dragons?" he asked casually, trying not to let his anger show through his voice.

"We ran into my father and about six others. They were surprised. I told him you would fill him in later," Nick said casually, as if taking a summer dragon with him was no big deal.

"Okay then. So I get to do the dirty work," Alex mumbled. "Are you not coming back with me?"

"I think I'll stay here another day or so," Nick said, leaning over and kissing Sadie. She smiled and then wrapped her arms around him, beaming at him happily.

"Send my regards to your father. Make sure he knows I am not completely happy with this situation myself," Cleon said, glaring at the lovebirds and their open affection.

"I will do so, Your Majesty," Alex said, shaking his head. "We will be off then. I do need to get back to Dumara. You know, duty." He looked pointedly at his brother, who ignored him. Shaking his head, they made their way to the ascender, where they found Tyson and his young son waiting for them.

"This is my son, Michael. You have inspired me to start training him. I guess it's never too early, really, and I've been preoccupied with my work."

"Hi, Michael," Mila said graciously. "Did you have fun this morning?"

"Oh yes! Father let me help him with the dragons. I didn't know the Kings were actually dragons, it was amazing! Father says I can ride them, once I become a real Dragon Keeper. Do you ride dragons, Ms. Fletcher?"

"Yes, Michael. But you have to keep the secret, okay? Don't go telling all your friends King Cleon is really a dragon," she said, looking around. Luckily, there were no servants or guests in the foyer right now.

"I see Ms. Fletcher is up and moving this morning," Tyson said with a chuckle. "I hope you don't mind, I did your duties this morning. I gave Prince Nick astragenica once he returned. I didn't want to disturb you, my dear. You had a little too much to drink last night."

Mila was filled with shame. She should have been the one to attend to Prince Nick. Alex squeezed her shoulder. "Don't worry about it."

They headed down into the cavern. It was just as dark as Mila remembered it, but she found her eyes had gotten used to the darkness more quickly than they did yesterday. She found that they were surrounded by summer dragons, all staring at them as they made their way slowly to the entrance.

"Do you feel that? It's malice," Mila thought to Alex.

"I do. They are angry with us. Well, angry at my brother, anyway," Alex thought back to her. "I'm glad Tyson is with us. I don't think they would let us leave if he wasn't."

"Do you think the sunrise dragons are going to be this angry?" Mila thought.

"Maybe. We will have to see."

When they reached the entrance, Alex quickly took off his clothes and started to turn, shifting so quickly even Tyson was surprised. "Well, then. Safe travels you two. Be careful, some nightfall dragons were spotted this morning, on the northern border. They left us alone, though."

"Thank you for the warning, Dragon Keeper," Alex said with a low growl. Mila quickly secured their bags behind them, pulling out the belt and making sure they were secured around his chest. She climbed up and nodded goodbye to Tyson and his wide-eyed son, who stared at Alex in awe.

"Goodbye, Mila. Send my regards to your father and stay safe. In the future, remember iseiki is not your friend," Tyson said with a grin.

"Thank you, Tyson. I will do so." She waved as Alex leapt into the air and out the entrance. It was already midday, and she watched as the entrance to the underground caves grew smaller and smaller beneath them. She was glad she had remembered to wear her cloak today. The air was cold, and she could see her breath. It would be winter soon, and the Fresthav dragons would fly to greet it.

They leveled out, heading due west, into the wind. It would be a slower, longer flight this time around. The mountains loomed to her right, and she found herself anxiously scanning the horizon for signs of enemies.

"Good idea. Keep a sharp eye out," Alex thought to her, dipping lower to avoid flying through a flock of geese.

They flew and flew, and Mila found herself getting sleepy. She struggled to stay awake, and she found herself nodding off a few times. She slapped herself to wake up.

"I'm getting tired also. This headwind is a killer," Alex said. "Maybe we can stop and rest."

Just then, Mila spotted several dark dots. They seemed to be perched on the mountain top, and she watched as the dots seemed to fall off the rim of the mountain. Suddenly, the first one spread its wings, and she noted with horror that it was a purple nightfall dragon.

"Alex!" she said sharply, as one by one, the wings opened and the nightfall dragons turned toward them.

"I see them! Hold on!" he said. "I've got a trick up my sleeve." Alex started powerfully flapping his wings, gaining altitude quickly. He slipped into the clouds, where she lost sight of their pursuers.

"I can't see them!" she said, in a panic.

"They can't see us either."

He continued flapping his wings quickly and steadily, picking up speed as he went. They were now headed due south.

Mila dug her hands into his mane and leaned down low, burying her face into his side. She felt the wind over her back and hoped that it was helpful to their speed. She had spied six nightfall dragons, and if they caught them, she had a feeling it would be a fight to the death.

"There is a break in the clouds just ahead, Mila. See if you can spy them," Alex said. He was panting now, clearly tiring.

When they broke through the clouds, she turned quickly and looked over her left shoulder. Closing rapidly, she could see the nightfall dragons, still hot on their tail. The one in the lead, a huge male, opened his mouth and roared. Mila ducked low, and a beam of dark energy magic shot to the left of her. She felt a faint tingle as it went by.

"Dang it! They aren't breaking off. We are so far south, and yet still they pursue us. I'm headed for Tiago. I doubt they will follow us that far. I'm running out of steam, and they can sense it, I think. I'm going to dive, Mila. Crouch down, and hold on tight," Alex said.

She gasped as another beam of dark magic flew right over her head. She bent low, and she saw Alex tuck his wings. He began diving, and they went even faster. Mila closed her eyes against the speed. How they would ever manage to land without crashing into the ground, she didn't know, but if they could get away from these nightfall dragons, she supposed it was worth it.

They still felt like they were falling, and Mila opened her eyes. They were now over Sunrise Bay. She turned and stole a quick glance over her shoulder and saw the nightfall dragons retreating. They were too far south. To the east, she saw a glorious sight: a group of sunrise dragons, some twenty strong, turning to chase the nightfall dragons. She let out a whoop, throwing her fist into the air.

But she turned her attention to the rapidly approaching water. They were going too fast.

"Hold on tight, water landing," Alex said. She sensed great fatigue in his voice. He spread his wings to brake, and Mila was nearly thrown clean off. Only her strong grip on his mane kept her on his back.

They landed in the bay like a giant sea bird, salt water splashing out on both sides of them in a giant arch. As they came to rest, Alex bobbed in the water. He tucked his wings in, his huge legs moving in the water, keeping him afloat.

Mila quickly took stock of her surroundings. She was drenched with cold sea water, and she could taste the salt on her lips. "Alex, the shore isn't far, but we are going to have to swim."

"You're going to have to change me here, in the water," he said. He sounded exhausted. Mila began to worry he wouldn't have enough steam to make it to the shore.

She quickly located her bags. and grabbed a set of clothes for Alex and shoved them in her Dragon Keeper's bag. She would tow the keeper's bag behind her as she swam. Her father had designed these bags himself, and they were somewhat waterproof. They would float, hopefully. The other two bags she threw off the side. She loosened the belt and let it fall into the water. Then she threw off her jacket and shoes, as she didn't want them to drag her down. She dived into the water, shocked at the cold. Luckily, the water was mostly calm today, with only small waves. She was thankful her father had taught her to swim in the river by the castle. With strong strokes, she swam toward Alex, pulling her bag along with her.

Reaching his head, she held on with one arm to his neck. She pulled her bag closer to her. It was floating nicely on the water. She managed to undo the clasp with one hand and dug into the bottom, feeling for the astragenica tucked into its little compartments. Her fingers brushed a top, and she pulled one out. Not having enough hands, she stuck it in her mouth, holding the cork top with her teeth.

Letting go of Alex's neck, she kicked strongly with her legs. She struggled to close the top of the bag finally managing to get the clasp closed without losing the bottle or flooding the bag with water.

He had been watching this all as he tread water. He was tired, so tired. He looked at the shore, hoping he had enough left in him to make it to the sand. She hit him on the nose, and he realized she had the astragenica ready. He opened his mouth, and she tried to avoid his sharp teeth.

She held onto the cork with her teeth, and with her right hand she pulled on the bottle. The cork came free with a pop, and she threw the entire bottle into his mouth. There would be no pouring in this instance.

She quickly swam until she was a few feet away, watching the transformation carefully while she floated to save her energy.

Alex felt himself changing, and about halfway through, he spit out the glass potion bottle. Of course, he had never transformed in the water before, and he found himself sinking as his limbs shortened. There was no way he could swim and transform at the same time.

He felt a terrific yank on his hair, and it was Mila to the rescue. She had seen him struggling, and she quickly swam to him, pulling him up from the depths.

Fully transformed now, he sputtered out water. He rolled on his back, floating for a minute. His eyes closed. "Thank you," he muttered.

"Are you good?" she asked, her teeth chattering now in the cold water.

"Yeah, let's get going," he said, rolling back over on his stomach and beginning to make his way to the shore. He didn't feel the cold, and he thought it was probably his dragon magic keeping him warm. He didn't even get very cold in the winter. He took the bag from Mila and began to move with strong strokes. She followed.

Within ten minutes, they fought through the waves and were standing on the shore. Well, more like laying on the shore. They were both gasping and panting and lacking the energy to stand.

He was still nude, and he really needed to find his clothing before a villager happened by. But they were still about a mile from the town, and the only people out this way would be farmers or fishermen.

With a groan, he scrambled to his knees and pulled the Dragon Keeper's bag to him.

Mila brought herself to a sitting position. Her lips looked blue, and her teeth were chattering violently. She brought her knees to her chest and wrapped her arms around them. Her hair hung in tangles around her face, and bits of seaweed were stuck in her brown locks.

"We need to get you warmed up," Alex said, unlatching the clasp. His clothes were soaked. He wrung them out and put them on quickly. He was covered with sand, wet and exhausted. Night was falling, and there was no way they could make it back to Dumara castle before moonrise. They would stay here on the beach for the night.

Mila cried out. "Oh, no! Water got in the bag!" She scampered across the sand, quickly digging into her bag. "Well, the astragenica is fine, but some of these herbs and powders are trashed. I have more in the workshop, so I can easily replace them, but it's just frustrating!"

"I mean, I don't know what you expect. I crash landed in the bay. Yet, you somehow managed to change me, and then swam through shark-infested waters to the shore. I'm surprised you even managed to keep a hold of your bag," Alex said.

"Shark infested?" she asked, looking back at the dark, cold water, fear in her eyes.

"Yep. Although it is the wrong time of year for sharks. They like the summer, when the waters are nice and warm. Now come here," Alex demanded, holding out his arms.

"What?" she asked. "You want to hug me?"

"I want to warm you up. You're freezing."

She put her bag down, realizing she was chilled to the bone. She took a few hesitant steps toward Alex. As soon as she was in reach, he wrapped his long arms around her and pulled her close.

"You're warm!" she exclaimed, tucking her head into his

neck. He smelled of the sea and also like the sweet, gentle scent of an astra flower, which was interesting. She had seen no perfume in his bags. He held her to his chest, and the warmth coming off him was almost better than a fire.

He smiled and put his chin on top of her head. She was the perfect size, and so soft. He closed his eyes as she warmed up. "I'm a dragon, Mila. A sunrise dragon. Our power is light. We don't really get cold. Not even in the coldest of winters."

She didn't say a word as the cold left her limbs. She could feel his heart thumping under her ear. They were together, as one, and he held her tightly as the sound of the waves crashed in his ears. The sun started to set, its glorious colors of pink, purple, yellow, and orange filling the sky.

Back at the dragon caves, the dragons landed at the entrance to the caves, flying in one after another. Aswin was waiting for them. He quickly strode over to Rand and delivered the astragenica.

Within minutes, Rand stood before him, and Aswin handed him his clothing.

"Trouble, Aswin," Rand said, looking concerned. "A pack of nightfall dragons were in hot pursuit of Alex and Mila. They must have been returning already from Terrak. Either their trip went very well and they left early, or it went very badly and they were sent away. Either way, it looks like my son was smart and headed due south. They are probably somewhere near Tiago for the night. I hate to think what would have happened if we hadn't chased the nightfall dragons away. Six against one is poor odds."

"They have never been so bold as to come that far south before," Aswin said, looking concerned.

"I know. We will have to keep up the patrols. Hopefully, Alex and Mila will arrive tomorrow. We will fly out at midday, and escort them back. Nick is missing, and his friend Ray told me that he left just after Alex yesterday. He went to Terrak himself against my wishes. That boy …," Rand said, exasperated. He followed Aswin as he started checking in with all the dragons that had been on patrol, making sure they had no injuries.

"He is very jealous of Alex, that is apparent. He's been acting sneaky as of late, Rand," Aswin said, looking at his King and friend, hoping he took no offense.

Rand pursed his lips, refusing to discuss his younger son. He looked out the cave entrance to the setting sun. Night was falling, and he hoped Alex and Mila had found somewhere safe to stay tonight and would hurry home tomorrow.

Back on the beach, Mila had warmed up and was now mostly dry. She was sitting on a driftwood log, watching the sunset. Little crabs played at the water's edge, and the surf crashed on the shore. Seaweed and shells littered the beach.

Alex threw another piece of driftwood onto the pile he had been collecting. He scowled. He was not happy he would have to spend a night camping on the beach. It was just too dangerous to fly at night. Nightfall dragons, with their dark coloring, were very hard to spot, and it would be a moonless night.

"Can I help with anything?" Mila asked, scrambling to her feet.

"Got anything to eat in that bag of yours?" he asked, his stomach grumbling. It had been a long time since those biscuits in the morning.

She tilted her head. With a pensive look on her face, she turned back to the waves, considering them. All of the sudden, she took off at a sprint down the beach, leaving Alex watching her in amusement.

He was amazed when Mila picked up a crab, and then another, holding her prizes high in the air. The crabs where the size of her hand, and their pincers and feet waved fruitlessly in the air as they tried to get away.

With a giggle, she brought back the crabs, throwing them on their backs in the sand. "Now, how are you going to light that fire without matches?" she asked, a grin on her face.

"I bet you didn't know this, but I retain my power in human form," he said, crossing his arms across his broad chest.

"Really? Show me," Mila said, not really believing him. Although, he had been deliciously warm when he hugged her.

"Stand back," he said with a grin, and she took a few steps back. His eyes narrowed as he looked hard at the driftwood. It would be hard to light on a good day, as it was slightly damp. His mouth opened, and light burst out, covering the wood in brilliance, and lighting up the campsite like it was high noon.

Mila gasped as the logs began to smolder and char, finally bursting into flames under the onslaught of light magic. With a snap, Alex closed his mouth, and the light disappeared.

Mila was dazzled, just for a moment. In a quiet voice, she said, "Oh."

Without a word or a glance at her, Alex strode over, throwing the crabs on the fire. Soon, they were dead, and roasting quite nicely.

"I wish we had some butter and salt," Mila said, avoiding the subject before her.

But Alex wouldn't let her. "And now I just made it clear, I'm not quite human."

"Well, I think I knew that," Mila said softly, looking at him, and his strong jaw, golden hair, longer at the neck, his intensely blue eyes, and his strong arms and legs.

He laughed and shrugged. "Point taken. I guess you do. I just don't like to make it obvious."

"So you can burn things with your breath. So what?" Mila said, moving closer to the fire.

"I can also see in the dark, I am stronger than a normal man,

I have a long life, and I can read your mind," he moved next to her, and put his arm around her.

She put her head on his shoulder and sighed. She was falling for this Dragon Prince and was quite vexed about it. She had promised herself she would never fall for a boy, and yet here she was. It was better that they stay friends. They would have to work together all their lives. He would marry some beautiful drakaina, and Mila would be dedicated to her work, serving him and his family. That is the way it was, and that was the way it had always been.

They sat like that for a while, words unspoken, while their dinner cooked. Finally, Alex got up and pushed the steaming crab out of the fire with a stick. He took a rock he found nearby and smashed the crab, handing it to her with his bare hands. "Careful, it's hot," he said, placing her portion next to her.

He sat down with his portion and started picking out the meat. Mila did the same, a smile on her face. "You cooked me dinner."

"Well, it was a team effort. You caught it, I cooked it," he laughed, considering his already empty shell. Well, he was still hungry, but at least it took the edge off.

"I'll do the dishes then," she said, picking up the broken shells and throwing them into the night.

"Come here," Alex requested, patting the sand next to him. "You'll get cold tonight, while we are sleeping. We will sleep here on the sand and by the fire."

She hesitantly sat next to him, and he wrapped his arms around her again. He leaned up against the log, and she sat between his legs, wrapped in his warm arms. Soon, her head dipped down, and her chin rested on her chest. She was tired, so tired. It had been such a long day. He held her a little tighter and sighed. Soon, his chin dipped down, resting on her shoulder. They slept like that for some time until they both woke up from cricks in their necks. Alex got up, threw another piece of driftwood on the fire, and then laid down on his side in the sand. He pulled Mila close so that her back was to his chest and held her tight. This was even better, and soon they fell asleep again, until the morning light hit their faces and they awoke, eager to be off and find their way home to Dumara.

Chapter 13

A Meeting in Murdad

Nick's plan was going perfectly. He had left Dumara a few hours after Alex and Mila had left, nearly being spotted as they took off from the sorcerer's tower. But Alex and his Dragon Keeper were in such great haste to get away from the nightfall dragons, they didn't notice that a red sunrise dragon had joined the group of purple dragons.

"Nick," the royal purple dragon on his right hailed him. "We are giving your brother a bit of a chase. But it looks like he's going to get away."

Nick recognized the dragon immediately. "Grenadier! Giving my brother chase, excellent. I do find that Alex likes to run away from a fair fight."

"One of these days we will catch him," Grenadier chuckled as he flew tip to tip with Nick, his almost black wings beating the air in syncopation. Four other dragons flew to his left. They all turned their eyes on Nick. It was well known he was a traitor, working with them to undermine his own family.

"You'll certainly make my job easier if you do."

"We were told to look out for you. King Ibis would like to

meet with you, if you can manage to sneak away," Grenadier said. He started to turn back to the north. He was getting too far from the mountains, and it would do no good to be caught by other sunrise dragons talking to the Prince.

Nick thought for a moment. "I can meet in two days' time. We will meet at sunset, above the waterfall that is right on our borders. I may have Sadie with me, depending on how things go in Terrak."

"You have put that part of the plan in motion already? The lesser son will become the greater in no time at all," Grenadier said, giving a little roar. The four other dragons with him joined him, and wildlife in the fields below them shook with fear.

"I have. Soon Sadie and I will be mates, regardless of what her father thinks. I hope I have his blessing, but if I don't, there is not much he can do to stop us. I have already taken her."

"Ho ho ho. So, she is your mate already?"

"In everything but name. We will seal it in front of the sorcerer very soon."

"Ahhhh, I wish I could be there. What a delightful turn of events. I will pass the news on to King Ibis," Grenadier said. He turned firmly to the north now, making haste. "Goodbye, I will see you soon, my little Princeling."

Nick wasn't sure he approved of being called a "little Princling," but the nightfall dragons were integral to his plan. Everything was falling into place. He just had to figure out how to get his father and brother out of his way, so he could claim the throne rightfully. If he could do it without the suspicion of his people, or the dragon clan, all the better. He turned directly to the east, headed straight toward his destiny.

Darius Fletcher came to his senses nearly two days later by a loud knocking on his door. He lifted his pounding head from the cold flagstones, his utensils and cauldron surrounding him with the water and soap long since dried.

The knock pounded again, and with a groan, he rose from the floor. Every bone in his body ached, and the visions he had seen were still forefront in his mind.

"One minute!" he shouted. "I'm coming!" He managed to grab his staff and hobble to the door. He flung it open angrily.

"Darius," Nick Chuvash stood there, looking at him with a twinkle in his eye. He had his arm around Sadie Dayia. "Did I wake you?" He looked Darius up and down.

Darius realized that he must look even more disheveled than normal. His hair was unkempt, and his eyes felt like they had sand in them, which meant they were probably bloodshot. His robes were rumpled, and he had to admit he smelled a little rank. But he looked back and forth between the two. This was not right. "What is the meaning of THIS?" He pointed back and forth between them and spoke in an angry tone.

"Well, sorcerer, we came to give you a wedding invitation in person. I have taken Sadie as my mate. We will be married in one month's time. I demand your presence at Dumara castle to perform the ceremony."

Sadie smiled at Darius and batted her long lashes. "I would love it if you would perform the ceremony, Darius. We really do want to make this legal in front of the Dragon God. And the clan."

"IT IS FORBIDDEN!" Darius roared, slamming his staff down. A beam of light shot out of the top, hitting his ceiling with a crack. Small stones tinkled down, and the floor where he hit his staff was now charred in a star shape.

"Come now. Both our fathers have given their blessing. It is just a formality, really. She is already with my child," Nick said, a twisted smile on his face.

"You are a conniving mongrel," Darius said, glaring at him. "Come in!" he demanded, pointing at his table. The three chairs were already set up around, although one was tipped over.

"Did you have a little party here, Darius?" Nick asked, wrinkling up his nose.

"Where is it? What have I done with it? Oh, I have such a headache," Darius mumbled to himself, looking through a pile of papers and books. Dust motes flew through the air, and various documents in leather bindings fell onto the floor, joining the mess in progress. "Here it is!" he exclaimed, holding up an ancient looking, cracked leather tome. Pages were falling out, but he took the book and slammed it on the desk.

"What is it?" Sadie asked, her eyes wide with curiosity.

"It is the word of the Dragon Lord. My employment contact really, and the laws that lay out the land. It was given to the first sorcerer, hundreds of years ago."

"So what? I have a copy at home. I had to study it in great detail with my tutors. Very dry stuff," Nick shrugged.

"Then you remember, Nick Chuvash, the part where it explicitly prohibits the royal families and dragon clans from intermingling! In fact, it's such an important rule, it is placed in the first chapter!" Darius said, his voice rising.

"It's just historical rubbish. What's going to happen, Darius? Am I going to be smote down by an errant lightning bolt? These rules were written hundreds of years ago. Who really cares about the old rules anymore? It also says to not eat the flesh of cloven animals, yet we hunt wild boars. It's all a bunch of rubbish really."

From out of nowhere, the ground started to shake. Slowly at first, but then faster. Darius looked at his walls, terrified the stones would crumble on his head, but just as soon as it had started, it stopped.

"Been a lot of earthquakes lately," Nick said, looking at the ceiling, which now had a large crack in it.

"Nick Chuvash! That is a warning directly from the Dragon

God. You are playing with powers you do not understand. I will not marry you, for fear the Dragon God will strike me down!"

"You will marry us, or I will bring down a dragon attack on you and this tower so fearsome, you will weep," Nick warned.

"Helping us will be in your best interests, Darius," Sadie said coldly. He had never liked this one. She was calculating, and the pair of them together could be very dangerous.

"You do not scare me, young pup," Darius said. "This scares me!" he said, pointing at the book.

"Be in Dumara in one month's time, or I will string you up in my dungeon with all the mentally ill criminals," Nick warned. He turned, pulling Sadie along with him. He slammed the door, and the tower shook. More dust and pebbles trickled down from the crack in the ceiling.

"Oh, what have I done?" Darius said, slamming his fist down on the table. His visions of the past few days came flooding back, and he heard a voice in his head. Whether it was the last vestiges of the effects of noctum, he did not know, but the voice clearly said, "The wheels are in motion. Marry the willful and the ignorant, the child is destined. Do as I bid, for I am coming."

He heard a boom that sounded like a drum. A prickle of ice went down his spine, and he looked back up at the crack. He would have to find some way to stabilize the ceiling, and soon. He didn't want his lovely tower to collapse on his head while he was sleeping. First, he needed a wash, and something to eat and drink.

Outside, Nick and Sadie changed into their dragon forms. They had a meeting to make, and would have to fly as quickly as possible.

They had one big problem: no Dragon Keeper. Sadie had demanded Tyson hand over to her a bottle of astragenica, which she had used on her beloved when they had arrived, but he had only given them one, citing a low supply.

It was a problem they had to solve before the final part of their plan could come into motion. That, and getting the sunrise dragons to accept her, but she had a plan for that. For if she won the hearts of the drakaina, the rest of the clan would follow. "Let's go love," she purred as they rose into the air. They headed due north to the waterfall and their date with King Ibis, a necessary evil in their grand plan.

It was a long flight, and they flew wingtip to wingtip to the waterfall. They traveled over the lake, and what she considered her island. The palace where they had met, fallen in love, and conceived their dragonling.

By the time they had arrived at the waterfall, the darkness had come, and it was a new moon, so the night was deep. She heard the sound of the waterfall before she saw it, rushing over the edge and tumbling into the lake, pounding the stones on the bottom. They flew up and over, landing at the edge of the cliff, just upstream from the cliff's edge.

King Ibis stood in his dragon form, regal and fearsome. His deep purple scales made him hard to see in the darkness, but his yellow eyes glowed as he stared at Nick and Sadie, unblinking. He moved out of the shadows of the tree line, and his immense form was revealed. His long horns, nearly a meter long, twisted up above his head.

Doyle stepped out of the shadows at his King's side. He nodded to the pair. "I see you are together."

"We are to be married next month. It has been arranged," Nick said in dragon tongue, staring back at the King with his blue eyes.

"Congratulations," Ibis hissed. "I am pleased to tell you that I have arranged for my son to marry a Princess of Fresthav. Soon, we will have a dragon child of night and ice, and a dragon child of fire and light. We will marry them and create our own Dragon Lord."

"A worthy plan. And together, our children will rule all," Sadie said with a smile.

"Until then, we must keep rebellion down, we must continue the secrecy until the time is right to strike."

"All this secrecy, Ibis. I think my brother suspects."

"We will take your brother and your father out of the picture," Ibis nodded to Doyle.

Doyle reached into his robes and pulled out a bottle of deep black, evil looking liquid.

"Noctum. This is the elixir of night and death. There should be just enough for what you need to do. One drop will give you powerful visions. Two drops will take you to the edge of death, but you will see the future. More than that will kill a man quickly and relatively painlessly. Be very, very careful. Do not get any on your skin. Destroy or boil any dishes it touches." Doyle wrapped the bottle in a bit of felt, knelt down and tied it tightly to Sadie's front ankle.

"My spies tell me your brother has secured an alliance with Terrak," Ibis said, his scales scraping on the hard ground. He inched closer to Nick, his eyes not missing anything.

"He did, but when Sadie and I take the throne of Dumara, we can take Terrak, and then our plan can come to fruition."

"You mean my plan," Ibis said, looking at Nick with dangerous, narrow eyes.

"OUR plan," Nick said, taking a step forward. The two dragons locked eyes, neither of them looking away.

"Yesssssss." Ibis hissed in a very reptilian way. "That's what I like about you, Nick Chuvash. You don't back down from me. You are a very good partner." With a chuckle, he took a step back. "Good luck, young Princeling. The next time I see you, I expect you'll be a King. Don't fail me."

"You need to find yourself a Dragon Keeper as soon as you

become King," Doyle said. "I doubt Aswin will consent to serve you, and Mila will probably follow her father. Both of their bonds will be broken when the King and Crown Prince die. Either you force one of them to serve you, or you find another. Visit the sorcerer, bring a necklace. Any old piece of jewelry will do."

"What are you carrying on about, old man? Visit the sorcerer with a necklace? Why would I do that?"

"It is an ancient ritual between the Dragon Keeper and his King. It will bind him to your service," Doyle explained, frustrated. "Any human can become a Dragon Keeper, it's just a matter of the ceremony. Of course, it helps if they know HOW to be a Dragon Keeper."

"The Fletchers are loyal to my father. I do not want them in MY service," Nick said firmly.

"You may not have a choice, unless you are going to force Sadie here to be your Dragon Keeper indefinitely. But I think she will be busy raising your son."

"How do you know the future?" Sadie asked, looking at Doyle closely.

"I had to test the noctum. Saw some good visions, but the future is still unclear. It all hinges on Nick getting rid of both his father and brother. If you do that, our path is clear," Doyle said.

"I will not fail," Nick said, looking at Sadie. If a dragon could smile, he would have been. A son! She would be anxious to make her nest for their egg soon, deep in his dragon caves. Just around the time of their wedding, the nest would be ready, and then his son could stay safe and warm until the spring, when the miracle would be born. Plenty of time to get rid of his family, cement his hold on the clan, and take the throne.

Chapter 14

The Calm

Mila blinked against the light hitting her face, and she felt Alex behind her stirring. He sat up and rolled his neck.

"I've got a crick," he said, rubbing his neck and blinking. Then he looked down at her, and a slow smile hit his face. He never realized how beautiful Mila Fletcher was. Her hair surrounded her in glorious curls. She stretched, and she was like a cat, long and lean.

"So do I," she said, sitting up. She glanced over at him with her own shy smile. It was like they had shared something special last night. "Oh, my hair. What a state," she laughed as she tried to run her fingers through her hair. "Oh well. It's not like either of us are fit to be seen in public."

"Well, at least you saved my favorite shirt," he said, looking down at his simple linen shirt, now covered with dirt and sand.

"Well, it did seem more practical than silk, and plus, it was on top," she giggled. "Now, what should we have for breakfast? Nothing with a side of nothing?"

"Hoy there!" A voice called out from down the shore. Mila

and Alex turned with surprise and saw a local fisherman walking down the beach. He was a simple man, carrying a tackle box and a fishing pole. "Where are you two from? You look like you washed up on the shore."

Alex stood with a grin and held out his hand. "Prince Alex Chuvash, sir. We did have a bit of trouble last night. My lady friend and I were out for a leisurely cruise yesterday. We hit a rogue wave, and our ship capsized. Before you knew it, it had sunk with all our provisions. We were planning on heading back to Dumara castle today."

"Your Majesty," the man said, shocked. He dropped his fishing supplies and bowed low. "The name's Guin. I be a simple fisherman from Tiago. Is there anything I can do to be of service?"

"No, Guin. We just borrowed a bit of driftwood and a spot of your beach last night."

'Well, it's not my beach," Guin said. "It be public like. I live nearby. Could I invite you to my humble home for a spot of brekky? The wife would love to meet you, and who is your lady friend?"

Mila blushed deeply. "A pleasure to meet you Guin. I am not the Prince's lady friend. I am a Dragon Keeper of Dumara. We were out on the bay, watching the dragons. Did you see them?"

"Oh yes, I spotted them last night. A group of those purple dragons front he north, looked like they were chasing one of our sun dragons. I hope he got away. Sun dragons are lucky, they say."

"Oh yes, very lucky," Mila said, giving a pointed look at Alex. He grinned.

"He got away, that's what we were doing, making sure one of our dragons wasn't hurt," Alex said, filling in the story nicely.

"We would hate to impose. We will just be on our way this morning," Mila said, trying to brush off the sand from her clothing.

Guin looked at them, slightly rumbled, no shoes, no desirable provisions. "Are ye sure?" he said in disbelief.

"Oh yes, I'm sure my father will send someone along shortly to pick us up," Alex said. "It was a pleasure to meet you, sir." He shook the man's hand, and Guin shrugged and picked up his tackle box again. He made his way down the beach, turning back and looking at the strange pair over his shoulder. They both grinned and waved at him.

Once Guin was out of sight, Alex gave a chuckle and quickly changed. Soon, Alex stood before her. Mila quickly stuffed his clothes in her keeper's bag, making sure she didn't forget his favorite shirt. Quickly, she swung up on his back, holding tight to her bag with one hand, and his mane the other.

"Let's go home, Alex," she said, tossing her hair into the wind. What she wouldn't give for a hair tie right about now.

He leapt up into the air, following the shore line. He saw Guin the fisherman, standing knee deep with his line in the water. Mila could see his surprised face as Alex dipped his golden wings and then turned to head straight north to Dumara.

He was flying low, just a few hundred feet over the whitecap waves, hoping to avoid any nightfall dragons. They passed a ship, and all the sailors stood on the deck next to the wooden rails and waved as they flew by. Mila waved back, and they all clapped and yelled enthusiastically.

It seemed like the ship was trying to race them, and Mila spied its name on the bow, The Southern Pearl. "I think that's a Norda ship!"

"Ahhh, that makes sense. It's one of the trading ships, trying to get in a final voyage before the winter storms. They are pushing it a bit," Alex said. Without even trying, he was pulling ahead. His strong dragon wings flapped steadily, his neck stretching long as he raced into the wind. The sailors tried to keep up with him by letting out their sails and turning the boat to pick up speed. The men on deck were singing a sea shanty, and Mila could just make out the words.

Our anchor's aweigh and our sails are all set
Bold Riley, oh, boom-a-lay
The folks we are leaving, we'll never forget
Bold Riley, oh, gone away
Goodbye, me darling. Goodbye, me dear, oh
Bold Riley, oh, boom-a-lay
Goodbye, me darling. Goodbye, me dear, oh
Bold Riley, oh, gone away
Wake up Mary Ellen and don't look so glum
By Whitestocking time you'll be drinking hot rum
The rain it is raining now all the day long
And the northerly wind, it does blow so strong
We're outward and bound for Sunrise Bay
Get bending, me boys, it's a hell of a way

Mila was tapping her fingers on the top of her keeper's bag, drumming along with the music, bobbing her head. Long after the ship had passed out of earshot, she was still humming along.

"Mila, dragons ahead, but they are friends," Alex rumbled. She gazed up and saw a half dozen sunrise dragons on the horizon. She could make out a man on the back of one and started waving, "It's my dad!" she said with delight.

Alex started gaining altitude, and before long, he had joined the group. They all turned around and placed him firmly in the middle. Mila waved at her father. The wind was blowing too strong today for her to hear him speak, but Rand growled, "Where have you been? We were worried. We've been hunting the bay for hours looking for you."

"Sorry, Father. We were chased far south yesterday by a pack of nightfall dragons. I had a headwind and was exhausted. They would have taken me. We almost didn't make it, to be honest. I had to dive and ended up landing in the bay." Alex recounted their terrifying escape.

"The nightfall dragons are becoming bolder. Did you make an agreement with Terrak?"

"I did. They will help us patrol the north. Oh yeah, Nick showed up, convinced King Dayia to let them wed. I'll let him tell you the good news. Is he home yet?" Alex asked, noticing his brother wasn't in the guard.

"No. He has not arrived. What good news?" Rand growled.

"Well, I hate to break it to you first, but you're going to be a grandfather," Alex said, staring straight ahead as he flew.

"Hades. This is moving too fast. You know what this means, son," Rand said, trying to catch his son's eye as he flew.

"Yes," Alex said simply. He stared straight ahead, trying to focus, trying to not let Mila read his thoughts, but it was too late.

"You'll have to marry, won't you? Because your brother is going to have a dragonling, and you need your own heir," she thought to him.

He didn't respond, still trying to keep his thoughts clear. He had no idea who he would pick. He supposed it didn't matter much, he might as well let his father make the arrangements.

Rand noticed his son's quietness and was disturbed. Was there something Alex wasn't telling him? His son had never been excited about marriage, but now it was necessary. It was sad he couldn't trust Nick, his own son, but he had some disturbing reports about him, from his spies in the clan. Whispers that he wished for his father's throne. Mutterings that he was trying to sow dissent among his own clan's people. Outright accusations from Nick, which Rand had brushed off at the time as teenage angst, that Alex was not fit to rule. The best course of action would be for Alex to marry and to cement his legacy as soon as possible. Then, Nick would have to be content to be the spare. Perhaps he could appoint him as a diplomat, as he seemed to have connections everywhere. Sometimes, Rand wondered if his youngest son was more connected than he was. If he could only develop that skill in him, put him to use. He would have to try harder when he returned to connect with Nick.

Mila had never been happier to see the rooftops of Dumara in the distance. Even though she had only been gone a few days, it seemed like a lifetime. In the caves, she attended to Alex, delivering his potion and taking his favorite shirt out of her bag. He didn't look at her, and he seemed angry at something. Without a word, he hurried off with his father, deep in discussion about a suitable bride.

Mila was left staring after him. A goodbye would have been nice. She shrugged and joined her father.

Before they could leave, they went to check on an injured dragon. Yesterday, during the dawn patrol, there had been a mild scuffle with some nightfall dragons. It was six against six, so the fight had quickly broken up, but in the initial attack, a dragon named Plume had suffered a wing tear.

They entered his cave, and his mate, Apple, was fussing over him. "Now, what did I tell you! Eat that venison! You need to keep your strength up!" she said, her yellow eyes glinting. She was literally perched over him, her yellow and orange body balancing on the edge of their nest, her claws digging into the stone wall.

Plume, for his part, rolled over on his side, his deep burgundy body sighing under her attention. Mila could see his injured wing. A long tear down the middle, stitched up with spider thread. "Listen, I'm trying to sleep. Your nagging isn't helping me heal."

Apple noticed the keepers come into their cave. "Oh, Aswin and Mila. He's being impossible! He won't listen to me, and I'm so afraid he's going to try to go hunting before his wing is ready," she cried, tears dripping out of the corners of her eyes and streaming down her yellow face.

Mila consoled Apple, patting the sides of her face and giving her praise for taking care of her mate. Apple seemed to settle, and she stood back as Aswin approached Plume and gently rubbed his side. "Mila, help me hold his wing out, please. I had to have Sam help me yesterday when I stitched it. He loved coming up here. He's a good lad," Aswin said.

Gently and carefully, she picked up the leading edge of Plume's wing. She could feel the strong bones in her hands. Luckily, he had not broken a wing bone. Dragons could be crippled for life if it was not set properly.

But the injury still gave Plume pain, and he groaned when Mila helped him carefully extend the wing fully. Her father took out a tin of healing balm and rubbed it over the injury, making sure the rent in the wing was healing together. "Very good, Plume. You should be back in the air in a week's time. But I want you to be careful. Stay out of the border patrol until it's 100 percent. We don't want a secondary tear."

"Aswin, I could go out today. I'm feeling much better!" Plume insisted as Mila gently helped him tuck his wing back into his side.

"Well, you still have visible pain, so I don't quite believe that. You had to be carried home, which indicates to me that it was a major tear, if you couldn't fly," Mila said.

"Worst day of my life. The humiliation of being carried as if I was dead into my own caves," Plume said glumly. Apple grumbled at him, giving him an evil look. "Listen, my mate, you are lucky you made it home. If you would have left me a widow with two dragonlings to feed, I would have haunted you forever. You listen to the Dragon Keepers and rest."

Plume sighed. "Stop nagging me. You'll be the death me of me yet." He rolled over on his side, and turned his head away, done with this conversation.

With a laugh, Aswin patted Plume, then headed for the exit. Aswin traveled down the main corridor, which was lined with dragon caves leading to the nests of the highest ranking dragons. They heard a huge roar from ahead, and it shook the walls.

"Where is the Dragon Keeper? Send for him at once!"

"Nick," Aswin said, his steps picking up. Mila hurried to keep up, hitching her bag on her shoulder.

"I see he finally made it home," Mila said sarcastically.

"Yes, a day late. One wonders what he does with all his extra time," Aswin said, pondering.

They entered the wide chamber and saw Nick standing there, red and fearsome. His chest was flexed, and he shook his mane. A group of angry dragons had gathered around him, roaring and grumbling. Sadie's dark green scales looked out of place, and apparently, she felt the hostility. She lowered her head and took another step back.

Aswin stopped and crossed his arms. Mila nearly crashed into him, he stopped so suddenly.

"Watch. It is a test," he whispered to Mila. He felt Rand watching the scene through his eyes, and next to him, Mila felt Alex watching also.

Nick stomped his feet and bellowed, and then started grunting as he moved forward in a sign of aggression.

The dragons of the clan stood their ground, their yellow eyes looking at him and Sadie in anger. "You have brought a summer dragon into our home! Why have you brought here a dragon from another clan? You have defiled Dumara."

"This is my mate! I have taken her and chosen."

Shocked mutters ran through the group, and more and more dragons started to gather, the hostility in the cave growing.

"Oh, let's see how brother gets out of this little predicament," Alex chuckled in her thoughts.

"We will let him settle this matter himself. Do not intervene, Aswin," Rand said in his head. "This is what he wanted, so he needs to deal with it."

"You have mated a summer dragon! It is forbidden!" The shocked voices ran through the group.

"I have chosen!" Nick roared so loudly, the cave shook. He emitted a light ray in his anger, and it hit the far wall.

"You could choose any drakaina in this cave, and yet you choose an inferior!" Torrid, a huge pale yellow dragon roared. His scales were the color of butter. He was a respected hunter in the clan, and he was larger than most dragons, his powerful chest and huge claws a sign of his dominance.

"She is not inferior. She is a Princess of Terrak. A marriage with her will only benefit our kingdom!" Nick roared, stamping his foot in anger.

Sadie stayed quiet behind him, lowering her belly to the ground in a submissive pose. Now was not the time for her to talk.

The group mumbled among themselves. Someone interjected, "Does Rand know about this?"

"My father has given his approval. My brother, Alex and I managed to secure an alliance with Terrak. They will help us patrol the border. But as part of that deal, we had to agree to this union. It was shocking to us, but I expect you all to treat my new mate as an equal," Nick said, stretching the truth about the wedding arrangements as far as it could go.

There was more mumbling among the dragon clans. More and more dragons were joining the group. The cave was so full that one could barely walk through the crowd now, and Aswin and Mila were nearly knocked over several times as drakaina started to join them.

"This is blasphemy. The Dragon God will smite you down!" One drakaina, known as Dahlia, roared. She was the daughter of Torrid and not yet mated. She was known for being outspoken and independent. Dragon males were attracted to submissive dragons, which was why Sadie was laying on the ground, refusing to look any sunrise dragon in the eye.

Mila felt Alex examine Sadie through her eyes. She sensed that he was curious about the drakaina.

"The sorcerer will arrive in one month's time and sanctify our union in front of the Dragon God," Nick roared at Dahlia, gnashing his teeth in her direction. He hated Dahlia. She was everything he disliked in a drakaina, but he knew better than to try to put her in her place. Her father, Torrid, would fight him before he could blink an eye, not caring that he was a Prince of Dumara.

More muttering from the crowd. Finally, one of Nick's friends, Sumac, stepped forward. Sumac was a thin, small dragon, who was a poor hunter and generally thought of as worthless in the clan. Which is why Nick had befriended him. He had made a point to befriend as many of the outcasts, rejects, and misfits he could find. The ones who felt dissatisfaction with the way things were. The dragons who dreamed of glory, but because of poor social standing in the clan, terrible genetics that made them weak, or just disagreeable dispositions, were good candidates for Nick's project.

Sumac took a deep breath. He was not a good public speaker, and no one really cared what he said anyway, but he tried. "I think that if Rand has given his blessing, we should too. Nick is a Prince of Dumara, and sometimes, a Prince must do his duty to the clan."

Surprisingly, he heard mutters of approval. Some of his friends, the other misfits shouted, "Yes! We agree! We welcome Nick's mate!"

"But it is forbidden!" Dahlia, cried, stamping her foot again.

"Oh shut it, Dahlia!" Sumac muttered. Before he could even get the words out, her father Torrid flew across the room, clawing at him. His open mouth with teeth dripping saliva came inches from Sumac's face.

"Do not disrespect my daughter, you scum! Return to your little cave, in the deepest darkest parts of the mountain, where you belong! Mateless, worthless cuss!" Torrid said. He swiped at Sumac. His claws tore at Sumac, but not enough to break the skin.

Sumac whimpered and dropped into a submissive pose. But the words had been said, and most seemed to agree with him.

Holly, a prominent female, stepped forward. "The females of this clan recognize a hard decision has been made. We welcome Princess Sadie of Terrak into our fold. May we learn to live in peace."

"Yes, we agree." Their mates mumbled, and dragons started to leave the cave. Sumac slinked away down to his cave, where he licked his wounds by himself.

Soon, all that were left in the darkness were the Dragon Keepers, Nick and Sadie.

Silence fell between them all. Finally, Sadie rose from the ground, picking her head up and looking around.

From the stairwell in the corner, Alex appeared. He had a stack of clothing, which he laid wordlessly at his brother's feet. Mila noticed there was some women's clothing which had been quickly procured from somewhere.

Without a word, Alex turned and went back up the stairs.

"Turn us, Dragon Keeper! What are you waiting for?"

Aswin sighed and flipped open his bag. "I only have one left. Do you have any, Mila?"

She opened her bag to check. She was glad she had managed to keep a hold of her bag. "I do."

Aswin nodded and strode forward to Nick. Mila grabbed one of her potions and walked to Sadie, her green sides breathing heavily. She must have been more nervous than she let on.

"Since you're official, I guess I'll have to give you a dragon name. It's the sort of thing I do," she said. She considered Sadie's dark green coloring. Her belly was black, and her eyes were orange. She was hard to see in the gloom.

Mila uncorked the potion, and Sadie opened her mouth, her

sharp teeth just inches from Mila's face. It suddenly came to her. "Ivy. Welcome to, Dumara, Ivy."

As Ivy changed into Sadie, Nick dressed. "Why did you have to go give her one of your stupid names?"

"I don't know, love. It's okay. Plus, if the Dragon Keeper has named me, it sort of makes it official, doesn't it?" Sadie took the simple dress from Mila's hands, looking at it with obvious distaste.

"I guess you have a point," Nick grumbled, kissing her forehead.

"I'm going to find a tailor as soon as possible," Sadie said, tying the dress at her waist.

"I know a great one! My friend, Kiara! Her father's shop has the finest, most up-to-date styles."

"And he does your clothes?" she asked with scorn, looking at Mila's disheveled appearance.

"Well, yes. But I lost my jacket in the sea, nearly drowned, and slept on a beach last night, so this is not a good representation of his work."

"I think you will find him adequate, dear. He is the King's official tailor."

"Anything's better than these rags," she said, holding her arms out and considering the rough homespun fabric.

Nick turned and led her to the stairs. It had been a long day, and he was sure his father would want to talk with them after dinner.

Aswin was crouched down, going through Mila's bag. "I'm glad you managed to save the bag. They are custom. I had them specially made by the leather craftsman. Seemed to keep out most of the water, just a bit of damage. You have some things in here that need replacement, and we will need to make a batch of astragenica tonight. We've been going through it."

Suddenly, exhaustion caught up with Mila. She felt bone tired. She nodded and took her bag from her father.

They made their way outside and down the steep path. Mila's

legs felt heavy. She nearly cried when they got back to the shop and found Sam waiting for them.

"I made up another batch of astragenica for you. Figured you would need it," Sam said, looking up from behind the counter. He was going through the accounts books, making the day's entries, and he looked studious as he tucked the pencil behind his ear.

"Thank you so much Sam!" Mila said, plopping her bag down on the counter. She pulled up a stool, and started going through the bag, pulling out the wet and ruined things and setting then aside.

"What happened?" Sam asked, looking at alarm at her growing pile.

"We sort of crashed landed in the bay and had to swim to shore. Lost the rest my bags but managed to hold on to this one. It floats, mostly," she said with a sigh. She put her hand on her chin and sat for a moment, as Alex's thoughts were intruding on her own. They were having a heated discussion up at the castle. So heated it was coming through, loud and clear.

Even Aswin stopped what he was doing, and looked lost in thought, his hand paused in mid-air as he reached for a shop apron on the hook. Sam looked back and forth between the two, realizing something was happening.

"I'll take care of this mess, Mila. Why don't you get some rest?" Sam said, pulling her bag closer to him. He picked up the pile of discards and threw them into the bin.

"Yeah. I think I will," Mila said, sounding like she was a million miles away. She stood up and made her way upstairs. She needed some food, a bath, and her bed. She found some bread and cheese in the kitchen, and opened the taps to draw the water, listening to the argument in her head.

Chapter 15

The Storm

Nick entered his father's study, a smirk on his face. He had left Sadie in his room in the hands of a capable servant who had started fussing over her immediately.

Alex was sitting on a chair, looking out the window pensively. The late afternoon sunlight lit up his face and his silhouette, making him look like an angry god. He didn't turn when Nick entered the room but Rand, sitting next to him, did.

Rand got up, crossed his arms across his thick chest, and stared at Nick with real anger. He was dressed in a red jacket, his blue eyes almost crackling with rage. "I don't know what you were thinking with that stunt you pulled. I gave you permission to ask for her hand, not to fly immediately to Terrak, upstage your brother's negotiations, and then bring her directly to our caves." Rand angrily pointed to the now empty seat by Alex.

With a pout, Nick took the seat offered. He knew not to cross his father when he slipped into one of his tempers. Alex still wouldn't look at Nick. He could feel the animosity roll off his older brother. Nick thought maybe he had pushed too hard and fast. He might need to back off for a while, play the long game, at least until the clan fully accepted Sadie.

"Your brother was in the middle of a very sensitive diplomatic meeting, and you burst in. Your lucky King Dayia didn't throw you out right then and there. I'm honestly amazed he agreed to both the alliance and your marriage."

Nick shrugged, wondering if his brother had anything to say, or if he was just going to keep staring out the window. "Well, it worked out, didn't it?"

"And the pure audacity of bringing her straight here! There should have been an announcement. I could have prepared the clan, but no, you just had to go off all wild. You've put me in a very poor position with our own clan. I'm going to have to go down tonight and persuade them that I'm not crazy. You have also put your brother in a predicament." Rand banged his first on his desk, causing everything to jump. As he spoke, his voice got louder and louder until it carried through doors. Servants down the hall stopped what they were doing to listen.

"Yes, Nick. You have forced me into a decision I didn't want to make," Alex said in a deadly quiet voice.

"What? Are you actually going to do your duty and marry? You're two years older than me. You should have done this long ago. You should already have a dragonling heir," Nick sneered.

"Has it ever occurred to you, you conniving little toad, that I was waiting to meet the right person? I wished for a marriage of love," Alex said, rising to his feet, glaring at his brother with true hatred.

"Well, we can't always get what we want," Nick said, joining his brother by standing.

"Boys, sit down!" Rand demanded.

"I think my little brother needs a reminder of who is the oldest and who is the Crown Prince. He needs to remember his place," Alex said, placing his hands on his brother's chest and shoving.

"Maybe my older brother should act like a Crown Prince. He would be a leader, and take risks. Maybe he should be worried about the future, instead of his own selfish desires. Do your duty, brother!" Nick pushed him back.

"Let me tell you about duty, Nick. Duty is doing what is best for Dumara. It's keeping our legacy alive. It's not sneaking off to mate with the hot neighbor. It's not sneaking off and doing whatever it is you do when we should be hunting or patrolling. It's not spreading gossip and decisiveness with all your little outcast friends. Don't pretend I don't know what you're up to," Alex said, pushing him again.

Nick had enough. He drew his hand back and he formed it into a fist. He brought it down with great anger to his brother's jaw. It connected with a meaty sound.

Alex started swinging himself, hitting his brother again and again. They grappled and then fell on the coffee table with a crash.

Nick kicked and flopped as Alex got his arms around him.

"Boys! Stop this fighting!" Rand shouted. But the punches continued to fly.

Finally, Alex got the upper hand, and he put his brother in a headlock, smashing his already bruised face into the broken glass from the coffee table.

Rand had enough. He grabbed Alex by the hair, throwing him across the room. Alex landed hard against the wall, the wind knocked out of him.

Nick was moaning on the floor, and Rand helped him up, surveying the broken furniture and shaking his head. "It's been years since you two broke furniture. I wish your mother was still here. She was always a tempering force, and you both listened to her." Rand sat back down behind his desk, looking sad.

Alex managed to catch his breath and stood, glaring at his brother.

Both brothers were bruised and battered. Alex had a large

black bruise already forming on his cheek, and his nose was bloody.

Nick had an eye that was nearly swollen shut. It would be black tomorrow. He had multiple cuts on his face and red marks on his neck where his brother had nearly tried to strangle him.

"Don't you come near me again," Nick said, slowly rising to his feet and brushing glass off his pants.

"Same," Alex said, tightening his jaw and clenching his fists.

"I can't believe I have to say this to two grown men, but go to your rooms. Nick, please try to run things past me before you go off all willy-nilly with some crazy plan. I do have a kingdom to run. Alex, go think about what drakaina you're going to take as a mate. I'll have to approach her father. The sooner, the better. You both will marry on the same day, and I expect an heir soon, Alex."

"But Father, Sadie and I don't want to share a wedding day with him!" Nick whined, mad that his brother would upstage him again. This wedding day was supposed to show off his power and vitality.

"Tough. Like you just told your brother, it's your duty. I think you've done enough damage already, Nick."

"Fine!" Nick yelled, turning on his heel, marching out the door, and slamming it has hard as he could. Servants in the hall resumed their duties, shooting him a fearful glance.

Alex was looking at his father sadly as he rubbed his jaw. "You're making me pick, tonight?"

"Yes. You already know who is available. Pick one, preferably one well connected," Rand growled, almost dragon-like.

"Yes, Father," Alex said, grief crossing his face.

"I want an answer at breakfast."

"Yes. Now, if you'll excuse me. I haven't eaten all day, I'm exhausted, and I need a bath," Alex said, heading for the door himself. He left his father sitting there and went to his room. His servant was waiting for him.

He asked for some food to be brought to his room. He had a lot of thinking to do, and he really didn't want to deal with his brother again tonight. He pulled off his grubby clothes, smiling as he took off his favorite shirt and set it in the basket for the laundress. He sensed Mila's connection, and he knew she had heard that entire conversation. He sensed her sadness, and he felt it too.

He had been falling for his Dragon Keeper. His own Mother had been born a human and had only gained the ability to shift into a dragon after her marriage. Alex knew that this was not an option in any way. The clan needed him to pick a drakaina to ease some of the pain of his brother's actions. His choosing a daughter of a powerful warrior would smooth over many bad feelings.

He took a bath, washing away the salt from the sea, the sand from the beach, and the blood from his fight. It had been a very long day, and he was exhausted.

He put on his plush robe and his slippers and settled into his favorite overstuffed chair. It wasn't even four o'clock in the afternoon, and already his body ached for bed.

The servant brought him a tray of meats and cheese and a bottle of his favorite wine, setting it on the table next to him. He ate slowly, thinking of his choices.

"I'm sorry, Alex," Mila said in his thoughts.

"Nothing to be sorry about, Mila," Alex thought back. "I just have a hard choice to make. I wish things could be different." He thought of kissing her sweetly, and her head on his shoulder, and her body pressed against his as they slept last night on the beach. He knew she could read his thoughts because her thoughts were filled with him.

With a heart-wrenching cry, he pushed her out of his head, slowly and softly, so as not to hurt her. He picked up the bottle of red wine and started drinking. He began to think of the two dozen or so unmated drakaina's that were about his age. Which one would be a good partner, a good mother, and most importantly, make the clan happy?

Most he discarded immediately, due to a poor family, bad dispositions, or he thought, a poor ability to blend into the human world. By choosing a mate, he would be bestowing a drakaina the ability to shapeshift into a human.

The secret was that any dragon or human could transform with an astragenica potion. It was just a privilege reserved for royalty. The secret of astragenica was well guarded and protected by the keepers.

His mind finally settled on one. Yes, she would be fine. He even admired her spark. His glimpse of her earlier through Mila's eyes only confirmed his decision. She would stand up to his brother, and her father was nothing to be trifled with. Dahlia would give his brother and Sadie a run for their money, and the match would bring the most powerful warriors more firmly into his corner.

Mila caught his choice, and as he sipped his wine and finished his food, he caught her thought. "That is a good choice, Alex."

Her approval caused him to smile.

"Goodnight, dear Mila," he thought as he got up. He slipped between his sheets and looked out his window at the afternoon light. In the distance, he could see the trees wrapped in their fall colors. Reds, yellows, browns, and golds. The colors of the sunrise dragons.

Winter would be coming soon, and the ice dragons would fly.

Chapter 16

The Choice

After Rand called a servant to clean up the mess in his study, he connected with Aswin. "Did you catch all that, my friend?"

"I did," Aswin thought back to him. "Kids. You're going to need to redecorate your study."

That made Rand chuckle. When the boys were younger, they regularly destroyed rooms with their fighting. If it wasn't throwing each other into furniture, it was accidental light beam fires. As they grew older, he had been happy to see them get along better. Cassandra had always been the peace broker between the two, counseling them in their disagreements.

"I'm going downstairs, Aswin. I'll stay the night there and fly in the morning. Meet me just after sunrise," Rand thought, headed for the stairs.

"Should I bring Mila?"

"No, let her sleep in tomorrow. Her and Alex had a rough day, I think," Rand said, gazing toward his eldest son's room. He had seen the way the two of them had looked at each other earlier. There was obvious chemistry between the two. It had probably been amplified by the mind connection. He could truly call Aswin his best friend. They were closer in some ways than he and his own mate had been. They knew each other in a deeply personal way.

He was sorry he was making Alex pick a mate, but it was his son's duty. Besides, a match with his Dragon Keeper was impossible. Unheard of, and borderline scandalous.

He reached the bottom of the steps and threw off his clothing. He immediately transformed and strode into the main hall with calculated swagger, roaring for his clan. One by one, they emerged from the caves, slinking in the darkness, forming a circle around him.

He sat on his haunches, looking at them all with unblinking eyes. There were mutters in the crowd, as they all knew he was here to address the unrest that had been ripping though the caves since Nick and Sadie had arrived and made their surprise announcement.

"Sunrise dragons, thank you for answering my call. I know today has been upsetting for you. I apologize for surprising you all with the news of my youngest son's choice of mate. That is not how I intended for you to find out," he began, filling his chest with air and speaking slowly and with measure. He made eye contact with as many of his dragons as he could. Most stared at him coolly, listening intently. A few appeared openly hostile in their body language, and Rand could not blame them. What his son had done was unprecedented. It was a huge ask of his people.

He continued. "As you know, we have faced unprovoked attacks on our northern borders from the nightfall dragons. Their kingdom is barren, devoid of wildlife for hunting, and limited in resources for trading. The humans who live there are enslaved in the mines, the land is poor, and they have very little farming. The nightfall dragons seek to expand, I believe, into our lush and fertile valleys, into our flourishing hunting grounds."

"They make off with deer from our northern forests. I worry about over hunting." Robin, a light red dragon, spoke up.

"And of course, there is the horrifying attack on our Queen. She was killed in cold blood. I have reason to believe it was a plot, and I'm working to get to the bottom of it. I believe the assassination was meant for me," Rand went on.

Many dragons nodded, looking concerned as their King laid it all out before them. "We skirmish with the nightfall dragons daily now. Only going out in numbers has protected us. They grow bolder every day," said a voice from the back.

"I know. And there have been reports of the winter dragons to the east. With the season change coming, I fear they will be even more bold. There is evidence that they are working with Murdad and the nightfall dragons. We can't be two places at once."

"Yes, we saw four just a few days ago in our territories. They quickly left the area when they spotted us, but it was strange to see them in Dumara so early in the fall." Torrid spoke loudly, and everyone nodded in agreement.

"So that is why I sent Alex to Terrak. They have always been allies of ours. We share a close relationship. I consider Cleon a friend. Our children know each other well, and I'm sure you all recall fondly the visits from the King and his family." Rand reminded them of the times when Cleon would visit when their dragonlings were younger. They had always stayed in the upper castle, but he had entered through the caves, and had greeted them all warmly.

"Yes, he's a good sort," Holly agreed, and murmurs of approval rippled through the crowd.

"So, when it was suggested that the alliance would be strengthened with a marriage between Nick and his daughter, it occurred to me that this would not completely be a bad thing. And a mating would give us certain advantages."

"The children will have both fire and light."

"Exactly, and while some may point out it is forbidden by the Dragon God, there have been hybrids before. Never in a royal family, but it happens. Also, because Nick is my second son, I felt like it wouldn't impact the royal line."

"But Alex has not yet taken a mate. He has no heir," someone pointed out.

"Yes, I have spoken to my son. He will pick a mate soon, and soon he will have an heir. He will marry the same day as his brother," Rand announced.

The room erupted in chatter. Dragons with unmated daughters became excited, roaring their approval. There was much stamping and roaring.

"I thought that might make you all happy. I will be glad to announce his choice very soon, and I promise you that these two marriages will only bring safety and security to our clan. Terrak and Dumara will be united, and your Crown Prince and Princess will give us an heir," Rand promised, hoping that indeed, Alex and whomever he picked would have a dragonling by spring.

The roars echoed through the caves, and the drakainas, back in their nests, smiled. They heard the shouts and realized that for one of them, her life would change dramatically.

After the meeting, Rand picked up a fresh deer carcass from the pile by the door and tore into it. He was hungry, and he would not be returning to the castle. Tonight, he would return to a place he had been avoiding since Cassandra's death. The Chuvash cave.

He quickly tore all the good meat off the deer, relishing in the taste of fresh blood. Normally, he ate human food, but when in dragon form, he found deer meat delicious. He crushed the remaining bones with his teeth. He licked the blood from his jaw, turned, and made his way to his nest.

Their nest. Where his sons had been born, and where he and Cassandra had built their family. The stone ring, wide enough for them to lay side by side, was cold and empty. With a sigh, he settled in, laying on his side. The space, usually occupied by her, was empty and quiet. A lone tear squeezed out of his eye, and for a brief moment, he considered taking another mate. However, he decided that no drakaina could ever fill the hole in his heart. One day, he would die, and his soul would return to the Dragon God, and his beloved.

———

The next morning, he arose just before sunrise. He felt well rested and ready to face the day. He had been dreading returning to their nest, but it had not been as bad as he had anticipated. His dreams had been filled with sweet memories, and this morning, he greeted the other warriors who lined up at the entrance with him.

At the last minute, Alex joined them, taking his spot on the edge of the cave without a word. Rand looked over at his son and nodded. "I did not expect to see you this morning."

"I went to bed early," was all he said.

Rand spread his red wings and dropped off the edge of the entrance, followed by his son and four other warriors. It was still dark, and they winged over Dumara, the river a silver ribbon underneath them. A few lights twinkled from the windows, spilling their golden light into the night.

They headed due east to meet the sun, the ground rolling quickly beneath them. The cold morning air felt good on their faces. They encountered no nightfall dragons, and they greeted the sun successfully, turning on dragon wings back to the west, while the sun followed their path across the land.

On the way back, they ran across a large deer herd. "A little morning hunting for the clan?" Rand suggested.

"Yes!" They separated and approached the herd from multiple directions. The deer, frozen with fear and indecision, were easy picking. All the dragons flew back with a deer carcass in their sharp claws.

Entering the caves, they deposited their fresh kill in the now empty food spot near the entrance. Aswin was waiting for them, to turn them, but Alex turned to his father. "Could we talk, alone?"

"Yes, up top," Rand said, and they both dropped back out of the entrance.

Rand flew to the top of the cliffs. There was a large, flat space there. The top of the cliff was sacred ground to the dragon clan. Their history told that this was where the Dragon God had descended from the heavens and sent his dragon children to all four corners of this earth. This was also the spot where duels happened, although that had not happened in a very long time.

Now Alex landed, tucking his golden wings into this body. His blue eyes looked over the edge at the Kingdom of Dumara spread out before him.

Rand landed and moved up to his son. "Impressive up here, isn't it? This is all of our kingdom, as far as the eye can see. Our people and our dragon brothers, whom we must protect and serve. Have you made your choice?"

"I have. I have chosen Dahlia, daughter of Torrid," Alex said, not looking at him.

Rand was surprised but impressed. He had expected Alex to pick a pretty, young, submissive thing. Dahlia was practically a spinster at the ripe old age of twenty. She was known to be outspoken, a drakaina with strong thoughts and opinions. But her father, oh her father was fearsome. A warrior of great might. His strength rivaled Rand's own, and Rand considered Torrid a good friend. "That is a good choice. A very good choice. Your children will be strong and powerful."

"I know. That is why I choose her," Alex said, rather glumly.

"I know this isn't what you want, but love will grow," Rand said.

"You married for love, how do you know?" Alex said bitterly.

"I married your mother for love, but honestly, we barely knew each other. We had met in passing, and it was love at first sight. Yes, she was the daughter of a rich Norda jeweler, but we had only met a few times before I asked her to marry me. I had to explain the whole dragon king thing, and of course she was hesitant. But she married me, and changed her whole life for me, and our love grew and grew. I will never marry again," Rand said sadly.

"I'm sorry, Father. I hope I find that same happiness with Dahlia," Alex said. "I have barely spoken two sentences to her in my life."

"I will speak to her father today. You can court her before you are married, of course. I think it is a good match," Rand said, pleased his son had chosen her. Now that he thought about it, it was a perfect match. His son was a large dragon, inheriting his good genetics, and Rand had a feeling their dragonlings would be huge. Dragons respected huge.

Two days later, the arrangements had been made. Rand and Alex had met with Torrid, and he had consented. Now, all that was left was for Alex to ask Dahlia. He could have just married her, with only her father's approval, but he wanted her to at least consent.

They met awkwardly at the entrance to the dragon cave. Alex stood on the edge, nervously waiting for her.

She approached and looked him straight in the eye. "Alex. You wanted to discuss marriage with me?"

"Yes, would you fly with me?" he asked, standing on the edge.

"Of course," she answered, stepping up beside him. Soon, they were both in the air, and they flew silently, considering each other.

Dahlia was a fiery red dragon. She had a drakaina mane, which wasn't as full as a male's, with a shorter tuft of hair. Her wings were large and beat the air strongly, and she easily kept pace with Alex.

She considered the Crown Prince. He was a large dragon, almost as large as her father. He was powerful, and strong. She knew him in passing, and he had always been respectful to her. Frankly, she had never expected to marry, knowing that she wasn't submissive. She wondered why he had chosen her. She would have to lay down some ground rules before she would agree to this.

They flew to the south, and Dahlia enjoyed the sun on her wings. She had been out little in recent weeks, caring for her mother, who had been ill. Aswin had been called several times and had given her mother a tonic, but he said that she had a wasting illness and would not last until spring. She had been getting weaker every day. At the news that Alex wanted to marry her daughter, she had smiled for the first time in a while. "I knew you were special, Dahlia. See, someone noticed your spunk. I guarantee it, he chose you for that. He wants an equal, Dahlia, not some doormat for a mate. Step up and meet the challenge."

Alex took the lead and led her to the southernmost point in Dumara, aptly called The Point. It was a quiet place, and only sleepy fishing villages dotted the landscape. The winters were harsh here, and it was hard to carve out a living in the poor soil.

He landed on The Point, just below the lighthouse. Seagulls flew into the air, angry to be disturbed. Below on the beach, black, fat seals bathed in the sun, and their honking could be heard from this distance.

Dahlia landed gently beside him, tucking her wings. She sat on her haunches and considered him. She would let him talk. She was most curious as to what he had to say to her. She would marry him, of course, she would be crazy not to, but she hoped he was as kind as he seemed.

"Dahlia, thank you for coming out with me today," he said nervously, not knowing how to approach the topic of marriage. He had never really dated, so he didn't know how any of this really worked. He had always been somewhat shy. Mila had been the first girl he had kissed, and he sensed her now, quietly watching. He cleared his throat. "Uhhhh, I wanted to ask you if you will marry me. I know we don't really know each other, but my father wants me to marry, and you are my choice." His words tumbled out of his mouth, and he realized he sounded ridiculous.

She smiled. "Why did you choose me, Alex? I am honored, but I want to know. Why didn't you choose Prima, Shell, or Bell? They are all younger, prettier, and more submissive," she pointed out.

He looked at her intensely. "I don't want submissive. I want someone who can stand with me. I think you are that drakaina."

"Well, you've got me there. I'm not one to slink around with my head down. I've gotten myself in trouble countless times with my big mouth and strong opinion. My parents have told me time and time again I would never find a mate if I kept talking. I can't seem to stop though," she said, shrugging.

"I like outspoken. I need someone to be a leader. My brother …" He trailed off, leaving much left unsaid.

"Your brother is a problem, isn't he? Nick and that summer dragon have just arrived, and she is already building her own little clique. She has all the horrid dragons around her, the backstabbing little monsters who love to talk badly of others. They don't like me, of course. I don't fit their mold."

He tilted his head. "I didn't know this. How many friends does she have?"

"I don't know, a good amount." Dahlia considered a moment. "At least five already. Interestingly, she's also trying to find mates for Nick's little outcast friends. So far, Sumac has taken a mate, and there is talk that Plum and Thorn will be mated."

Alex looked pensive. "My brother is moving fast. He's rewarding his followers. This is alarming. You know all the drakaina, and you have connections I do not have. This is why I want to marry you. Will you accept?"

"You're asking me? I didn't know I had a choice."

"I'm giving you a choice. I know we don't really know each other, but I'm hoping we will come to love each other. We can't do that if I don't give you a choice, can we?"

She smiled, her fangs shining white in the sun. "Thank you. I accept," she said, and for the first time in her life, she lowered her body and head to the ground, settling into a submissive pose.

Alex moved near to her, rubbing his head on her hers. "You didn't have to do that, you know."

"I know, I wanted to," she said, rubbing his jaw with hers. She found this pleasant. She supposed it would be nice to share a nest with this dragon.

"Rise, chosen one," he said, pulling back and looking at her.

She rose to her feet and cocked her head, wondering what he was going to say next.

"If I take you as a mate, you will gain the ability to shift into a human. Do you realize that?"

She looked startled, as she had not considered that portion of the deal. "No, I didn't realize …," she trailed off. "How does that work?"

"The Dragon Keeper will give you a potion. You will shift to human form. You will live with me, part time, as a human, and rule the Kingdom of Dumara at my side. Do you consent to that portion of the marriage?" he asked, looking at her with concern. For some dragons, the thought of living as human disgusted them.

Dahlia thought for a minute. Cassandra and her mother had been close friends, and she had respected and loved the former Queen. She would be honored to try to follow in her footsteps, although she was anxious about how it would be to walk around on two legs and pretend she was human. "I am scared, but I will do it. You will be by my side to guide me."

"I will be. I promise you, I will be by your side," he said, fondly, in wonder at this strong drakaina before him. He knew he had made the right choice.

But in the back of his head, he could feel Mila's sadness, matched with his own. He pushed it away and considered the seals on the beach below him. "Should we hunt? Seal is a tasty treat I don't get often."

"Yes. I think we should," she said, and they launched themselves off the rim, bellowing in joy, before picking up fat seals with their claws, and dropping them from a good height to kill them. They would feast.

―――――

A week passed, and the news had not yet been announced to the citizens of Dumara. Rand planned to announce it tomorrow at noon in the town square. The market was in its last week before closing in the fall. And many people were traveling to visit it to stock up on supplies and goods before the first snow flew.

Aswin had closed the shop for the day, as it was Sunday. He knew they would be busy tomorrow, and the young ones had been looking as tired as he felt. "Take a day off, you two. You both have been working yourself to the bone. I'll go up to the castle and handle the dragons. Torrid's wife is still failing. I need to give her another potion today."

"Are you sure, Father? I can go with you," Mila said, feeling guilty.

"No, no. Go have some fun." He smiled, picked up his keeper's bag, and turned the door sign to closed.

"Want to go to the park with Kiara and me?" Sam asked cheerfully, picking up his cloak. "She's going to be excited I have the day off. It's been work work work for us all lately. Not that I don't love my job."

"Sure, Sam. I haven't had a chance to talk to Kiara in ages. How are things going between you two?" Mila asked, picking up a cloak. Her father had just purchased the most beautiful warm cloak for her. Made of thick wool, it had the coat of arms of Dumara on the back, and it was the same color as Alex, so that she would be camouflaged on his back.

"Very well, Mila. I see now why you thought we would be good for each other," Sam said with a smile. They both exited the shop and headed across the street, stepping into the tailor's shop. The tailor's had not closed for the Sunday. The store was empty, but Kiara and her mother Judith were hunched over their machines in the back, their feet pumping on the foot pedals, their machines eating fine silk faster than the eye could follow.

Kiara looked up with a smile. Her hair was slightly undone, and she looked tired. "Sam! Mila!" she exclaimed, stopping her work and rushing forward. She kissed Sam on the cheek and then hugged Mila.

"You look busy," Mila said, laughing at her friend's excitement. Kiara was practically bouncing up and down, and she had a glint of mischief in her eye.

"We are so busy. Princess Sadie has put in a huge order for her wardrobe. We had to go up to the castle yesterday to do measurements, and we started on the first pieces last night. We thought we would get an early start today, and we are nearly done with the first dress!" Kiara said, waving at the piles of material behind her. "We are expecting to do her wedding dress, so we want to get this done as soon as possible."

Mila nodded. "I expect you will be asked to do the dress for Alex's wedding also."

Kiara looked stunned. "He's getting married? What? We haven't been informed of that …," she trailed off, looking panicked.

"It's not announced yet. Don't spread it around," Mila said, realizing she may have spoken out of turn.

"Oh, no problem. I won't. I'm just worried. We have so much to do!" Kiara said, looking around desperately.

"This is probably a bad time to ask you if you want to go on a walk to the park with us," Sam said, looking sad.

"Go, Kiara," her mother said around a mouthful of pins. "I've got things covered here. Close the shop until you get back though. This will probably be your last chance to see your beau for a while."

"Are you sure, Mother?" Kiara asked anxiously.

"Yes. Go have a little fun this afternoon. We will work late tonight and all next week. Your father can get on the machine when he gets back from his buying trip. We will be fine. This is nothing compared to King Rand's wedding. That was a nightmare. The bride couldn't decide on her dress, and we had to sew a whole new wedding ensemble with only a week's notice. Back then, it was just your dad and I, and I slept for days after that project was done," she chuckled, waving them out.

Kiara didn't have to be told twice. She happily turned their shop sign to closed and grabbed her shawl from the hook by the door. Sam grabbed her hand, and they walked happily together, just the three of them, down the street to the nearby park.

The trees were in full color, and leaves covered the path of the park. A park keeper was raking the paths clear, creating huge piles that would be burned later. With a grin, Sam pushed Kiara into a huge pile, and then Mila. They three laughed, throwing handfuls of leaves at each other. The gardener glared at them, but then shrugged and moved along. The young ones were just having a little fun, who was he to ruin their day?

The musky smell of fall leaves was thick in Mila's nose as she tumbled in the pile, laughing so hard she nearly cried. Since becoming a Dragon Keeper, there hadn't been much time for fun, although she enjoyed every day.

She laid back on the leaves, looking up at the bare skeletons of tree branches above her. Just then, she saw a group of dragons flying to the north. She recognized a few of them by sight, Torrid, Holly, Ray, and interestingly, Nick. The younger Prince hadn't been out of the caves much since he had brought Sadie home, preferring to spend time in his nest with her, or conversing with his little gang of friends.

"I'm going to turn the tables on him today and follow him," Alex thought to her. In a few minutes, she spied Alex and Dahlia's forms above her, red and gold, heading in the same direction the main group had gone. She thought it was sweet they were doing things together, she and wished them the best.

She sat up, and gold leaves cascaded around her. She was surprised to see Sam and Kiara looking at her. They were sitting side by side, holding hands and grinning at her like crazy people. "What?" she asked laughing.

They glanced at each other, and then Kiara held up her hand, grinning. A simple ring was on her finger, sat with a small opal. "We're engaged! Sam asked me to marry him last weekend, when you were away on your trip to Terrak."

Mila threw back her head and laughed. "You didn't tell me! Congratulations you two! When is the wedding?"

"We wanted to tell you together, and we've all been so busy we just haven't had the time," Sam said shyly, hoping there were no bad feelings. He still loved Mila, he just realized now they would have to settle to be friends, and that was okay with him.

He had found a partner in Kiara, and he couldn't wait to start his life with her.

"Oh, you two! I'm so happy for you!" Mila said, moving over to sit next to Kiara. She gave her a big hug and then looked at the ring. "It's so pretty."

"Thanks. I love it." Kiara said, looking at her Sam with love in her eyes. "We want to get married as soon as possible, but with the royal wedding coming up, we are going to wait until a month later."

"I've been looking for a place for us to live. I've been saving up some money with your father. It's all tucked away in his safe," Sam said proudly. "Can't have my drunk of a father getting his hands on it. He's already been asking me how much I make. I can't wait to get out of that house."

"Please be my maid of honor," Kiara said, squeezing her hand.

"I would love to," Mila said, smiling happily. "But do I have to wear a dress?"

"No, of course not," Kiara said. "We will be happy to make you one of our signature pantsuits, free of charge. We've been selling a lot of them lately, and it's all because of you, you little trendsetter. People are asking for 'that woman's suit the Dragon Keeper wears.' Of course, they tend to get it in more expensive fabrics than you usually wear, but all the better."

"Are you going to keep working in the tailor's shop?" Mila asked, wondering what the Wrights were going to do without Kiara's capable hands.

"Yes, at least, until we start a family," she said, smiling up at Sam, who blushed and looked away.

They finished their walk in the park. It was a carefree moment at a time when everything had been stressful and busy. Mila was happy Sam and Kiara were getting married. They seemed so perfect for each other, and she couldn't wait for their wedding.

First though, was the royal wedding, and Mila knew that would be a busy time for them all. It was still weeks away, but she was mentally preparing to see the one she cared for marry another. She couldn't bring herself to say she loved Alex, but she certainly cared for him deeply. She didn't know if it was true love, or just her complicated emotions, but seeing him marry someone else would hurt a bit, she had to admit.

Chapter 17

Fresthav

Mila had been keeping her distance, going with her father to attend to the dragons. Since Sadie's arrival, the mood in the caves had changed. There were clearly two sides now. The royalist side, which sided with King Rand and Alex and Dahlia, and the outsiders, who sided with Sadie and Nick.

She had seen the drakainas flock around Sadie, but it was the shrewd ones, the lower ranking ones. She saw those that flocked around Dahlia, the more thoughtful ones, the ones who held high status. It was interesting, and Mila saw the competition growing.

That morning, Alex and Dahlia flew in together with the rest of the patrol. Today was a special day. Dahlia would transform into a human for the first time. She needed to be fitted for a wedding dress. It had been explained that she was from a far western province, and the dress there was different. She would need a whole new wardrobe fit for a Queen.

Mila stood ready and waiting as the warriors shuffled off. Dahlia stood next to her, her red scales gleaming in the morning sunrise. Aswin quickly changed Alex, and he threw a glance at Mila as he put his favorite shirt on. "Still got it," he said with a grin. Then he shot another glance at Dahlia, who waited patiently. "I'll wait for you at the stairs, to give you a little privacy," he said. He hurried off with Aswin, and Mila and Dahlia were left alone.

"Are you ready, Dahlia?" Mila asked softly, placing her hand on Dahlia's flank. The dragon was trembling.

"I think so," she said, softly. "Does it hurt?"

"I'm not sure. Alex has never complained. It only takes a minute. Look, I've already laid out some clothes for you. Of course, I had to guess on size, but as you are a big dragon, I went with something slightly larger than me."

"Okay, I'm ready." Dahlia squeezed her eyes shut and opened her mouth.

Mila unstopped the astragenica and poured it into Dahlia's mouth. She waited nearby as the drakaina transformed for the first time.

Dahlia felt warm all over, and then felt like she was going to be sick. It was a feeling of vertigo, of the world turning inside out. She was glad she had closed her eyes. She felt her limbs shortening, her spine squeezing, her body seeming to melt away around her. She whimpered at the uncomfortable feeling, but in a blink of her eye, the process was complete.

She felt a breeze on her skin, and she opened her eyes. She was on all fours, naked, with her hands touching the ground. She stood up and almost toppled over. Mila was there to steady her.

"Careful. I expect it's going to be an adjustment. Here, let me help you with these clothes." Mila put the dress on over her head, and Dahlia blinked. She looked at her hands, so small. And then down at herself. She seemed to be much taller than Mila, and fuller at the chest and hips. She had creamy white skin instead of red scales. She touched her face, and it felt weird. Her teeth were not sharp at all, and she wondered how humans managed to eat meat.

Mila looked her over and smiled. "By human standards, you are stunning, Dahlia. That auburn hair seems fitting."

Dahlia touched a strand of her hair and held it in her fingers. It looked like fire. This was all new to her.

"I remembered shoes. Although these might be hard for you to walk in, you're going to have to get used to them." Mila slipped some silk dress shoes on her feet. They were tight, and pinched.

"I don't think I like … shoes," Dahlia said, looking down at her feet. She tried to take a step and almost tripped. She slipped them off again and took another step. "Much better. I can walk without shoes." Her voice sounded strange to her, musical and higher pitched. It wasn't her deep drakaina growl, and she wasn't sure she liked it.

"We will keep them close. You will need them for dinner," Mila said, gently taking her arm and leading her to the stairs.

Dahlia was confused by stairs, but after a few steps, she got the hang of it. "I never thought I would be walking up these stairs," she said with a giggle.

"I bet this is strange for you. If you have any questions, I'm here," Mila said.

"Thank you, Dragon Keeper. I'm glad you're here with me."

They made their way up the stairs, and they were met by Alex and Rand. Aswin had already headed home, leaving Mila to help Dahlia today.

"Dahlia," Alex said, taking her hand and kissing it. "You are as pretty a Princess as you are a drakaina."

She blushed, and then Mila led her away. She was to be fitted today by Kiara.

"This is your room until the wedding," Mila said. "Alex asked that I attend to you, as he is more comfortable with me changing you than my father. He thought you would be more comfortable with me as well. Although I know dragons do not have the same body embarrassment that humans do."

Kiara looked back and forth between the two. She didn't really understand what was going on. "Hi, Dahlia. It's nice to meet you. I'm an old friend of Mila's. I'm the tailor's daughter, and my father sent me to measure you. I heard you had to pack light, and you need a wedding dress."

"Yes," Dahlia said, flashing a grin. "You could say that."

Mila settled into an armchair by the fire. A screen had been set up with a full-length mirror. Kiara helped Dahlia change into a silk robe. For the first time, Dahlia stood in front of the mirror, looking at herself.

She was tall, with dark auburn hair. She had brown eyes and a light splattering of freckles. She turned around, looking at her backside. She didn't know what accounted for beauty in humans, but she supposed this would do.

"Kiara, where Dahlia's from, they don't wear high heels. I think that flats, slippers, or even sandals are going to work better for her. And she's tall, so it's not like she needs the height," Mila pointed out.

"Good point. If you've never walked in heels before, we don't want to put you in them at your wedding."

"Thank you, Kiara," Dahlia said, standing still as Kiara went to work with the measuring tape.

"So, what kind of fashion do you like? My friend Mila here is the queen of pantsuits. I can count on one hand the days that girl has worn a dress," Kiara said with a slight grin, glancing at her friend.

"Oh, I don't know. Something simple, please," Dahlia said.

"She's not that into fashion, Kiara. We need to go with elegant, and simplicity," Mila said. Because of her connection with Alex, she knew exactly what he was thinking of. Even now, he was thinking that Dahlia would look one hundred times more regal than Sadie.

"I'm thinking of royal jewel tones, to set off her hair. Those will look great on her. Since it's winter, we are going to use brocade fabrics, and tiretaine of course. Maybe lined with ermine," Kiara said, rambling on with tailor speak. She had brought a few fabric samples, and she held them up to Dahlia's face to check the swatches.

After a while, she stood with her hands on her hips, surveying Dahlia. Something was not quite right with the girl. She acted like she had never been measured before. But maybe that was just because she was from a backwards province. That had to be it. "So, what are you thinking for a wedding dress?" Kiara asked, putting her hand on her chin.

Dahlia just shrugged. "I've never been to a wedding before. My wedding will be my first. What do brides usually wear?"

"What? You've never been to a wedding? My whole life has been about weddings lately. I've been working on Sadie's wedding dress, my wedding dress, Mila's dress…"

"You made me a dress?" Mila said, horrified.

"Yes, remember, you're my maid of honor. You don't have to wear it if you don't want to. I made you a suit in the same color. But I would be so happy if you would…"

"Maybe. We will see," Mila said, looking displeased.

"You are getting married also?" Dahlia asked, looking at the cute little tailor. She was a pretty girl, and by the blush on her cheeks, she could tell she was very much in love. She wished she felt that way about Alex, but she would settle for a good friend. She had grown to like him very much since agreeing to marry him, but she wouldn't say it was true love. She found him sometimes short with her, and very lost in his own thoughts much of the time. Sometimes she wanted to desperately ask him what he was thinking of, but she never did. She thought maybe she didn't want to know the answer.

"I am! Right after you. You've probably not met him, but he's the shop keeper at the Dragon Keeper's shop. He runs the store while Mila and Aswin are in the caves with the dragons. He's been just as busy as me, and we both have been working late into the night. It's worth it, though. Sam is saving up to buy us a house. We've located the perfect cottage, just outside the city. It's a bit of a walk, but it's in our price range, and the outside will be perfect for the children," Kiara rambled on.

"Children. I suppose I'll have those soon also," Dahlia said. "I hope my mother will be here to see my children. She's been very ill lately. Aswin said he doesn't know if she will make it to the wedding day."

Kiara wrinkled her forehead, wondering why the Dragon Keeper would be checking on Dahlia's mother, who supposedly lived in a far-off province.

She caught Mila's eye, and Mila just smiled. Kiara thought better than to ask. She knew Dragon Keepers had secrets, and flew all over the land with the dragons, on secret cloak and dagger missions they never talked about. Some things she would just never know. "I've been busy with the royal wedding, of course. You should see Sadie's dress! It's just too much. Yards and yards of taffeta and cendal, covered with crystals. She is going to shine like the sun!"

Alex laughed in Mila's head. He had been listening intently. "Perfect. I have an idea, see if you can get Dahlia to buy in." He relayed his plans, and Mila smiled. It was deliciously perfect.

"Dahlia. I'm wondering if you would like to do something a little nontraditional. Typically, a bride would wear white on her wedding day. It stands for purity. But what if you wore Chuvash colors? I'm thinking of gold. So much gold. We want you to outshine Sadie, so maybe we can even get a gold tiara for you to wear on your head."

Dahlia looked apprehensive. "I don't know. I don't want to disrespect Alex or his father."

"Yes, that's just what I had in mind. We can set the crown with sunstones. I'll even get a matching one!" Alex thought, excited for the visual they would make.

"Oh, trust me, Alex is on board with this. It's sort of his idea, he mentioned it to me … before," Mila said.

"Well, it does sound lovely. Can we add a little red in there, to represent my family?" Dahlia asked. Her family were all red sunrise dragons.

"Of course, I'm sure Rand will like that also," Mila said, reminding her that Rand's dragon form was red.

"Okay, girls. This is exciting. We've got a bolt of gold lamé. Very, very expensive stuff. I think we bought it for Queen Cassandra, but she never got to use it. So you'll be honoring her, also. We can incorporate some red lamé in there, and you will be stunning. You will shine like the sun, and all eyes will be on you!" Kiara said, clapping her hands in anticipation. Her father's shop would be the talk of the kingdom. Already, orders were flowing in. So many they had to hire women from the town to handle the more pedestrian jobs. Her father had even promised to give Kiara and Sam one thousand banknotes as a wedding present. It had been a good year at the Wright's Tailor Shop.

After the fitting, Alex met them in the hall. He kissed Dahlia's hand and told her again how pretty she was.

"Thank you, dear. It's been a very exhausting day. I think I'm going to go lay down," she said, as they led her back to her room.

"Do you want to go back downstairs? Mila can take you," Alex said, worry crossing his face.

"No, I would like to eat dinner with you tonight and experience your food, if that's okay. I want to try to sleep in a bed. You know, do human things, and maybe you could join me after dinner," she said with a slight smile.

"Uhhh, yeah. Okay," Alex said, blushing awkwardly. "Yes, yes. I will. And then we can meet the sun tomorrow, together. I need to speak to my Dragon Keeper, Dahlia. We will be going on another diplomatic trip soon, and we need to make plans."

"Okay, I'll be waiting for you," Dahlia said with a wink, closing the door behind her.

———

Alex smiled at Mila. "Thank you for doing that. You didn't have to, and I appreciate it."

"Dahlia is a pleasure, Alex. She is so nice. She was a good choice for you," Mila said, truthfully. She was feeling okay now about him marrying her. He would be in good hands.

"I need to talk to you. Father is in the throne room. He had court today, which is why he didn't join us. He should be about done by now, I think," Alex said. He put his hand on the small of her back and guided her downstairs. She tried not to think of his warm hand. She knew the rest of him was just as warm. He caught her thought and moved his hand as if she was fire. He cleared his throat awkwardly and kept walking.

This was so hard, this trying to pretend they didn't care for each other, that when they touched each other, they didn't burn with desire. She knew he felt it too, but she had a lot of practice lately, pretending these feelings didn't exist. She pushed them back down and raised her chin, looking him straight in the eye. "I'm going to have to buy some warmer clothes if we are going on a trip. I wouldn't want to get cold."

He laughed at her spunk, throwing his head back, his blue eyes crinkling up in mirth. Only Mila could make him laugh like that. "Oh, that's good, Mila. Yes, we are going to Fresthav."

They neared the throne room, and Alex addressed at the herald. "Is my father done for the day?"

"He is. I think he was getting his papers together," the herald said, standing at attention, his yellow tunic spotless and perfect. He was carrying a long sword on his side, like all the royal guards.

"Lock the door behind us. We are not to be disturbed," Alex said curtly, opening the door and entering the room.

The throne room was longer than it was wide. It had marble floors and was covered with a pale yellow silk. Two very large, oversized thrones stood on a dais on the end, covered with solid gold. The fabric on the chairs was also gold, and Mila wondered if that was the same fabric Dahlia's dress would be made of. If it was, it would certainly cause a stir at the wedding.

Rand was sitting on his throne, and a tray with a pile of papers and a quill rested on his lap. He was writing, but he looked up as the pair walked into the room. He looked tired after a long day of hearing complaints from his subjects. His crown was sitting on the empty throne next to him, taking up the seat where Cassandra had sat with him on court days. "Ahhh, just the pair I was looking for. I trust the day went well, Mila?"

"Yes, Your Majesty. We got Dahlia all squared away with the Royal Tailor. I think you will love the dress we have planned. It's really going to be a show stopper," Mila said, a glint of humor in her eye.

"Perfect. You know we are sending a message. A message of power and might. And that is why I've called you two here today. I need you both to go on a quick trip before the wedding. I want you to pay a visit to Fresthav for me," Rand said, pushing the papers aside. He folded his hands together and looked at her intently.

"Yes, Your Majesty. I will go where you need me," Mila said, bowing her head.

"Alex and I have been suspicious of Nick for some time. Recently, Alex followed him from a distance when he was supposed to be patrolling with the warriors. We caught him meeting with a Fresthav agent. We don't know why, because Nick must have sensed something was off and left hastily. The Fresthav dragon went on to the Kingdom of Murdad."

"So, you want us to talk to Fresthav?" Mila asked, looking at Alex. He nodded.

"We want you to talk with the Dragon Keeper. Her name is Gayle, and she is the only other female Dragon Keeper. She replaced the previous keeper a few years ago. Queen Stellen ate him. She's not fond of males, you see," Alex said, noticing the horrified look in Mila's eyes.

"She ate him? Do I need to be worried?" Mila asked, as visions of being eaten alive by a winter dragon crossed her thoughts.

"No, you are under my protection, of course. You will be an honored guest. I need to make a few things clear to the Queen. Winter is almost here, and they will be traveling across our land with the first snow. We want to sign a treaty with them, that they will not attack us or threaten us during this time. It would be a non-aggression treaty, giving them fair passage through our kingdom with the understanding they remain peaceful," Rand noted, watching her closely.

Mila felt better at this news. She thought it was interesting to meet other Dragon Keepers, and to meet another female Dragon Keeper would be an experience she didn't want to miss. "Oh, okay then. I assume this will be a quick trip like last time?"

"It has to be, as my wedding is just a week later. Don't forget to dress warm, and I don't need to tell you this, but be ready for cold," Alex said, trying not to think of the night on the beach.

"Will Dahlia be joining us for dinner? It might be nice to have some alternative conversation, rather than to listen to Sadie ramble on about cave gossip," Rand said, looking hopefully at Alex.

"Oh yes, she will be joining us. She also wanted to spend the night," Alex said, avoiding his father's eyes.

Rand broke out in a wide smile. "Very good. I trust she is comfortable in her quarters?"

"Yes, I think she will be," Mila said, rescuing Alex. "Goodnight. I hope you have a nice dinner. I'll be off now, to check in with my father. I hope he's cooked us something other than bean soup again."

———

When Mila got home, the store was already dark and closed. She opened the front door with her key and wondered where her father could be. The lights up the stairs were still dark, and she wondered if he had gone to the pub, something he rarely did these days. But she saw a thin line of light under the door that led to the basement, and she knew her father must be downstairs.

She locked the store door behind her, hung her cloak on the hook by the door, and went to join her father.

The basement was a bit of a catch-all. It had a dirt floor and was slightly cold, damp and musty. Bricks lined the walls. There were no windows down here, but there was a hidden door behind the bookshelves that lead into the sewers. A single lantern, held in her father's hand, was the only illumination.

Shelves lined one wall and were used for storing excess goods. Barrels lined the other wall and were filled with things like salted pork, beans, and dried apples. Her father liked to order in bulk, to save money, and their winter order had already arrived. That is why they ate so many beans.

"Ahhh, Mila. You're home. I've got a kettle of bean soup upstairs keeping warm. I had to put away the day's income," he said, moving to the far corner. He pushed over an empty crate, revealing a door set in the floor. He opened the cover and revealed a very large space, about four feet deep, filled with banknotes and bags of gold coins.

Whenever he had a chance, he traded his banknotes for gold, silver, or jewels, believing they were more secure than notes. He put a stack of banknotes into the crevasse and then slid the cover back into place.

He stood up and pushed the crate back into its spot, and then dusted his hands off. And then they went upstairs for dinner.

———

That night, Mila was picking at her dinner, trying as hard as she could to focus on her soup. Alex and Dahlia were … well, let's just say they were making sure they were compatible before marriage.

"What's on your mind, dear? You have been quiet this evening," Aswin said, pausing with a huge spoonful of bean soup halfway to his mouth. In his other hand, he held a crusty yeast roll that the baker included in his weekly delivery to the shop.

"Nothing," she said hastily, blushing.

"Oh," Aswin said, sitting back and putting his spoon down. He thought he knew what the problem was. He chuckled. "They don't tell you about that when you get bonded. That connection is there all the time, even at the most intimate. It feels very intrusive, doesn't it? I've been bonded with Rand for so long, we don't even pay attention to stuff like that anymore. I forget you've not been bonded with Alex that long. This whole wedding thing … and I forget you've never … dated," Aswin said, skirting around the issue.

Mila bushed even redder, if that was possible. She decided to change the subject. Maybe that would push Alex and Dahlia's fumbling explorations out of her head. "Alex and I have been asked by King Rand to visit Fresthav. We will be leaving next week," Mila announced, and then took a bite of her soup.

Aswin smiled. His daughter didn't want to talk about it. He could take a hint. "Yes, I'm aware, of course. You need to be careful around Gayle. She's a little too much to handle. She tried to seduce me the last time we visited her."

Mila looked shocked and shook her head. She didn't want to think of Alex and Dahlia, and she certainly didn't want to think of her father and this mysterious Gayle.

"You will find the Fresthav dragons have an interesting culture. They are primarily drakaina-based. There aren't many male dragons around. It's thought they kill boy dragons if the males don't meet certain criteria. All the men they do have are basically soldiers and breeding studs. The men have their own caves and are only called upon to 'do their duty,' so to speak. The drakainas outnumber the males by nearly two thirds," Aswin said, returning his attention to his soup bowl.

"King Rand wants me to connect with Gayle. I'm not sure if I can," Mila said miserably. She was starting to dread this trip. She had not ridden with Alex since the trip to Terrak.

"Don't sell yourself short dear, but remember, she will be trying to get as much information from you as you are from her."

"I'll remember that," Mila said, and then grimaced as a particularly lurid scene flashed into her thoughts.

"Here, daughter, at the worst of times, a shot of iseiki can dull the connection." Aswin got up and opened the tall cabinet. From the top shelf, he pulled down a bottle and poured her a measure.

"Okay, but just one shot. Anymore, and I'll be worthless tomorrow," Mila said. Her father raised an eyebrow. He wasn't aware Mila had been drinking such a strong spirit.

She threw the liquor back like a pro and then went straight to bed. Sleep would bring her blessed relief from their shared thoughts.

The day of their leaving finally arrived, and Mila met Alex at the caves. He was already in dragon form, and Dahlia was at his side. She nuzzled him on his face, and he reciprocated. It was obvious these two were mates, with or without a fancy ceremony.

"Be safe, my love," she grumbled, low in her chest, so that Mila could barely hear her.

"I will. Do not worry, I am in capable hands," he said.

"I'll be waiting here, in our nest, for your safe return. It will be cold without you," she said, slinking off toward the Chuvash cave. She had moved into the far end, while Sadie and Nick were on the other. They had an icy agreement to not cross Rand's nest, which was usually left empty.

"And when I return, we will be married," Alex said, reminding her.

"Of course. I have a fitting with Kiara while you are gone, and then Sadie and I are meeting jointly, with the florist. That should be good fun," she said sarcastically, moving off down the hallway.

"Well, Mila, are you ready for our trip?" Alex asked, turning his attention to her.

"I am," Mila said. "I got a new belt, to replace the old one that we lost in the sea."

"Good. I have my luggage over by the stairs," he said, nodding in the direction. Mila quickly wrapped the belt around his chest and attached their three bags firmly. She found her hat and gloves and buttoned her cloak. She was wearing thick woolen pants and a sweater. She hoped she would be warm enough. They were just days away from the first snow, and she had been told it was always cold in Fresthav. Even in the summer, a chill was in the air.

She swung on, and they quickly exited the caves. The wind bit into her, but she still felt warm. Her hands were protected by the gloves and by the warm hair of Alex's mane.

They headed due west, and Mila noticed the trees under them were already bare of leaves. Their branches rose dark and skeletal, reaching for the sky.

"It's a long trip to Fresthav. It will take us most of the day," Alex said. "But, it will give us time to talk."

Mila gulped. She wondered what Alex wanted to talk to her about. "What is it, Alex?"

"You know, things between us have been awkward since our last trip," he said, dancing around the issue.

"Yes, they have been. That's partially my fault. But I find Dahlia awesome, Alex. I really do. I know you have to do what you have to do, and I understand," Mila said quickly.

"Thank you. You are too kind. Dahlia is special, and I appreciate how you have made her feel welcome. She told me that you have helped her with human etiquette and the finer points. You didn't have to do that. She certainly isn't getting a warm welcome from my brother or Sadie. If they talk to her, it's with scorn and malice. My brother is driving a wedge between my people, Mila. I don't know if my marriage and future children will be enough," he sighed, his body dipping slightly in the wind.

"It will all work out, Alex. I know it will. Besides, her wedding dress is so fantastic, it's going to bring down the house. No one is going to be paying attention to Sadie," Mila said brightly.

They continued on for hours, chatting again like the tension between them never existed. They were back to being close friends. Mila was glad for this trip, because now the anxiety and awkwardness would disappear, and she could do her job again, without worrying now about how things stood between them.

They were greeted by a contingent of winter dragons, just a few miles into the border. When Alex spotted them, he immediately landed on the edge of a frozen lake. There was no snow yet, but it had turned bitterly cold.

The breath rose from Alex in giant clouds as the winter dragons settled in around them. These dragons were all different shades of blue, mixed with white underbellies or streaks on their sides.

A periwinkle-colored male dragon approached them, and Mila could see what her father described. Every dragon in this pack of winter dragons was as large or larger than Torrid, the largest summer dragon in their clan. They moved with lithe ease for their size, and their eyes had a hard look about them.

"A sunrise dragon in Fresthav," the periwinkle dragon said, slinking toward them dangerously. "And the Crown Prince. Tell me, Alex, what business do you have with us? We are preparing to greet the winter, we have no time for distractions."

"I come in peace. I won't take much of your time. I need to speak to Queen Stellen before you fly to greet the winter."

"Well, you had best hurry. We are leaving the day after tomorrow. And who is this you bring with you? A female? Where is Aswin Fletcher?"

"This is Mila Fletcher, his daughter. She is now a Dragon Keeper," Alex said firmly. He saw them all nod, and knew they approved.

"Come with us, we will take you to our Queen," the periwinkle dragon said. Mila held on tight as they rose into the air, this time surrounded by a half dozen dragons. They turned to the north now, skirting the final ranges of the Great Divide. As they turned past the mountains and lost their shielding from the wind, the full winds of Fresthav hit them head on, blowing straight from the north. It bit Mila to the core, and she hunched down, so she was almost laying on Alex, to try to stay out of the wind. He was warm as always, and she was glad. She wondered if winter dragons were always cold. She knew that instead of having the light magic that summer dragons had, they had an ice ray that froze solid anything it touched.

They flew and flew, and Mila could tell Alex was getting tired. His wings didn't beat as fast, and he tucked in behind one of the slower winter dragons to draft off of him. As they flew farther north, the land under them turned to ice and snow. Below, Mila could see polar bears and seals, the favorite hunting prey of the winter dragons.

Finally, the keep of Fresthav appeared. It arose suddenly out of a frozen plateau. Made of a solid gray granite, it looked forbidding and dark. Just behind it were the dragon caves, carved into the snow. Alex followed the dragons into the caves, and they landed with a soft thump on the solid ice floor of the cave.

Mila looked around her, and the ice crystals made the place look magical. Caves, carved into the natural earth and ice, branched off in an orderly manner. It was as cold as an icebox, but of course, these dragons liked the cold. She slid off Alex and waited for his direction.

"Welcome, Prince of Dumara." A dragon voice boomed from the far end of the cave. They turned, and a sky blue dragon with a white tail stood there, blinking her gray blue eyes at him. Next to her stood a tall and dark woman. She had dark hair, and dark eyes, and was dressed completely in white polar bear furs.

"Princess Linnea, thank you for welcoming us," Alex said, bowing his head. "With me today is our new Dragon Keeper, Mila Fletcher. Mila, this is the Princess and her Dragon Keeper, Gayle."

"A pleasure," Gayle said with clipped tones, looking at Mila like she was a specimen in a jar. "Now change, and I will lead us all to the Queen. You are just in time for dinner."

Gayle quickly pulled a potion of astragenica out of her bag, slung causally over her shoulder. Mila reached into her keeper's bag and pulled out her own. She quickly unlatched the belt and took the bags off Alex. She administered his potion and quickly handed him clothes. To a normal person, he had packed way too light, with just a dinner jacket, a silk shirt, and pants, but she knew he wouldn't get cold. He quickly changed, irritated that both the Princess and Gayle watched him silently the entire time. They didn't even bother to avert their eyes.

He turned up his collar and then moved closer to Mila. He felt protective of her. He knew that the Stellens were rough, and hoped they went easy on her.

They were led straight to dinner, and somewhere along the way, the message must have been passed that there were guests. Two extra plates had been set at the long table.

As they entered, a tall, pale old woman at the end, dressed all in white, looked up at them coldly. She had the same gray eyes as her daughter but had all white hair. Mila thought maybe she was wearing a white wig because it didn't quite look real. She had such heavy white powder on her face, she looked like a corpse.

"Alex Chuvash. We were just discussing you," she said, her voice dripping with malice.

"Go easy on me, Thora. I'm just here on a quick diplomatic visit," Alex said, pulling the chair out for Mila.

Mila sat stiffly, wondering what she had gotten herself into. The Princess took the seat across from Alex, and Gayle took the seat across from her.

"And what of your Dragon Keeper? Mila Fletcher, you are a young little thing. Naive and fresh, like I was a long time ago. Still very firm and supple. What this one needs is a man to show her a thing or too, ehhh Alex?" Thora chuckled, looking Mila up and down. Mila felt naked under the Queen's gaze and turned red.

"What a horrible woman," Mila thought to Alex, staring at the Queen's wrinkled hands, covered with so many jewels you could barely see her hand.

"She is just trying to get under your skin. Ignore that," Alex demanded of her, in her head.

"Mila," Gayle said kindly, "you haven't been a Dragon Keeper that long, have you?"

"No, I haven't. But I've been at my father's side since I could walk." She turned her attention to the woman, who had dark hair and eyes. She had taken off the white furs, and she now wore a simple pale blue dress, belted at the waist. She looked perhaps in her thirties, and Mila's first impression was that she had a kind soul.

As they sat, dinner began to be served. It was an elaborate meal, served on fine china and sat with the best silverware. Wine, pressed from frost berries, was served in crystal decanters.

Queen Thora picked up her glass, swirling the delicate wine as the first course was served, caviar roe on one cracker. "I hear you are finally getting married, Alex."

"I am, next week actually," Alex said, picking up his cracker and eating it in one bite. Mila took a small nibble. It tasted like the sea, and the eggs popped in her mouth. She didn't dislike it, but it wasn't her favorite. She politely finished it, hoping the next course would be better.

"Who is the lucky girl?" Princess Linnea said with a sly grin.

"You wouldn't know her. Her name is Dahlia. She is the daughter of one of our most esteemed warriors," Alex said as the servants took his plate. They replaced it with a plate of cold shrimp on a bed of lettuce.

"I also heard your brother is getting married to Princess Sadie of Terrak. That's a match."

Thora chuckled at her own joke. Her daughter Linnea had just given her a granddaughter. And she couldn't wait for Alex to find out what they had done.

"You understand, it is a marriage of duty, Thora. The clan was upset that my brother spit in the Dragon God's face."

"So, he will have a halfling. Do you know I have a halfling

granddaughter?" Thora asked, her voice dangerous. "I do not view halflings as an abomination, do you?"

Alex was stunned. "A halfling?" He put two and two together, and horror dawned across his face.

"I see you understand. My granddaughter is a half night dragon and half winter dragon, and she will rule Fresthav one day."

Alex nodded, suddenly very afraid. There were things going on here he didn't understand. He picked up a piece of his shrimp and ate it without saying a word.

Linnea smiled, twirling her knife in her long fingers. She would love to plunge it into Alex's neck right this minute, but it wasn't time to act. Although, her mate, Kai of Murdad, would probably approve.

Kai had wanted her to arrange for an accidental death for her mother. The old, overbearing witch was getting on in years. No one would know if she held a pillow over her face as she slept.

But she had decided to just wait until she died a natural death. She would be Queen regardless. Then she would marry Kai, something that her mother strictly prohibited. It was fine for her to have his dragonling, but at the mention of marriage, her mother had flown into a blind rage.

"Don't worry, Princeling. I won't hurt you. Just because I wanted my daughter to have dual powers doesn't mean I have declared you an enemy. You have safe passage."

"Thank you," Alex said, "I know you are getting ready to answer the call of winter. I've come to ask you for a peace alliance. As I'm sure you know, there have been a few skirmishes on the border. I ask that you pass through in peace and discontinue aggression." He pulled out the paper and laid it on the table with a pen as the servants came to deliver the main course, a slice of raw seal meat.

A male servant came out with a bottle of wine, refilling their glasses with a red wine for the next course. As he filled Queen

Thora's glass, a single drop of wine landed on the white sleeve of her dress. She looked at him coldly, and the servant's face drained of blood. "My Queen. I'm sorry, I truly am. Please ...," he begged, starting to back away.

Like lightning, her head whipped around to the female butler, who was standing at the far end of the room, supervising dinner. "Chain him downstairs. I'll be down later to take care of him. You know what we do to men who perform poorly."

"Your Majesty, I'm sorry. Please, please don't ...," he cried, falling to his knees, pleading. The butler snapped her fingers, and instantly two guards appeared and hauled the pleading man away.

"What will they do to him?" Mila thought to Alex with concern.

"Do you really want to know, Mila? Queen Thora rules Fresthav with an iron fist," Alex said, staring ahead. It would do no good to condemn the woman's actions. He was here to make an agreement with her, not instigate her.

"Please, tell me," Mila begged Alex.

"She will have him castrated. Most male servants here are." He looked at his main dish of seal. His mouth was watering.

Mila was horrified, and in that moment, she wished she had not asked. She considered her main dish and tried to push the thought of the condemned servant out of her mind. She tried to eat her dinner, but the seal meat was disgusting, and it slid down her throat. She almost choked, and she quickly took a drink of her wine. Alex ate it no problem, but then again, he was a dragon, and he sometimes ate seal.

Gayle pushed her main course away and gave Mila a little smile. At least she wasn't the only one not eating the fatty, gamey substance.

Alex pushed the paper down the table to Thora, who took out a pair of reading glasses and studied it carefully. She looked at Alex over her glasses, looking very much like a strict librarian.

"I have no problem agreeing to this. I'll tell the warriors to stop their nonsense, you know how the males get, all full of hormones and rage. I haven't approved these actions at all," she said, pulling out a pen and signing the paper.

Alex didn't quite believe her, but he took the paper and tucked it into this breast pocket. Dessert was served, a fruit mousse of cloudberries. It was the most delicious thing served tonight, and Mila wished she could pick up her bowl and lick it clean.

"Mila, I would love to talk shop with you, if you don't mind. We will leave Alex and Queen Stellen to discuss their own topics," Gayle said, rising from the table and placing her napkin down.

"Of course," Mila said, standing. They left the Queen and Alex in deep discussion about summer trade agreements, and Gayle led her down the hall to a small entrance. The stairs curved up, and Mila realized that they were in a tower.

"This reminds me of my uncle's tower, but cleaner, of course," Mila said, as they climbed up into a workshop. Unlike her uncle's tower, everything was in its place. Books were neatly lined up on shelves, and herbs and ingredients very familiar to Mila were neatly labeled in bins behind the workspace.

"Fletcher, of course. The sorcerer, Darius Fletcher is your uncle?. I never made that connection before. I've met your uncle. He was very fun and … attentive."

Mila looked at her, not understanding, and then it dawned on her. "Oh," she said, her eyes going wide.

"Yes, Mila. Your uncle and I had a little fling. I became the Dragon Keeper suddenly, you see. Queen Thora got tired of Flynn. She is not a fan of men really, except for when she needs an heir. She picked me from the village, she said she liked my ambition. I had to learn quickly, and the best way to do that was to get some lessons from the sorcerer. He was adamant that he didn't work for free, so I paid him in my only currency," she said, sitting down at her workspace.

"Well, that was more information than I needed to know," Mila said truthfully. "To be honest, I just met my uncle. He never has really been around much. You know, doing sorcerer things. I don't know that I would call him fun."

Gayle threw back her head and laughed. "You seem very naive, Mila. Let me tell you, in ten years, you'll be much more worldly. But I understand, you are young. So tell me, what is in your astragenica potion?" Gayle pulled out a pencil. "I've been studying regional differences in potions."

"Wormwood, nightshade, iodine, saltpeter, carbon, and dried or fresh astra flower petals, and a pinch of anise. You bring up a good point, do astra flowers grow this far north?" Mila asked as she watched Gayle take notes.

"Oh yes, but only for one week in summer. The fields are covered with the large blooms. It looks like snow, in the middle of summer."

"Interesting. Our flowers only grow in caves, and they are quite small. I wonder if they are a different variety."

"They may be. You also use anise. We use rose hips. Doyle in Murdad uses cloves. Tyson in Terrak uses ginger."

"I always assumed the anise was to make it taste better," Mila admitted. "But, I've never tried leaving it out. I don't know if it's necessary or not."

"It makes sense, but I have a hypothesis. Every potion is exactly the same, except for that one ingredient. What if that one ingredient is a key? I've never tried, but I wonder if the potions would work the same if I tried to use my astragenica on a summer dragon? What if that one ingredient was essential? I'll have to test it later. Now, tell me, what do you use in dragon balm?"

They shared notes for some time, and Mila even took some

notes of her own. She found Gayle fascinating. A glimpse of what her life may be in ten years' time.

"So tell me, how it is to be connected with Alex? It is as vexing as it sounds? He is quite handsome, I think it would be hard to avoid his charms," Gayle said, holding her chin in her hand as she sat on her stool and considered this young girl. She caught the slight blush and the avoidance of eye contact.

"It's been difficult. I wasn't expecting it. The mind connection has come quite in useful, but there have been some awkward moments," Mila admitted candidly.

"I bet there were honey, and I would have paid good money for that mind link." Gayle threw back her head and laughed, and before she knew it, it was time to say good night.

A servant led Mila to her room, and she was surprised to find nearly the same set up as in Terrak. Didn't anyone besides them believe in private rooms? Alex was sitting with his shirt off, taking some notes. Mila tried to avoid looking at him as she said good night, grabbed her bag, and headed for the bathroom to freshen up and change.

She splashed some water on her face and considered her face in the mirror. No longer an ungainly ugly duckling, she had come into her own these last few months. She looked like a woman now, and not a little girl. She sighed and slipped out of her warm clothes and into the nightdress. She put on her dressing gown and exited the bathroom carrying her pile of clothing. Alex was standing right in front of her, blocking her exit.

"Uhh, hi. I'm going to bed," she said, moving to get by him.

"No, you're not," he said, taking her clothes out of her hands and then setting them aside. He stared at her hungrily.

"What do you want?" she asked, throwing up her hands in exasperation.

"I want you," he said, longing in his eyes.

"You're practically a married man, Alex Chuvash. I don't

think that's appropriate," she said sharply, putting her hand on her hip.

"I know. I'm sorry. I don't mean to act on my feelings. I just wanted to let you know how I felt. I'm getting married next week, and I feel trapped. Dahlia and I, we just don't have the connection you and I have. I feel like I'm making a big mistake," Alex said, his voice rapid and urgent. "And I just had to tell you, before it's too late, that I love you." He moved in closer to her, his eyes soft and pleading.

Before she realized what she was doing, she was in his arms. He started kissing her, passionately. The feelings they had both been pushing down bubbled over, and then she slowly dropped her robe to the floor.

Alex couldn't help himself. The dragon part of him took over, picked her up and threw her on the bed. She laughed, and then he gave her his full attention.

Later, in the darkness, he looked at her figure in the moonlight, shining in through the window. She gave him a kiss and sat up, leaving his warm body. Mila turned to look at him, sadness on her face. "It's too late for us, Alex. I love you. I want to be with you, that's why I'm here, in your bed. I didn't have to sleep with you, but I wanted to. I wanted to know what I would be missing. It breaks my heart, but I think we have to let each other go. You have to do your duty."

He sighed, and then pulled her closer. He kissed her neck. "I know I do. Can't we just have this one night? I'll marry Dahlia, and we will have a passel of dragonlings, but at least I'll know what *we* have is true love, even if we can't …," his voice broke.

"Be together," Mila finished for him, her eyes filling with tears.

"Dammit. Why am I crying? This is impossible," Alex said, wiping the tears from his eyes.

"Impossible," she repeated, kissing him deeply as she pressed against him. He moaned, his eyes closing. Their mind connection made this intense. He knew instantly what she wanted, and she wanted him. He didn't know if tonight would be enough, but it would have to be. Damn his brother. If not for him ruining everything, he might have been able to marry her. Sure, it had never been done before, but it seemed like the Chuvashes liked to break the rules.

Early the next morning, Queen Thora stood in her dragon form, fearsome and cold in front of her drakainas. She was almost all white, with a dark blue underbelly. Gayle was on her back, wrapped up tight in her furs against the cold, with her bag slung across her chest. Linnea stood next to her, sky blue with her white tail that twitched in anticipation. Behind them, the entire clan of winter dragons waited for the signal, every shade of blue and white. Princess Linnea watched her mother Thora tear up her copy of the alliance agreement with Dumara. "Just because I signed it, doesn't mean I'm going to abide by it. What do I care for a piece of paper? We will push up our greeting of winter and fly this morning. Prince Alex will have a little surprise waiting for him at the border."

"I did like Mila Fletcher. Too bad we can't spare her," Gayle said, her mouth turning down in a frown, hoping that the pair got her warning. She had tried, and that would have to be enough.

"There are always innocent casualties of war, Gayle," Thora said coldly, then leapt into the air, snow immediately surrounding her. With a communal roar, the entire clan joined her, moving en masse to the skies, snow billowing from around them, and coating the land with its first substantial snow of the winter. They would fly from one end of the world to the other, welcoming winter's icy embrace. They would arrive back tomorrow morning, exhausted and spent, but then curl up in their caves for a long winter's rest.

A handful of male warriors had been ordered to stay at the border and attack Prince Alex as he returned home. Periwinkle was sulking with his friends. "Of course, she left us behind to clean up Prince Alex. If we kill him over the village of Sala, we can lure him into the sea. Maybe his body will fall into the ocean and never be found."

Chapter 18

The Blessing

Mila woke up the next morning, and the first thing she did was reach for Alex, but the bed was empty and cold. She sat up and found she had three quilts covering her, but the fire had died down overnight. It seemed like the Queen really didn't care about the warmth of the humans here, and she supposed that they all got used to the cold anyway.

Alex was leaning against the wall, one hand on the door frame. "Mila, are you going to sleep all day? We've got to get going." Alex was already dressed. His hair was still messy though, and he looked like he hadn't slept well.

"You just woke up," she guessed, crossing her hands over her chest and looking at him with a slight smile.

"Okay, I admit it. I couldn't sleep at all. I was just staring at you," he said, avoiding her eyes.

She sighed and stood up, the cold from the room hitting her bare skin. She grabbed her robe, and quickly put it on. She crossed to him and gave him a kiss on the cheek. "Thank you," was all she said, and then she went to get dressed.

She could feel his torment in her head. His sense of duty

combined with his feelings for her. Shaking her head at him, she quickly got dressed, pushing her feelings out of her head. Last night, they had shared something beautiful and precious. But it was the next day, and they had work to do. It would be better if they pretended their night of passion had never happened.

Alex nodded, picking up on her thought. He ran a hand through his golden hair. It was shoulder length now, as he hadn't cut it once the entire time Mila had known him. "A servant delivered us breakfast and a note from the Dragon Keeper." Alex held up a note, with a big flourishing signature that read "Gayle Hutchins, Dragon Keeper of Fresthav."

"Just curious, are you ever going to cut your hair? Your brother wears his shorter?" Mila asked, joining him in the common area between their rooms. Tea, a plate of breakfast sausage, toast, and a bowl of cloudberries was set out on a table. She sat down and poured them both a steaming mug of tea.

"Probably not. There is an old legend that says a dragon becomes stronger the longer his mane is. I kind of like it. It speaks to me. And the Dragon Lord knows I have no desire to look like my brother." He took a mug of tea and took a sip, then grabbed a slice of toast and a sausage.

"You like your tea black. I'm learning more things about you every day, Alex," Mila said, pouring cream and spooning a little sugar into her tea. She sat back with her legs tucked under her, holding a slice of toast that she wrapped her sausage in. There was a fire roaring in this room at least. She took a sip of her own drink, happy that it was hot. "What did this letter from Gayle say?"

Alex opened it and read it out loud.

Dear Mila and Alex -

I like you, and I'm rooting for you. Because I'm fond of you two, I'm leaving you this warning. Queen Thora has unexpectedly decided this morning to welcome the winter. We ride at sunrise. You will find the castle mostly empty. But I warn you, she's laid traps. Prince Kai Monserrat is here lurking in the castle somewhere, waiting to attack you. To the east, she has set an ambush.

I suggest leaving by the south gate instead of the tunnels. I have a feeling he's lurking below. I don't know what to tell you about the route home. You'll have to do your best. Of course, the weather will be raging. Queen Thora has taken nearly every winter dragon, so the full power of winter will descend upon you. I have prayed to the Dragon God this morning, that he would deliver you safely home.

I hope sometime you return a favor to me when I am in need.

Your friend,

Gayle Hutchins

Dragon Keeper of Fresthav

"This is treachery," Alex said, putting the letter down. A worried look came over his face.

"I don't understand why Gayle would warn us." Mila jumped up and ran to the window. There was indeed snow. In fact, it was so snowy, she could barely make out the courtyard below. A good couple of inches had already fallen.

"You apparently made an impression on her, Mila. You *are* the only other female Dragon Keeper," Alex smiled, taking another slow sip of his tea. He liked to enjoy his first cup of the day. He didn't guzzle it down one after the other, like his father.

Mila looked at the accumulation of white on the windowsill. She could see the wind was strong, and the snow was blowing fiercely across the courtyard, already drifting in the far corner. Her mind was spinning. "Queen Stellen made our journey home difficult on purpose. It will be easy for the winter dragons to hide in a white out."

Alex smiled at her. "I see we are thinking along the same lines. The wind and blowing snow will make visibility very difficult."

He saw Mila's eyes get wide with understanding. "She's set the trap to kill us?"

"Thora obviously wants us out of the way. If she kills me,

all alone in the wilderness, then her job is just made easier. She's proven herself to be as sneaky as it comes. She admitted last night Linnea had birthed a hybrid. That means she is closer to Murdad and the nightfall dragons than we even thought."

"And the letter said that Kai lurks below, waiting to attack us! It was a mistake to come here then," Mila said, starting to panic.

"Perhaps, but now we have a clear view of where they stand, and I'm not going to fly home the way they expect." He picked up two more sausages. He would need the energy to fly the route he had started to think about late last night, before he even knew the snow was going to fall.

Mila's forehead crinkled, thinking of the map in her mind. She sighed and decided to peek inside Alex's head. She saw the route laid out. He would go straight east, over the fjord and the Dead Plains of Murdad, before dropping down over the mountain pass near Dorado. "Isn't that dangerous? Going into nightfall dragon territory?"

"It can be, but we are going to be flying over the dead plains. No one lives there, and not even animals roam. With the snow, we shouldn't encounter any nightfall dragons. They will all be tucked away in their volcano caves, keeping happily warm," Alex said, grabbing a few more pieces of toast.

"Okay, then. I trust you," Mila said, watching him eat in fascination. She had never seen him eat like this. It was like he was famished.

"It's going to be a rough flight. I've got to store up energy. In fact, I'm going to need you to look in your little bag of goodies and see if you've got what you need for an energy potion."

"Good idea. I'll go get my bag." She jumped up and went quickly to her cold bedroom. She took a minute to get dressed, braiding her unruly hair. She grabbed her keeper's bag and went back into the common area. She put it on the table and began rummaging through it. Sam kept it well stocked for her, and she was happy to see she had everything she needed, except for a mixing bowl.

She spied a metal vase on the fireplace mantle filled with a dead, dried flower arrangement. She threw the flowers in the trash and then rinsed the vase with some water from the bathroom. "I've never made keeper potions in a vase before, but we do what we have to do," she laughed, plopping the vase down on the coffee table in front of them. She pulled out the herbs that she would need, still in their neat packets. Ginseng, sage, pennywort, golden root, and peppermint. Alex watched her closely. He was always fascinated to watch a Dragon Keeper work.

She placed her one clean potion bottle she had with her on the table and got to work. She had a small flask of mineral oil in her bag, and she poured that into the vase. She ripped open the pre-measured packets of herbs and poured them in, leaving some peppermint in the packet. She didn't need that much. Then, she took the vase over to the fireplace, wrapping her hand in a towel to protect against the flames. She warmed the oil, and the strong scent of the herbs filled the room. After a few minutes, and only one burnt finger, she sat the still hot vase on the table. "We will let it cool, and then I can cork it into the bottle."

"Thank you. I'll use that when I run out of energy, somewhere in the middle of the Dead Plains, I think," Alex said, looking at her fondly. "I'll finish packing while that cools, and then we will be off."

―――

They made their way out of the castle, encountering no one but servants. It was silent and eerie, as if the whole castle had just up and left.

"We are not exiting through their caves. I don't trust it," Alex said, as they made their way to the courtyard. There were not even soldiers at the gates. They walked down the road for a while, trudging throughout the deepening snow. They made sure the city was out of sight, lost in the snowstorm, before slipping into a strand of snow covered pines.

"I feel like we are outlaws or something, sneaking around like this," Mila laughed, her cheeks rosy from the wind and the snow. She was well bundled up with the hood of her cloak pulled over her head, a warm scarf around her neck, and her warm gloves. Her feet could be warmer, she supposed, but soon they would be in the air, and her whole being would be cold.

Alex disrobed quickly, not feeling the cold at all. Steam rose from his body, proving that he was indeed a sunrise dragon. Mila hurried and tucked his clothes away as he changed, and then tied their bags to the belt, making sure her Dragon Keeper's bag was secure. She placed the energy potion just inside her bag, but on top, wrapped in a felt rag, so that it was within quick reach. Climbing onto his back, she wrapped her fingers into his mane, being careful not to pull.

In the snow, Alex's golden body stood out like a sore thumb. The only thing that would make him more obvious was red scales like his father. She realized that the winter dragons would be all but invisible in this weather and she shivered, not only from the cold.

But there was nothing to be done besides changing their route. With the storm raging around them, Alex took to the skies, and soon they became totally surrounded by white.

Mila didn't know how he managed to navigate because she couldn't see a thing. She was soon blinded by the driving snow, and she buried her head into his mane, his golden hair keeping her warm.

Alex himself was having a hard time seeing, but his vision was better than Mila's. He could make out the faint white orb of the sun in the distance and knew he was heading due east. Under him, he could just make out the dark water of the fjord.

It was so hard to fly in the wind. It battered him from all sides, and the wind was relentless. Several times a gust blew him so hard, he was tossed sideways. He was happy Mila was hanging on tight. He didn't think he could catch her if she fell off in this weather. He struggled on, and he was glad he had eaten a big breakfast. Already, he could feel his energy flagging, and he wondered if he could even make it across the water without having to find a desolate rock somewhere to rest for a few moments.

———

Meanwhile, Periwinkle and his crew perched on the mountain ridge just above Vassa, watching to the south. "What if he decided to wait out the storm? What if we don't see him?" A light turquoise warrior named Betta asked.

"If he waits another day, we will wait here. We can be patient, can't we, or is that a simple concept you can't understand? We aren't going to miss him. We will see him from miles away. He's golden, he'll light up like a beacon."

Betta glanced around the small group. "I hope you're right boss, if we miss him, Thora is going to be angry. You know how she gets when she's angry."

"We aren't going to miss him!" Periwinkle roared, and the other dragons cowered and scanned the horizon, hoping the sunrise dragon and his keeper would show up soon.

"Boss! I think I see him! But he's way far north. See that golden flash over there?" Betta roared.

"I do! Dang it, I don't know if we can catch him. He's moving fast, but we've got to try," Periwinkle said. He launched himself off the mountain, followed by his group of four in hot pursuit.

———

"Alex, to the south. I think I saw four dragons at the top of that mountain, and now they're gone," Mila said, near hysteria in her voice.

"I saw them. They are going to have a hard time catching me. I'm going to dive again, to gain even more speed," he said, his voice sounding strained. Mila hung on tight as he tucked his wings. She laid down low again on his back, but still the wind bit into her. She was cold, so cold. But being cold was better than being dead.

"Watch this, I'm going to make them think twice," Alex panted, turning his head toward the approaching dragons. He roared, and a light beam shot through the storm, directly into the middle of the approaching group. They had plenty of time to avoid it, but it caused them to break up and deviate from the straight path.

Alex continued to roar and send light beams in their direction, and soon he was well ahead of them. Mila was watching them closely and whooped with joy as she saw them turn back. Alex was just going too fast, and he was already too far away from them. They had given up, realizing that there was no way they could catch them.

But the storm intensified. "I think they have made the storm worse, on purpose, to try to slow me down," Alex panted, his sides heaving. Every wing stroke now was pain, and he was almost delirious from exhaustion.

He made it to the Dead Plains, his chest muscles screaming as his wind speed slowed. The ground beneath him was dry and dead and hadn't seen vegetation in years, if not decades. It was warmer here, and the snow was just beginning to stick to the ground, but it was not yet inches deep.

His claws found purchase in the hard rocky ground, and he nearly collapsed, his sides heaving and clouds of steam billowing from his nose. That had been the most difficult flight of his life.

"Mila," he gasped, trying to catch his breath. "Be a lookout just in case they turn back."

Mila had already been scanning the area. It was miles upon miles of flat, unbroken land. Nothing but dead trees, rocks, and the mountains looming to her right. She had never been on this side of the mountains. She found she much preferred Dumara over this dead wasteland.

She saw no movement anywhere, not an animal or even a bird. She could see no cute little homesteads or farms. It was like everything here had died, which she supposed gave the Dead Plains their name. She wondered if all of Murdad was like this, or only this small corner. She settled down on the ground and rested against Alex's heaving flank. He was so warm, he felt like a fire. She pulled her knees up to her chin but continued to scan the horizon.

Alex rested for nearly twenty minutes, slowing his breath, regaining his strength. "Do you have that potion?" he asked, blinking and looking around for the first time. The storm was growing stronger, and the land was turning white.

"Yes, I have it right here," she said, reaching into her bag. She uncorked it and poured it in his mouth. The strong scent of peppermint filled the air.

"Delicious. Tastes like candy," he joked as the warmth and energy flowed back into his wings. Within minutes, he was standing, ready to go.

"Let's go, I don't want to linger here too long," Alex said as Mila climbed back on his back. She glanced fearfully around again. She was just as concerned as Alex about running into nightfall dragons.

Soon, he was flying, stronger than ever. They flew low, hoping to keep out of sight, and the snow was thick again. Alex's wings beat the air, and he picked up speed. He wasn't far now, and he could make out the gap of the pass in the distance.

His heart started to thump as he neared the pass, hoping that he didn't run into some kind of ambush. He was too deep into Murdad territory, and he hoped his hunch was right, and that the nightfall dragons stayed home today.

They both held their breath as they sailed through the pass, the Dumara mining town of Dorado below them. The gold mines were silent today, as the workers stayed home by their warm fires.

"We've made it," Alex said with a roar, announcing his arrival to the townspeople in their houses below, and Mila could feel his elation as they turned due south for home.

———

They arrived, and Dumara castle looked like a postcard below them. The turrets of the castle were frosted with snow, and the light shone through its windows, making it look inviting and warm. They swooped into the cave, finding it nearly empty. This second leg had been much easier on Alex, but the potion had started to wear off toward the end, and an even greater exhaustion had filled his body. With everything, there was a price to pay, and he knew from previous experiences using energy potions that he would sleep for days.

Alerted that they had arrived, Aswin hurried down the hall. They were back too soon, and worry crossed his face, but he relaxed when he saw Mila taking the bags off Alex.

"Did everything go okay?" he asked, concern filling his voice.

"Is Father listening?" Alex asked. He shook his head when Mila offered him a potion. He would sleep in his nest with Dahlia tonight.

Aswin paused for a moment, his eyes becoming unfocused, and then he turned his attention back to Alex. "He is now."

"Thora signed the treaty without blinking, but she revealed that she has a hybrid dragonling granddaughter—half winter dragon, half nightfall. When we awoke this morning, the winter dragons were gone. Thora welcomed winter early and left us alone in the castle. I was worried about ambush, so we took the northern route and encountered no one. I don't know if that was the right choice, to be honest, but we made it back."

"How did you make it that far, in the blizzard? It's raging outside," Aswin said, looking at the pair. Mila was shivering. She was wet through from the snow, and she leaned against Alex for warmth.

"I made an energy potion. We stopped briefly on the Dead Plains to rest," Mila said, her teeth chattering.

"Good job," Aswin said proudly. "Now, let's get you home. You are chilled to the bone."

"Yes, and I'm going to rest," Alex said, moving to his nest. A voice from the hallway stopped him.

"Brother. You have returned. Curious. Your trip went well?" Nick said, moving slowly. Two of his lackeys slunk behind him, their heads down, their eyes blazing.

"It went very well, thank you. Now, if you will excuse me, I need to rest," Alex said, pushing past his brother and his friends.

Nick hissed. "You'll get no sleep in there, Sadie and her friends have been up all night, she says it's called a bachelorette party. Dahlia already went upstairs."

With a sigh, he turned to Mila. "I'll take that potion then. I need to rest."

"Of course," she said, hurrying forward. He changed, and then turned to go up the stairs, his steps slow and his eyes heavy.

"Well, now I know what to do to get him to leave. I'll tell Sadie to have more parties. I'm sure she won't mind," Nick said with a chuckle. He turned. He had been kicked out of his nest tonight. He would stay with Sumac and his wife, they had extra space.

He didn't catch the look Mila and Aswin gave him as he turned and left. Aswin shook his head and then headed home.

Once home, Mila changed out of her wet clothes and let Sam

and her father fuss over her. She sat in front of the fire, wrapped in a big quilt. She held a mug of chicken noodle soup, feeling its warmth seeping into her bones. She went to bed soon after, but when she woke in the morning, she had a high fever and a terrible cough. Her father gave her a tonic and sent her back to bed, and she tossed and turned with fever dreams. Her mind was filled with nightmares of getting caught by winter dragons and being blasted with their ice power. In every dream, she was caught in ice, forced to watch Alex killed, and unable to do anything about it.

It had been days, but Mila was finally feeling better. She woke that morning and heard unfamiliar chatting coming from their common room. She dressed and struck her head out.

She saw the sorcerer drinking tea at their table with her father. His hat lay next to him, and his staff leaned against the wall. "Uncle Darius, is that you?" she asked, wondering if her eyes were deceiving her.

"It is, Mila. You know, I've got a little wedding to officiate. Every inn in the city is filled to the brim, so I took a chance that your father would let me sleep on his couch."

"You had other options, Darius," Aswin said with a trace of anger. He wasn't happy his brother had turned up on his doorstep this morning, but he was family, and he couldn't turn him away, no matter how much he wanted.

"My choices were sleeping on a bench in the cathedral, sleeping out in the street with the drunks, or knocking on my childhood home," Darius said, with a glint of fun in his eyes. Mila could tell he was enjoying the banter.

"You could have stayed at the castle. You are officiating the wedding after all," Aswin said stiffly. He looked at his brother's ratty robes. "I do hope you've brought something besides that to wear."

"What's wrong with my robes?" Darius said, looking down at himself. He guessed maybe they weren't that dressy, and he had a few stains and a small hole in the sleeve.

"Oh, dear lord. Mila, could you run over to the tailor's real quick. I'm sure they are swamped, but tell them it's an emergency."

"Uhhh, sure Dad. Good thing this wedding isn't until the evening," Mila said, moving to the door.

"Make sure you take a cloak! You are just getting better!" her father demanded, pointing to her outwear she had left hanging on the back of her chair.

"Oh, sorry. Yeah, I guess I'll need it," Mila said, glancing out the window. It had snowed again last night, and fresh powder lined the walks. She hastily buttoned up her cloak and slipped on her boots. Giving her uncle a quick welcome kiss on the cheek, she ran out the front door. They were closed for the day, of course, like nearly everyone on the street except the tailor's.

She burst into the shop. There were already a few people there picking up last minute alterations. Kiara was behind the counter, smiling and serving customers. Her face lit up when she saw Mila.

"Feeling better today, Mila? Good timing," Kiara said while handing a brown wrapped package to an older woman, who scowled at Mila.

"I'm feeling much better! My uncle Darius has arrived, to officiate the wedding. You've never met him, but he's interesting, to say the least. Think of what your vision of a cranky old sorcerer who lives in a dusty old tower is, and there you have it. The problem is that he didn't bring any nice-looking robes, or vestments. We are going to need a rush job, Kiara. A real rush job."

In her head, she could feel that Alex was awakening. His

chest was bare, and his sheets were wrapped around him. Dahlia was still sleeping on her side. "Are you kidding me? He didn't bring anything nice to wear? That man, I swear!" he thought to her, shaking his head.

"I know. I'm taking care of it. Don't worry. He'll be ready for the wedding. You go do whatever it is male dragons do on the day of their wedding," Mila thought back to him.

Meanwhile, Kiara looked worried. She finished with the last customer and then tapped her fingers on the desk. Her mother looked up from her sewing, while her father kept his machine going next to her. He looked up, his glasses perched low on his nose. "What is it, dear? A problem?"

"The sorcerer didn't bring anything to wear to the ceremony!" Kiara shouted back to them.

Franklin stopped sewing and threw back his head and laughed. "Oh, that sounds like Darius all right. Hold on, I've got some robes the clergy ordered in the back. They were going to pick them up later today. I can probably whip one out in an hour or so, I've got time. They aren't that hard. Not even fitted," he mumbled to himself, flipping through his racks.

"Thank you so much, Mr. Wright," Mila said, "You should see the state of his robes. If I didn't know better, I would say he was homeless."

"Is he still about the same size as your father?" Franklin asked, his hand on a hanger.

"He's just a little thinner. I don't think he eats much."

"Probably too busy making trouble," Franklin said, flipping through what he had. "This will do. Made it for the head priest for midwinter services. He's not even scheduled to pick it up until next week, so that's good."

"Thank you so much! Oh, and maybe a new pair of shoes. Probably size 10. He can borrow some socks from my father. Charge it to my father's bill," Mila demanded.

Franklin nodded, placing a pair of dress shoes from his

display on top, and then wrapping the package in paper. Mila took the package and hurried back across the street.

Sam had arrived, and he joined the Fletchers at the table. He was dressed already for the wedding, in a nice black suit and tie. He would be joining them today with Kiara at his side. Dahlia loved the dress Kiara had made so much, she invited her and her soon-to-be husband to the ceremony.

Mila plopped the package down on the table. "Speedy delivery!" she said, giggling. Her father poured her a cup of tea and passed her a danish.

Darius reached for the package. "That was quick."

Aswin slapped his hand away, "You're filthy. Wash before you even touch that."

Darius looked slightly hurt but stopped opening the package.

"I got you shoes also. You might need to borrow a pair of socks from father," Mila said between bites.

They all looked down at Darius' shoes. Brown and worn almost through, his shoelaces knotted to hold them together in several places. "Wow, thank you. I haven't had new shoes since I can't remember."

"I charged to your account, Father," Mila said, taking another bite of her sweet roll. It was delicious.

"I expect a discount on my next services, Darius," her father said, looking at his brother grumpily. His brother had always been a freeloader, and now was no exception.

"Of course," Darius said with a nod. "Tell me, young, Sam, how do you like working for my brother? A bit of a taskmaster, isn't he? Always worried about the bottom line. I bet the safe downstairs is overflowing with money. Does he pay you enough for your services, young man?"

"Enough of this, I'm going to check on the dragons this morning. Make sure I have a full dozen astragenica. They are all going to fly tomorrow morning in celebration, and it's better to prepare now."

"Of course, boss," Sam said, nodding his head. He hadn't expected to make potions today, or he wouldn't have dressed up, but he could take off the jacket Kiara had so lovingly made him and put on an apron.

Mila heard Sam talking to Darius as she and her father hurried out the door, grabbing their dragon bags. They would come back around lunch time to change and get ready for the big event.

"Well sir, your brother pays me very well. I love working here in the shop. I've learned so much already. I'm getting married soon, and I hope to buy a house in the spring. We will live with her parents just across this street until then. I had a house all picked out, but my father's house needed a new roof, it was leaking like a sieve. He hasn't worked in years, and I owe it to my mother to make sure she has a decent roof over her head."

"You're a good boy, Sam. Family is so important, isn't it?" she heard Darius say, before they turned down the street toward the river path.

On the morning of the dual wedding, Dahlia got ready, and then went downstairs and visited her parents. She appeared before them in her human form, the first time they had laid eyes on her as a human. Alex accompanied her, with his hand on her lower back. His soon-to-be wife was beautiful, her dark auburn hair piled on top of her head, winter roses tucked into the hair.

Torrid greeted them, but her mother was so ill, she stayed in the nest. She had lost a lot of weight, and for a dragon, she was incredibly skinny. She had cried when she saw her daughter in her glimmering sheath wedding dress that hugged every human curve she had. Dahlia wore a mink-lined cape of red, and she had finally managed to learn to walk properly in shoes, so today she wore a golden slipper with a slight heel.

Upon her head was a golden tiara, with three large inset sunstones.

Her mother looked at her fondly, a sparkle in her eye for the first time in quite a while. "You will be our Queen. I will probably not live to see it, but you have made your father and I proud. You make a beautiful bride."

Dahlia stood on her tiptoes and kissed her mother gently on her cheek, and Alex followed. She smiled at her father, who had tears in his eyes. Alex bowed to her father and thanked him for allowing the marriage. Torrid nodded. "I am proud to call the Crown Prince a son-in-law. You will always have my backing, and the backing of all the warriors."

They then made their way back upstairs, managing to avoid running into Nick and Sadie, who were apparently running late. Aswin and Rand were already there, waiting for both wedding couples to leave in the carriages that would take them through the streets, now lined with cheering citizens, to the Cathedral of the Dragon God, located in the heart of the city.

The day was cold, but a recent warm snap had melted all the snow. Three carriages stood waiting, along with a hundred soldiers on horses to lead the wedding parade.

Alex helped Dahlia into the first carriage, which was pulled by two white horses. It was the grand carriage, reserved for state events like these. The last time it had been used was his father's coronation, some twenty years ago. But it had been polished for this wedding until the ornate carvings of dragons on the doors shone gold again. The leather seats inside had been dusted, and the windows of clear crystal shone, casting prismatic rainbows across them both. He settled in beside her, unbuttoning his suit coat for the ride while they waited for his brother to appear. Rand and Aswin took the final carriage, leaving the middle one for the late couple.

Dahlia smiled and placed her hand in his, and they sat like that for a moment, looking at each other's conjoined hands. He smiled. She would make a beautiful Queen, and she was everything he needed. She just wasn't everything he wanted. His heart longed for Mila, but since coming back from Fresthav, they had both put their night of passion out of their minds and slipped back into their familiar ways, studiously avoiding touching each other if not necessary. The minute their hands did touch, sparks and heat flew between them.

But Dahlia and Alex had found, if not passion, mutual respect and enjoyment of each other's company. He looked back behind him and saw Nick and Sadie finally getting into their smaller and less elaborate carriage and rolled his eyes. Sadie's wedding dress barely fit into the carriage, it was so voluminous. The yards and yards of white taffeta had to be stuffed into the carriage, and as his brother took his seat next to his bride, he looked very uncomfortable.

Alex reached up and adjusted his crown. He had it commissioned from the royal jeweler as soon as the dual wedding date had been set. It was a small golden crown, with one giant sunstone set in the temple. It purposely was a smaller replica of his father's crown, and it would be a surprise to Nick and Sadie, who wore no such regalia.

He was the Crown Prince, and not his brother. That was the message they were sending today, and a message that he was sure would rankle Nick. But his brother had set this day in motion, with all his scheming and planning, and now he would have to face the humiliation of being the lesser brother, sharing his wedding day with his hated older brother.

"He's been insufferable lately," Alex commented as the horses pulled away from the castle. Their driver was dressed in the royal colors, looking smart up on the driver's seat. The entire parade started moving, winding slowly past the onlookers. Dahlia waved and smiled. Alex joined her, looking out onto the sea of people. Today would be a holiday, and there would be many parties and much drinking this evening. Tomorrow, they would wake early, and the entire dragon clan would greet the sun. Even Sadie would join them, as much of a travesty as some of them thought that was.

Dahlia tried to keep a smile on her face as she waved out the window. The crowd were here to see them, the Chuvashes, and the new brides. "I know. I was thinking of moving our nest. There is a large family chamber, just down the hallway, that has become vacant. It's closer to my family's chamber, and more importantly, will give us privacy. I can't stand Sadie's constant stream of visitors, and she can't stand mine. It's really not working out well, there is much snipping at each other back and forth. Of course, she only really acts up when you and your father are upstairs on business. She dare not say mean things to me when you two are present."

"I am not opposed to that idea. Father rarely sleeps downstairs much anyway, and some privacy would be nice," he said, giving her a little smile.

"Okay then, we will announce it tomorrow after the clan flies. I have already made it known that I want it."

It took them some time to make their way to the city, but finally, the Cathedral of the Dragon God came into view. It was a huge limestone building with two towers rising from each side. An iron spire, seemingly delicate, rose from the center. Colorful stained glass windows depicting the origin story of the dragons filled its arches. The cathedral was ancient and had been there as long as anyone could remember. Inside, pillars reaching for the vaulted roof were intricately carved with natural scenes, and the dark wood beams and furnishings gleamed under thousands of candles, lit for the ceremony.

The steps of the cathedral were lined with the priests, all wearing white robes. They stood at attention, their hands clasped in prayer, their eyes turned to the floor. The sorcerer, Darius, stood at the top of the steps to greet both wedding couples.

Alex and Dahlia would be married first, so they were the first to exit. When the crowd caught sight of the Crown Prince and his beautiful bride, attired in such striking colors of the kingdom, they roared their approval. The sound of adoration swelled, as he turned and helped his bride down from the carriage. She beamed as she took his hand, and they made their way up the steps.

"Welcome, dragons of the sun. Today is your wedding day, and I am happy to be here to give you the blessing of the Dragon God," Darius said. Alex noticed that he had cleaned up well, wearing new robes for the occasion. He had even trimmed his hair and beard. He looked, well, almost respectable. Darius stepped aside, and the pair entered the cathedral.

The invited guests had already arrived. Alex left Dahlia at the door and gave her a quick kiss on the cheek before walking into the church and taking his spot at the front of the aisle. He spied Mila, but she was keeping her thoughts to herself. She waved and gave him a little smile. She looked beautiful today, and his greatest wish was that he could take her as his mate.

She must have caught that thought because she looked away and frowned. The girl sitting next to her gave her a squeeze, and he realized that was the tailor's daughter, Kiara was her name, and Sam was sitting next to her.

Outside, the second wedding couple had arrived. Sadie and Nick managed to extract themselves from the carriage. The crowd cheered loudly for them also, and Nick took a few extra minutes to smile and wave at the people. Finally, they made their way up to the sorcerer, who greeted him in almost the same manner.

"Welcome dragon of the sun, and of summer. Today is your wedding day, and I am happy to be here to join you in marriage."

Sadie gave him a curt little smile, and the two brushed past him. Nick joined his brother at the altar. Sadie stood just behind Dahlia. The two girls did not talk, and did not even look at each other. The tension was thick.

These two had fought over every detail of the dual wedding, finally deciding to have their own flowers, their own invitations, and to host their own receptions afterwards. For convenience's sake, it was for all intents and purposes the same reception, to be held in the grand ballroom of the castle, but half of the room would be in red and gold, and the other half white. The florist appeared and handed the brides their flowers. Dahlia held a huge bouquet of red roses, and Sadie held an even larger bouquet of white roses.

Dahlia had asked Rand to walk her down the aisle, and he had accepted happily. It would indicate that he accepted this union, and that they were indeed his heirs. He looked regal today, his large crown on his head, his royal robes of red velvet looking splendid. He offered her his arm, and they began to walk down the aisle.

Behind her, Aswin was doing his duty. Sadie's parents had declined to attend their daughter's wedding, a huge slap to her. The Dragon Keeper was dressed in a simple black suit with his red tie, and she glanced at him scornfully. "Couldn't you have worn something nicer?"

"I think this is quite appropriate," was all Aswin said, smoothing his hand on his hair. The last wedding he had been in had been Rand and Cassandra's, here in this very spot. It had been a joyous affair, not strained and ceremonial like this one was. He led her down the aisle, and she smiled at the crowd as the wedding march swelled. Aswin gladly left her next to Nick. He had done his duty for the day.

The assembled guests only had eyes for Dahlia and Alex. Of course, her choice of colors helped. She was a majestically beautiful bride, with her auburn hair and vibrant choice of colors, which were the royal colors of Dumara. Alex was next to her, handsome and tall. His stood with his back straight, a slight smile on his face. The pair were perfectly matched, and the crowd couldn't get enough of them.

On the other hand, Sadie was a beautiful bride, but she was certainly trying too hard in all the wrong ways. Her wedding dress was too big, her makeup too much, her smile too forced. Nick just looked angry. He was scowling at his brother, and his hands were shoved into his pockets in fists.

Darius began, one hand on his staff, which now glowed with a large stone on the end. The other hand he held in the air. "Please be seated."

The mass of invited guests sat as one, their attention on the front of church. The wedding of Alex and Dahlia would be performed first, followed immediately after by the vows of Nick and Sadie. A double wedding had never been performed in Dumara, but as they were proving, there was a first time for everything.

"We are here today to bind these couples together and to bestow upon them our blessings. Today, these couples will be bound by marriage with a sacred seal. And so, in the presence of the Dragon God, I ask you each your intentions. Do you, Alex Chuvash, Crown Prince of Dumara, come here freely to enter into marriage, do you promise to be faithful to your bride, and assume all the responsibilities of married life?"

"I do," Alex answered truthfully, holding both of Dahlia's hands in his tightly. No matter how much his heart loved Mila, he would be faithful.

"Do you, Dahlia, daughter of Torrid, enter into this marriage freely, do you promise to be faithful to your husband, and assume all responsibilities of married life? Are you prepared to become the Queen of Dumara, when your husband takes his throne?"

"I do, and I am prepared," she answered, squeezing Alex's hands.

"I now bless you with the spirit of the Dragon God," Darius said, and held his staff out. A blue glow emitted from the end and settled around the couple like a misty cloud. Alex felt warmth fill his body, and he bent down and kissed his bride.

The audience erupted, and the freshly married couple sat down next to Aswin and Rand. Suddenly, all the joy was sucked out of the room as Sadie and Nick stood to take their vows.

As they approached the altar, Nick noticed a tremble under his feet. It was as if the very earth was tensing, and he looked around him with concern. He noticed the chandelier swaying ever so slightly. He glanced at his father, who nodded slightly. He had noticed it too.

The crowd was silent as they watched the sorcerer repeat the wedding ceremony with Sadie and Nick. Sadie was smiling widely, while Nick was looking at the crowd, trying to read the room. He felt the odd tension and was wondering what was happening.

As Darius got to the end, he looked up, hoping that the Dragon God didn't decide to smite him down for officiating such a travesty of a marriage.

"I know bless you with the spirit of the Dragon God," he repeated, holding his staff out over the heads of the pair, grimacing a little. But nothing happened. No light of any color emitted from his staff. He looked at it in disbelief. His staff had never failed him.

"One moment," he said, as the crowd started to mutter. Nick looked at him angrily, and Sadie tapped her foot impatiently, scowling in his direction.

He looked at his staff, gave it a few good taps on the floor, and tried again. He cleared his throat, "I now bless you with the spirit of the Dragon God." Instead of blue light, a thick, black, choking smoke poured out of the tip of his staff, causing the bridal couple to cough and wave it out of their faces.

Immediately, the ground began to shake, slowly at first, and then faster. People began shrieking as the chandeliers began to swing, dripping hot wax out of the drip trays on the audience below. Dust and the sound of cracking filled the air, and Rand closed his eyes and prayed. Large stones from the ceiling dropped with a crash, somehow managing to not crush anyone in the process. People screamed as the ground continued to rock.

Dahlia grabbed Alex, looking at the ceiling fearfully. "It's okay," he whispered into her ear, holding her close. Behind him, Sam was standing in front of Kiara and Mila, holding out his hands as if that would protect them somehow. Guests started making for the exit, but were stopped in their tracks by a sudden voice that filled the spaces of the church.

"I WITHHOLD MY BLESSING. I AM ANGRY. I AM COMING," the voice boomed. Two solid beats, that sounded like a death drum reverberated through the room. BOOM BOOM.

After the drumbeats, all was still. You could have heard a pin drop in the cathedral, as they all looked at the couple who had brought down the wrath of the Dragon God.

Read Dane and the Sea Monster, a free prequel short story to The Dragon Keepers series. Claim it here!

Want to find out what happens next? Read book two, *The Sorcerer's Absolution*, for more sassy sorcerer and dragon adventures.

Next In Series

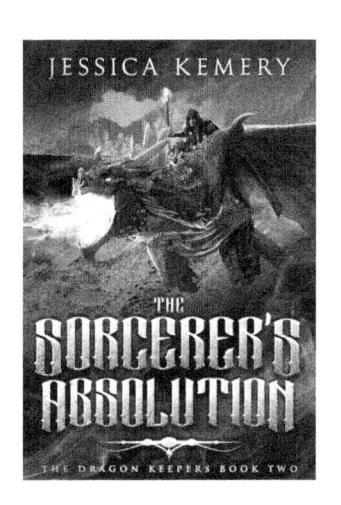

The fate of the realm rests in the king's hands. Will a corrupt successor with a thirst for power send the dragon world to its doom?

The Sorcerer's Absolution is the action-packed second book in The Dragon Keepers fantasy series. If you like intricate magic, rich backdrops, and classic battles, then you'll love Jessica Kemery's fight for morality.

About the Author

Called by some a multi-tasking ninja, Jessica Kemery lives in Crystal Lake, Illinois, where she works a day job so that her dog, Rocky, can live a life of pampered luxury. *The Hobbit* is the first book she read, and she has been searching for dragons ever since. Powered by caffeine and the bare minimum of sleep on a nightly basis, she thinks the world's greatest invention is meal delivery services.

She has a habit of dabbling in all different kinds of fantasy, but all of her stories have strong female characters, sweet romance, action and adventure, deep world building, and maps. Visit https://www.hotmessexpresspublishing.com/works for a complete list of her books and make sure to follow her on Facebook, Instagram, Twitter, and TikTok at Author Jessica Kemery.

Printed in Great Britain
by Amazon